Most Hated

Most Hated

A Novel

By Kara Alloway

Toronto, 2023

RE: Books

Copyright © Kara Alloway.

All rights reserved.

www.rebooks.ca

Published in Canada by RE: Books.

ADDRESS:
re:books
380 Macpherson Ave. Suite 306
Toronto ON
M4V 3E3
www.rebooks.ca

First RE: Books Edition: May 2023

ISBN: 978-1-7386702-2-2
eBook ISBN: 978-1-7386702-3-9

RE: Books and all associated logos are trademarks and/or registered marks of RE: Books.

Library and Archives Canada Cataloguing in Publication
Title: Most hated : a novel / Kara Alloway.
Names: Alloway, Kara, author.
Identifiers: Canadiana (print) 20230151590 | Canadiana (ebook) 20230151655 | ISBN 9781738670222 (softcover) | ISBN 9781738670239 (EPUB)
Classification: LCC PS8601.L5535 M67 2023 | DDC C813/.6—dc23
Printed and bound in Canada.
1 3 5 7 9 10 8 6 4 2

Cover design by: Jordan Lunn

For my boys, Baron, Hunter & Christian,
and my husband Graham.

"Frankly, Mr. Shankly, this position I've held
It pays my way and it corrodes my soul."

–The Smith's "Frankly Mr. Shankly"

Subject: FW: Casting Attractive, Wealthy, Glamourous women for TV Series

From: fpoke@cpmedia.com>

To: fpoke@cpmedia.com>

CASTING CALL
"ARE YOU THE *TALK OF THE TOWN...*"

DO YOU LIVE A FABULOUS GLAMOROUS LIFE...

A celebrated series about real women, living fabulous *real* lives, is currently casting.

The hit docu-soap TV series will give viewers an inside look at the most glamorous women.

For **this** version of the franchise, chosen participants will have the opportunity to work with an internationally acclaimed, award-winning director.

We are looking for outgoing, exciting, strong, focused women who reside in New York City and want to share their lives with us—and the world.

They should be lively and energetic, with defined opinions and views. The women will have busy lives, strong work ethic, an active social calendar, and an enjoyment of the good life.

We love glamorous women who are self-confident and happy with who they are.

This is FANTASTIC exposure for anyone involved.

The women, their significant others, and their families must be open to sharing their experiences with the producers and the television audience.

If you are interested, please reply to this email with your name, age, contact information, recent photos, and brief bio.

T he woman was responsive. Beneath the non-rebreather mask, she was mumbling and moving her head from side to side. Her eyes blinked repeatedly—all good indicators the naloxone had done its job and she'd be okay. Despite the unknown quantity of Vicodin she'd ingested, she wasn't going to die of an overdose. The paramedic silenced the volume on the cardiac monitor and spoke into his device.

"Truck 7737, coming in with a female, conscious, opioid overdose. Narcan is onboard, patient on high oxygen and we have obtained IV access." He tucked her arm, the one without the line, under the beige blanket and noticed it was very cold. Her low body temperature was not surprising.

The boxy vehicle maneuvered through the streets of Upper Manhattan, battling the gridlock like the red plastic car in a sliding block puzzle, and took an aggressive corner. Items rattled and jostled in the storage cupboards behind him, and the paramedic reached to steady the IV bag atop the pole that emerged from the stretcher. Glancing over his shoulder, he peered out the small rear window to see where they were. He knew every bump, every building along the way. The pyramidical glass awning he spotted, looming over the entrance to the condo building on Fifth, indicated they were very close to the hospital.

Back to his radio, he continued, "We're about two minutes out. ETA…." Here he paused to look at his watch because those clocks in the rig were never correct "ETA 9:10."

Retuning the device to the holster on his uniform, he made eye contact with his passenger. They shared a look of reassurance before he continued his work documenting her vitals on his ePCR tablet. Empathy was an important but potentially problematic part of the job.

2

Zoe

Eight Weeks Earlier

Zoe shifted in her chair, untucked one leg, and checked the time on her laptop: 10:12 a.m. As the lead talent producer on *Talk of the Town*, this was her deal. The other production assistants she had hired, Fiona and Milo, were assembled around the table in this poorly furnished rental office that smelled like a dirty hamster cage. The film companies always rented the crappiest places for their staff to do pre-production. Zoe wondered if they got together with the network and determined it essential that the mental and physical abuse of the crew begin immediately once employment contracts were signed. The three were immersed in discussing the minutia of the candidates' lives since the primary agenda for the day was to review possible filming locations and finalize casting for network approval. Potential cast members had delivered lists of restaurants they frequented, salons they visited, vacation properties they owned, their neighborhood cutesy coffee shops, boutiques where they were known (smaller ones were more agreeable and easier for filming), routes for their walks around the city, and any other camera-ready conceivable locales for their filming.

Privileged bitches, Zoe thought.

"Courtney P. is out." Milo said as he read an email aloud in his best impression, "The fact that you would even consider asking me to postpone *my* important surgery to accommodate your filming schedule indicates to me that my health and well-being are of little consequence to your production company. And for that reason, I will not be signing the participant agreement. *Your* lucky…"

3

"She did a Y-O-U-R here people," Milo interjected, "…I'm not taking this to a lawyer to share with the Department of Labor."

"Wasn't it fibroid surgery?" Zoe asked.

Fiona shrugged. "I thought it was a cancer scare and that's why I asked to hold off till filming. The hospital scene, waiting for results, such good content there."

"Guys," Milo rationalized, "the bigger point is she made the 'YOUR/YOU ARE' mistake. These women think they're Mensa because they did an online test once, but the reality is they are the most insecure and easiest to handle."

Zoe shot him a look.

Milo sat back in his chair, raising his hands in surrender, "Hey I'm only speaking from experience."

"Forget about her," Zoë said. "If they're difficult before filming they'll be impossible once we start. She's out. I hope she turns up as a charter guest on *Below Deck*. That'll run her around fifty grand but at least she showed us."

Redirecting her energy to the task at hand she continued, "Where are we at as of now. Who's in, and who needs a little push over the edge?"

Fiona stood up, removed the pushpin holding Courtney's photo to the board and threw it in the garbage. She plucked off a few Post-Its with production notes scribbled on them from under the picture and dropped them in the same can. With her back still to the two, she began.

"We have the larger-than-life Ms. Budgie Verroye confirmed."

Larger-than-life was a reference to both the size and personality of the Broadway producer. They had yet to come up with a bona fide nickname for her.

"The unholy mess that is Nicole Trace, fading popstar, also confirmed. Let's hope she doesn't get another DUI between now and filming." Fiona paused, likely expecting something back from the group. But since another DUI was an obvious possibility for Ms. Trace, nobody laughed.

"And when I say confirmed, I mean they are signed and sealed. They've both completed their psych evaluation, and physical," she added.

Every participant was to undergo a psychiatric evaluation and a medical exam with a doctor hired by production before being officially contracted. Zoe explained it to the participants as both an insurance must and a mental health safety precaution to make sure they could withstand any harsh criticism from fans without crumbling. The truth? It was a fast and easy way to get the inside track on the participants' triggers, phobias, past surgeries, and medications. This intel, alongside Fiona's exceptional cyberspace investigation skills, was the reason Zoe had recruited her for this project, which resulted in a complete dossier on each potential "star."

"The sex toy woman?" Zoe asked.

"Mariana? Hadn't gotten there yet," Fiona answered.

Zoe knew Fiona thought she was rude—and pushy. She kept the meeting moving because the other PAs had this annoying habit of dissecting and analyzing the minutia of everything. Zoe had determined their liberal arts minds were stuck in some first-year university discussion group where you were given extra credit for the quality and quantity of contribution.

Fiona tapped the photos as she mentioned the women's names. "Right, Mariana, aka 'the sex toy woman'," she looked over her shoulder at Zoe and tilted her head, "Mariana is in. And there's Lexi, she said she's speaking to the lawyers today. She will sign. I mean this show is an influencer's dream gig."

There was general nodding and sounds of agreement at this statement.

"With Courtney out that leaves The Countess of Controversy and the WAG."

Milo repeated, "WAG?"

"Dahlia Irvine?" Fiona feigned shock. Then she explained, "As in *wives and girlfriends* ... as in a sport star's significant other. Victoria Beckham was the original back in the height of WAG mania!"

Ah yes, should anyone forget that Fiona was from London, she always had to drop some dopey reference. Zoe wondered how long she'd had this one ready and waiting.

"Okay, what about these two?" Zoe asked. "Do we have any feedback? Any idea what they're thinking? Did they answer the survey for locations?"

Milo scanned his email and read, "Budgie's convinced her cousin Sabrina will do it. *She'll put up an 'I could never' but she'll come around*. Her words," he added. "Oh, and *she may have some tweaks to her contract*."

"Not gonna happen." Zoe replied, "But that's for legal not me. Everyone signs the same contract. No exceptions. Let's have the cousin think we're passing on Sabrina the Countess. Fake her out and tell her not to worry 'because casting is more or less complete'."

Milo nodded and made a note in his off-brand Moleskin.

"And Mick Irvine's wife, our '*WAG*'?" Zoe asked. "Do we know where she's at?"

This would appear to be the real fake out of the day, since Zoe knew exactly how the negotiations with Dahlia Irvine were going. The wife of the hot, entertaining, NFL tight end was undoubtedly hanging out somewhere between bored to tears and at the end of her rope. Zoe had it on good authority that she was spending most of her days alone, trying not to feel empty, abandoned, and irrelevant—like the old building near Zoe's apartment with the Blockbuster façade. Yes! That was a far better nickname for her; Dahlia Irvine was "*Blockbuster*." Purposeless and out of date. Perfect for the show.

3
Dahlia

I didn't want to let go of Mick when I left for Day One with the show. Homesick kid off to the first day of camp.

To my surprise, when offered, he had agreed to participate in filming. Clocking in at six feet, five inches, with features so perfect they seemed illegal and a great sense of humor, my husband was a score for production. Thanks to a Super Bowl three years ago, a slew of endorsements that followed, a mention in a Lil' Wayne song, and a special touchdown dance, he was the one not-a-quarterback football player every non-footballer could name.

"I can't leave you to it alone," he had said. "I'm your partner and this sounds like something you would have done a few years ago." Whether he knew it or not, those were the magic words. The show had been his idea, but I didn't need much convincing.

"This is a step in new direction for us." I had replied. *This* was something, for the first time in a while, that was for *me*. An exciting project for the one who took photos for the fans and who held the stuff when he posed for those photos. There's no way he was excited by the idea of reality TV. "And I see what you're doing here ... you're taking one for the team." A concept, very familiar to me.

Being Mick Irvine's wife meant giving 100 percent to him. His physical and mental needs always trumped mine; it went Mick, then the team, then Dahlia. Football dictated what we ate, when we ate, how we slept, when we celebrated, where we lived, who we socialized with, when we argued, even when we had sex.

7

I could not depend on him for anything, but he had to be able to depend on me for everything. The game was blameless, perfect, and beyond reproach. I knew all this before I married him, and I'd have to be pathological to resent something that had done so much for him, for his family, and, honestly, for us.

But today was not about football.

I wondered how many other husbands or partners would make appearances. I hoped the more, the better. There's something backward about the idea of getting a bunch of women together and demanding television-worthy drama.

That being said, Sabrina Verroye was somewhat of a lightning rod. Any Verroye wedding would make the news, of course, but she had continually made headlines.

For one thing, the guy she married was a straight-up hottie. For years, trashy magazines featured grainy photos of Earl Robert Stanhope—better known as Racy Robbie—emerging from crystal clear waters in the sunshine, his eight-pack glistening in all its glory. He dated every beautiful actress and model at some point or another. Always top five on those *Hottest Royals Ranked* lists, he was the party boy, the titled disappointment; no one could get enough. A Bond villain smirk made him look sweet and youthful, but without the smile, he was fiercely beautiful.

Okay, full disclosure? I met my own prince charming, one that other women drool over. But the good-looking guys were never my thing. My friends used to try to figure me out, pointing out this guy or that guy, asking, *what about him? Do you think he's hot?*

My answer was usually a shrug. A *meh*. Because it always took more than nice eyes and chiseled features to interest me. Physical attractiveness was always a plus, and I never hooked up with—well, I never *dated* anyone who was hideous. But something about Robbie—he was captivating. He was the exception to the rule.

A gorgeous specimen.

The tabloids went *mad* when he started hanging around Sabrina Verroye, the original celebutante. Already an American princess, her family had been rich since the railroads. They had their name on a line at Tiffany's—one piece even called *Sabrina's Key*. They owned Michelin-rated restaurants, apparently for fun. Her aunt was the founder of a massive fashion line that had been known for bringing Old Hollywood to the modern runway. Her cousin Budgie was the Queen of Broadway—producing hit after hit. From banking to real estate, without question the Verroye family was one of America's most storied dynasties with a white-gloved hand in almost everything. Sabrina was the It Girl, the prettiest family member by far (even though their glamour did more of the work than most natural good looks could), and she was an actress.

Her first movie was *Lily of the Alley*. It should have been a massive failure. But it was too intoxicating. I saw it (for the first time) when I was twelve years old, when my best friend, Cassie, and I snuck into the theater and watched, mesmerized, as a dazzling, gorgeous Sabrina Verroye—only nineteen—played a teenage prostitute who witnesses a murder and falls in love with the killer. It was steamy and dark, intriguing, and romantic. The film took place in a hot summer in New York in the 1940s, and she looked so flawless that it seemed she'd been born in the wrong era.

I could recite all the dialogue to that movie by heart, and that goes for most girls my age—and all the guys who watched it for the nude scenes. Critics hated her for it, calling the plot atrocious and sexist, saying it was passing off pathological behavior as romance. Still, it crushed the box office.

After that, Sabrina Verroye skyrocketed in popularity. She was on the back of every locker door and on every magazine cover. Everyone wanted her shade of shimmering, shiny red hair, and I was long jealous of the contrast between her mane and her bright blue eyes.

And then … nothing. Hollywood forgot about her. The references to her character—Lily Lowe—never stopped, especially from those of us who'd experienced a sexual awakening. But Sabrina was never in much of anything again. She vanished from the social radar. And it was such a waste because it wasn't like she went down some drug spiral or anything like that—she simply went away.

But right when she had been gone long enough that no one seemed to think she'd come back again, there she was frolicking in the Mediterranean surf alongside Earl Stanhope—a guy ten years older than her. He wasn't royalty—"he's a titled aristocrat" as my gran used to tell me. But he was a perfect fit for the Park Avenue Princess.

All this *fantastic* gossip happened during my freshman high school year. Half the world hated her for being the "entitled rich girl who played a hooker when she was a kid"—again, she was nineteen, not exactly a kid. And the other half loved her because she was *Lily Lowe* and because who better to keep Rascal Robbie in line?

This is why it was such a big production when their wedding came around.

The drama never ended. Sabrina in those monarch-worthy outfits and getting married in a million-dollar gown. She wasn't frequenting Soho House anymore; instead, she was in third world countries, holding babies and feeding children.

It might sound rude, but following the intimate details of her day to day wasn't quite as interesting once she shifted into the Mother Teresa role. I wanted them to get married and live an unapologetically lavish and decadent jet-set life instead of settling down and saving the world.

For many years after that, no one was looking in their fishbowl, interest waned, and the gossip stuttered until it stopped. They showed up every now and then in those *Hello! Magazine* holiday celebu-space spreads with their daughter, but their lives seemed way too ordinary to merit any more attention. And then, out of nowhere the tranquil hush of years of obscurity was broken when Robbie got accused of sexual misconduct from a female staff member. Then another woman came forward. Then another.

Until the number of women surpassed four and the scandal started to seem beyond reality. This, then, became the official line. The women were lying. Lying and looking for a payout.

The anonymity of the women made it impossible to count the exact number of accusers, and maybe not every allegation was true, but to say that every woman was lying was ridiculous. And while Robbie acknowledged two of the encounters, labeling them "consensual infidelities," there were never any criminal investigations.

That's when Sabrina, who had been quiet for much of the frenzy, spoke up in a massively controversial article wherein she announced her pending divorce from Robert, her shock and horror at the whole experience, and her solid support of the women who had come forward.

Everyone *hated* her for it. She had made the cover of *Vanity Fair*, and suddenly she was deemed every bit in the wrong as him. "She must have known, how could she *not* have known?" was the general consensus, along with the sister judgment "That's on her if she didn't know."

"I intentionally kept silent to protect my family from further embarrassment and to restore a small degree of the privacy we have lost. But recent circumstances now require me to speak up," said Robbie in a retaliating interview. "I fully acknowledge that I acted inappropriately as a husband, father, and public figure. However, I am devastated to discover that my remorse and desire to privately repair and reconcile what was broken is not a shared objective."

His campaign for sympathy and forgiveness didn't end there. He did tearful interviews with respected journalists. He took over the charities that Sabrina had walked away from—and succeeded in convincing people she had "deserted" her philanthropic efforts, while the truth was that she had only stopped because she was no longer associated with his family, who founded them. But then, to cement her *most hated* status, their fourteen-year-old daughter, Lady Aubrey, stayed in the UK to live with her father and his parents, while Sabrina returned to America.

The world went nuts. Support for *Repentant Rob* went up like surrender flags. *Sabrina's Choice* to abandon her daughter and flee back to America had sparked debate from everyone, everywhere. News channels hired expert panelists to comment with authoritative opinions, late-night talk show hosts delivered monologue after monologue filled with Sabrina jokes, and social media was flooded with runaway-Sabrina-themed memes. Robbie's rebuttal had revealed many *real* problems with his marriage, including years of feeling ignored and used by his wife as a means to her ends and his longing for genuine attentiveness that sent him seeking relationships with other women; the general public seemed to accept the "truth" he had presented. And Sabrina, the "failed actress," who would do anything for attention, including taking her clothes off on camera, was now seen as a master manipulator who managed to weasel her way into a title and give birth to a child who was clearly a retirement fund—since she had no other way to succeed.

After that article, Sabrina disappeared. I didn't blame her.

But when I heard that *she* was doing this show, I was equal parts confused and intrigued—there was no way I was going to pass up a chance to be a part of it.

The first meeting was in the penthouse suite of a hotel I was pretty sure Sabrina's family owned.

Yikes, I thought, pressing the PH button in the elevator, *I am going to have to sit on my gossip-column knowledge of all things Sabrina Verroye or she's going to think I'm a stalker.*

It took everything I had to hide the twelve-year-old in me that wanted to squeal at the sight of Sabrina's gleaming, copper head.

★★★

"Dahlia! Welcome! I'm Fiona. We've been emailing and texting so much it's nice to finally catch up in person." The PA's accent was stronger in person. We'd talked a lot on the phone and discussed her growing up in England and me having spent a year in Geneva playing professional soccer, "football" as they call it over there.

She shook my hand enthusiastically. "Oh my gosh, I'm excited that you're here. Can I get you anything? I have a bottle of bubbly open if that would help take the edge off."

She gestured at Sabrina, who had not turned toward me yet, still sitting in the high-backed armchair like some sort of animated villain. In front of her, there was not one but two glasses of champagne.

"That would be awesome," I whispered.

She gave me the "I got you girl" look and scooted off.

Someone outfitted me with a microphone and transmitter without acknowledging that I was a human being or giving me the opportunity to acknowledge him. It was an intimate procedure, and I tried to make small talk while he helped me thread a wire up the inside of my top.

"Wait, we're not filming today, are we?"

"We need to get soundbites and measure your voice."

"Measure my voice?"

He did not say anything else.

I looked up at a sound, expecting pleasant little Fiona and my glass of liquid courage; I started a little when it was not her but Budgie Verroye. The room filled with her energy when she came out of one of the bedrooms, clicking the screen off on her phone.

She had on an ostrich feather shrug and an amount of jewelry that might have been gaudy on someone else. I learned later that her real name was Bernadette, but that had never suited her. *Ette* implied small, and Budgie was in no way small. She was the sort of woman who would be described as big boned since no part of her seemed drooped with fat. Instead her wrists, legs, and bust were all practically magnified. She reminded me of Kathy Bates' Unsinkable Molly Brown in *Titanic*—what I pictured when someone used the word "flamboyant."

"Can't take the afternoon off without something going wrong. Hiya darling, which one are you?"

It might have offended me, but her frankness was funny.

If my husband was the athlete everyone knew, no matter how little they cared about sports, Budgie Verroye was the Broadway producer/director that everyone knew about—no matter how little they cared about *the theater*.

"Which one am I? I'm the gold digger married to the football player."

"Ha! I like this one already," she put a hand on my shoulder, speaking across the room to her cousin. "Are you still on that phone, Sabrina?"

"No," came a silken, full voice that was immediately recognizable.

Budgie gave me a look and put a finger to her lips. *Shh*.

She snuck around the chair. Catching Sabrina in the act, she yelled, "Gotcha."

Budgie snatched the phone, and Sabrina put up a brief fight, like they were sisters, then remembered herself and saw me for the first time. I wasn't sure if I measured up.

Fiona returned with my glass of champagne. "Here you are, Dahlia. Cheers love."

"Thanks."

There was an awkward pause as I stood there, not knowing if I should sit or what I should do next.

"Come join us over here; what's your name again?" Budgie said, saving me. "I might know every word to *Hamilton*'s opening number but I'm helpless with names. Remind me yours?"

"Dahlia."

"Dahlia! Interesting name. Why did your parents saddle you with that? Tough come up to be named after a dead starlet, isn't it?"

"One part my mom's favorite flower, but she's always been a junkie for unsolved mysteries."

Sabrina gave a flick of her eyebrow. Budgie glanced at her. Did anything get by Budgie?

"Let's have a toast before the other girls get here and we have to start deciding who to hate." She lifted her glass in the air, and I imitated.

Sabrina hesitated and then lifted hers.

"To guts and glamour, and to never losing either," said Budgie with great vigor.

"To guts and glamour," I repeated.

We clinked glasses. I took a sip and thought, "I cannot believe I'm drinking champagne with Lily Lowe." Sabrina downed the rest of her glass and then held it up for Fiona to refill, which she did without hesitation. We were drinking Cristal, and I made a note to appreciate it more.

There was a knock on the propped-open door, and in came a girl who looked familiar, but I couldn't quite place her. She looked like *a lot* of people.

Her brows were bold, dark, squared, and structured. Her face was contoured and smooth; she looked like a walking *Maxim* cover. She had shining, puffy lips and long, straight, shining black hair. Her boobs were pushed up to her collarbone, her waist was tiny, her hips disproportionate. She was in fashion-athletic clothes, all one brand. Her nails were long, neon yellow and decorated with crystal charms.

I found it hard to look away from her. Her whole presentation was confusing, I decided, because she didn't seem real. She looked like a filtered, photoshopped Instagram picture or maybe too much like a Bratz doll that was somehow balancing five feet, two inches, on six-inch stilettos.

She went through the mic hookup without a blink like it happened every day, which maybe it did.

"Hey," she said, voice painfully cool.

I waved, smiled, wondered what her deal was. What got her to this room. I imagined hundreds of thousands of followers, endorsements, and likes. Maybe we could bond over the haters.

Fiona gave her the welcome spiel and handed her a glass of Cristal.

"Do you have any tequila?" Fiona stood statue-still for a moment. "A few slices of lime with a splash of soda and tequila on the rocks would be great, thank you."

When Fiona walked away, the tequila drinker smiled and said, "I didn't get this body putting away two hundred calories a drink. You know?" She gave an empty laugh, then sat down with us, at home right away.

"A glass of champagne is only around ninety calories." I said, "Tequila is closer to sixty-five. Still more, but it's not bad, all things considered." My knowledge of worthless trivia was going to out me as a fraud in this group.

"That's twenty-five calories I don't need, right? Gotta keep it tight."

There was a silence from us, the three women drinking the glasses of flab her body couldn't afford. As if on cue, we all took a sip.

The tequila arrived in a heavy, leaded glass, the limes in a napkin, almost right away, and she said, "Oh my god you're my best friend, thank you so much, you're the best ever."

She fished in her bag and whipped out and assembled a two-part stainless straw, which she slid into the glass. Then she started squeezing in the limes, delicately, with her plastic-tipped fingers. Once squeezed, the limes were placed on the wooden end table.

She pulled out her phone and started clicking away at the drink in the air in her hand, adjusting the angle to capture her bracelets, rings, and three of her electric bejeweled talons.

Budgie said, "What's your name honey?"

She took a few seconds too long to respond, moving her head but not her eyes toward Budgie and the question, before looking at her with a big, huge smile and holding out a slim arm.

Budgie took her hand.

"I'm Lexi. With an 'i.'"

"Budgie Verroye."

"I'm sorry, say it again?" Lexi leaned in and moved her sheet of hair aside.

From the look on her face, I could tell Budgie didn't get asked to repeat herself very often.

"Budgie Verroye."

"Vair-*wha*," she repeated. "Is that French?"

"It is," Budgie said with narrowed eyes, but no less enjoyment.

Sabrina was staring daggers at her. I didn't blame her. How could this girl not recognize the last name?

"And you said Budgie? That's so cute. You're so cute, oh my god, I love you already."

She sank back into her chair and back onto her phone.

Reading—at least—my mind, she sat back up and said, "Oh my gosh, how rude am I? My best friend is freaking out because somebody *hacked* her Insta and stole a bunch of her photos. And the account already has like four thousand followers so it's legit a disaster. And my man is being, *ugh*," she rolled her eyes and splayed the fingers in her free hand. "Anyway, you are?"

She extended her hand in my direction.

"I'm Dahlia Irvine. Nice to meet you, Alexa."

Budgie's smile and eyes moved to me.

"It's Lexi. With an 'i'." The brief look of irritation on her face said far more than the returning grin.

"Lexi, sorry."

"Don't worry about it! No worries, no worries. And…," she looked to Sabrina. "Oh, *shit*, wait a minute, you're that rich actress that married the English guy, right?"

Instead of shaking Sabrina's hand, she got back on her phone and said, "I know I saved one of your looks. Hold up, I'll find it."

Lexi swiped through her phone, her middle finger, ring finger, and pinky spread in the air. She had no self-consciousness about dominating the conversation, no worry that she was annoying us. She swiped and swiped with complete faith in our attention.

She found the picture and said, "Sorry the one I thought was you wasn't you, but this is, right?"

She held her phone out.

Sabrina's glass was empty again, as was her expression when she confirmed that yes, that picture was of her.

"I thought so, that's *in-sane*. You're like super famous! Ew, I was on my phone, I didn't even know who I was sitting with. Can we take a selfie? It'll be great branding for the show."

She stood, not waiting for an answer, and teetered over to Sabrina. Once there, she crouched beside her and held a well-practiced arm out and cocked her head to the side—her good angle—and snapped.

"Oh my god, it's so adorable. Look at us. What's your Insta?"

"I don't do my own social—"

"Of course. Here, I'll tag you if I can find it…," then, in a sing-song voice, she said, "there you are!"

"What perfume are you wearing? Those are Cartier right," she gestured at the bracelets on Sabrina's left wrist. "Let's see, Cartier… and… ah, Creed. Must be. Right?"

Sabrina shook her head. "These are custom and my perfume is Baccarat. And … why?"

"Tagging? Duh? Sorry not duh, but you know what I mean."

It was clear that Sabrina did not.

Lexi clicked away again, before holding her phone out to me and showing it to me and asking if I thought it was cute.

"Excuse me, sorry," said Fiona, appearing out of nowhere and positioned trying to make the least fuss of herself as she could. "I need to remind everyone that a few teaser photos for your social media accounts are okay, but you are to say nothing about Aleksandr Borrow. If asked, you are to state that you can neither confirm nor deny your involvement in any upcoming project."

She cringed. "I'm sorry! It's in the participant agreement."

"Oh, no, I read that contract!" said Lexi. "I was pre-law, so…"

Her sentence faded away as did her interest, though mine was piqued. She was pre-law? And until when?

The caption read: *New friends bring energy to the soul. Love this girl!*

My cringe showed, but Lexi did not notice. She looked like she found a winning lottery ticket as she sat back down and waited for the likes to roll in.

4

Sabrina

She should have eaten. She knew she should have eaten. She should have known the liquor would be free flowing.

But it wasn't her imagination that this Lexi girl was the worst sort of girl, right?

The other one, Dahlia, seemed alright. Nervous, new, but *normal*. Probably an easy woman to like. The type who reeled people in with her friendliness but kept trust because of her honesty.

Because she didn't seem to be one of those saccharine sweethearts, not at all. She, for instance, seemed to see the problem with *Lexi*.

Sabrina knew she was being judgmental. But Lexi was awful. She shouldn't have let her take the picture. Though, what was she supposed to do, say, *no, sorry, being associated with you will hurt an already bad news cycle for me.*

And if that was true, what was she doing here?

According to Budgie, what she made of this was up to her. *This* was Sabrina's opportunity to take control, turn the narrative, and maybe in the process win back her daughter's approval. If the world was going to talk, Budgie had suggested Sabrina should be the one writing the script.

There had to be a better way.

And yet here she was, the contract signed. The network's lawyer had seemed bewildered when she endorsed it because the agreement made it impossible to revoke her appearance. After the movie, the drugs, the marriage, could the court of public opinion acquit her from yet another mistake?

She had to make the best of this.

More champagne.

She held up her glass to Fiona, who refilled it with a wink and a smile.

At least she was getting paid well for whatever *this* was about to become. And right now, that was something. This show was the first thing that had been hers in as long as she could remember.

The hotel room door opened again, and in came a woman who could be recognized by anyone. Sabrina looked to Lexi to see if she—

Lexi flew up out of her chair with a squeal that would have been at home in the orchestra of background noise at a college bar, and ran to her, arms outstretched.

"I'm Lexi, oh my god, it's crazy to meet you!"

"Nicole," said the newcomer, extracting her hand from the sudden proximity between the two of them.

A mic pack was attached, and she showed a true and genuine familiarity with the routine.

"I grew up listen-*ing* to your albums *nonstop*, full disclosure, I was a little young for them. But I didn't even care, I was ob*sessed*. You're a total icon. Seriously. *Obviously*, but you know what I mean."

Lexi had that habit of pronouncing "ing" like "een" and had something Budgie told Sabrina was called a vocal fry.

Between the obnoxious limes on the table, the *selfie*, and the affectation, this girl was going to be hard to stand. Either that or Sabrina had spent too much time in a bubble, feeling too comfortable saying the people around her were crossing lines.

She took another sip.

Nicole was given a glass of champagne, too. She looked nervous. Or maybe "nervous" wasn't the right word. Dahlia was nervous. Nicole looked uncomfortable and fidgety. If she had to guess, Sabrina would say the fan-girl encounter had caught her off guard and distracted Nicole from completing a more pressing task, like the bank robber whose heist is thwarted by a chatty cop.

Sabrina was sick to death of her suspicious self. Or whatever this cobbled together version of her was.

5
Dahlia

Okay, Nicole is, as Lexi said, an icon.

A former popstar. A *mega* popstar. Girls my age spent the summer of age ten creating dance moves to her music. To this day I remember every word to her biggest hits. She did the Super Bowl. She did *SNL*—host and musical act (she was a bad actress, but no one cared). She was briefly married to her male equivalent in the pop star world. But after eight years of togetherness, it took only one year to break the marriage. That was when she went downhill.

She *lost her shit*.

She was photographed taking her top off in the middle of the day at a bar in Nolita. She was the kind of drunk where she keeps *saying* she's having a good time, but it's *very* clear that she is hysterically unhappy. She was filmed getting kicked out of The San Vicente Bungalows for skinny dipping. She punched a paparazzo. She was in rehab a few times. She went radio silent. The photos have been dragged out as proof of *what can happen*.

Nicole's sanity break involved a lot of booze, a lot of exhibitionism, and a whole lot of cameras. It also included one rough mugshot for a DUI in Vegas, where she mowed down a road sign.

And here she was now, in the same hotel room as me. If you had told me in fifth grade, when I was listening to her music at the park on my portable discman, I'd be here with her, I would have screamed like Lexi did.

Nicole sat down with us and gave the awkward *I just got here* wave.

It was strange seeing her in real life. To be honest, Sabrina looked exactly how she did in pictures. Completely put together. Smooth skin, perfect hair. Like a modern-day Katharine Hepburn. The only difference between her and the photos were that she looked tired and weary. Dark circles under her eyes and a deep exhaustion that permeated the room.

But Nicole looked different in a whole other way. It was like she was the knock-off, lower-priced version of Nicole Trace. The Nicole Trace from Wish. The blonde wasn't quite as shimmering or icy; it was brassy. Her makeup looked hurried, and her clothes looked inexpensive and ill-fitting. Her phone had a crack down the center of the screen. And she had the confidence of a new kid in middle school. The worst part was that she looked like she knew we were all thinking that her best days were behind her.

Nicole might have been right in that assessment, except for Lexi, who seemed to be looking for another *in* for a boost in her social media presence. Lexi had a hungry look in her eyes when she asked, "Okay, Nicole, can we take a selfie? I'm posting for my followers, and this will make their heads explode."

"Can we not do that? I'm not feeling a hundred percent and I'd rather not."

Lexi looked stunned. Sabrina did a finger gun at Nicole.

Budgie chuckled, and I watched in wonder.

The door opened again, and Fiona scurried over saying, "You made it! How was the flight?"

We all turned our attention to the attractive, shrewd-looking woman with the intense hazel eyes who had entered the room. She was very done up, lots of makeup, long fake lashes, glistening glossed lips. She looked almost like she could be Lexi's pushy stage mom.

And then … she spoke.

How to describe it?

You know Janice on *Friends*? Or Fran Drescher? Her voice was hybrid of those but an octave higher at the same decibel. She had this baby voice I cannot quite put into words. Loud and unique.

"Of course I made it! Oh my gosh, you are so sweet. Hi all! I'm Mariana." She said the first part to Fiona, shaking her bangled wrists before taking the champagne flute. "Do you have any mineral water? I'd kill for a mineral water. They only had those awful cans of water on the plane. Who*ever* okayed canned water?"

She came over to us and flumped down onto the couch beside me, a smidge too close.

She shook her hair back and out of her face and let out a coo of what I would call privilege-tired. It's specific. The sort of tired someone gets after planning a vacation wardrobe.

"I flew right in from Miami. I don't know how much time you've all spent down there, but the airport is abysmal. Such a zoo. Anyhoo, I get there a few minutes later than I wanted to," she paused, "Classic Mariana. The driver drops me off at the wrong door, which I don't even realize until it's already too late. I get in and I've left my purse in the car. Such an idiot. Luckily, I had my ID and my AMEX with me in my phone wallet." She held up the card, it was black. "I always have to have it on me like this because I lose my purse *all the time* but never my phone. But I needed the purse, I mean it has everything in it, including my Xanax, which I don't like to go *anywhere* without, much less on a plane," she said. "I shit you not, I buy the cheapest flight I can for the driver and call him and say, 'Romeo, I know you're going to absolutely *hate* me, but I need you to park and bring me my purse, I'll be at gate B16, I bought you a ticket to, I don't even know where, Orlando or something, so get that cute butt in here!' Long story short—"

Too late.

"He gets in *as* I'm about to board. I am the last person in line and he races over and starts apologizing, bless his heart. It was *such* a scene."

"That must have been hard," said Sabrina.

"You wouldn't even believe. I swear I feel like I climbed Everest. And the worst part was, I ended up realizing after all that? The Xanax was in my carryon."

"That's the *worst*, oh my god, it's lucky you have such a dependable driver," Lexi laughed.

"Tell me about it." She remembered another thought mid-sip, swallowed, and continued. "All this, I look like a maniac, but the poor TSA attendant who went through my carry-on at security must have thought I'm even crazier than that. I own a sex toy company, so when I travel with my samples, I'm always worrying, what is the TSA going to think about me if they go through my bag? They'll assume I'm some sort of sex-crazed psychopath!"

"A sex toy company? Tell us more." Budgie settled into her chair to listen to what was undoubtedly going to be a whole thing.

"At first it was a fun hobby, you know all my friends were talking about their marriages and wanting to spice things up and some of them—believe it or not—had never even used a *toy* before, and I thought, what the hell? I knew a guy who knew a guy, and bing, bang, boom, a year later I was off and running!"

"Bing, bang, boom!" I echoed.

She pushed me on the leg, laughing, and said, "Pun intended of course. It's taken off and been *so* rewarding. Enough to keep me busy, that's for sure. We've got all kinds of fun new designs coming out. It's all sustainable, made in the USA, all the leather stuff is vegan—

Oh, and we also contribute to a charity to stop female circumcision."

There was a general murmur of *that's nice, at least*.

"How are you ladies? God, I always do this, I go on and on about myself, my husband is always giving me crap for it. Tell me, tell me! I obviously recognize you, Ms. Sabrina, and you, Nicole. Such a pleasure!"

But we didn't get the chance; the door opened again, and this time brought with it a gust of an efficient, fast film crew, all very focused and falling into step behind one man.

Aleksandr Borrow. He was the quintessential off-kilter film director, screenwriter, producer, author, and I believe at one time, actor. His movies were not my thing, although Mick loved the dark humor and kick-the-shit-out-of-them violence.

"How is my beautiful cast doing on this fine afternoon?" he asked.

A cameraman followed him, and filmed him, and he appeared to be comfortable with the process.

"Sorry, I was told that we weren't filming yet." Nicole said brushing a self-conscious hand over her hair.

"Not to worry, this is behind the scenes content. Much more for me than for you, the guts of the show we'll get to this week. Although I might add, for the next six weeks, if we're around, we're filming. Yes? Alright," he clapped his hands together once. "Today is our meet and greet, a chance for you all to get acquainted before we start, since the implication once we get going will be that you have all met before. Has anyone met before? Besides Sabrina and Budgie, of course?"

"I've met Budgie a few times and I think I met Sabrina at the Met Gala once, but that's it for me," said Nicole.

Sabrina added, "That's right, we did meet at the Met Gala. You looked lovely."

"Thanks," said Nicole. There was a touch of irritability in her response, I couldn't imagine why. And I noticed that she didn't give the polite and obligatory *as did you* response.

"My goal here," said Aleksandr, pulling out the office chair from the desk, turning it around, and straddling it backward, "is to showcase some humanity. I don't merely want to demonstrate how women can be crazy. I don't want ratings from viewers who watch in order to feel sane by comparison. I want you all to demonstrate the ins and outs of female friendships, even if they are new."

He narrowed his eyes at us and nodded, like he'd put it perfectly, "And let's be frank here. May I be frank?"

There was a murmur of *sure* and *yes*, and Mariana who said a loud, "Yes, *please!*"

"You're all here for a reason. Consider that reason. Know what it's going to take to get you where you need to be. Redemption?

A second chance? Perhaps you love a risk? Is it to become someone? To prove something? Is it because you're bored?"

Because you're bored was directed at me, and he was right about that one.

"If you're bored," he said, like he was reading my mind, "then what will keep your story interesting for the viewer? And … why are you bored? Can you fix that here? *Think* about it."

He looked behind him and a woman stepped forward. She had straight hair, thick glasses, a plump face that hadn't let go of the baby fat, was wearing a cardigan despite the warm weather, with a defensive stance like she dared any of us to come at her.

"This here is Zoe. I believe you have all spoken with her before."

We'd emailed back and forth almost every day for the past month. She, Milo, and Fiona had coordinated everything, from setting me up with the entertainment lawyers to organizing my car for today. I would have thought she'd be the one greeting us at the door rather than lurking in the background. I tried to make eye contact, but she was glued to her iPad.

Aleksandr continued, "As I won't be around all the time, please consider Zoe my ambassador. Fiona and Milo will also be here for you. Is Milo here? Did he come?" He looked around and a slight, young guy stepped forward and did an index finger wave. "Here he is. Listen, this is going to be fun. Try to work with us and if you're afraid something will be taken out of context, my best advice is to watch what you say. Because it will."

He winked then, and I wondered if I was the only one who heard that as a somewhat ominous threat.

6
Sabrina

If the house did not feel like her own before, it felt even less so now. A crew of people with a clear set of instructions came in with heavy plastic milk crates and a game plan. They walked around Sabrina's house, looking for the right place to set up. They ended up picking the area between the front hallway and the living room. They blocked off the big windows with foggy mylar paper and relit the room with bright, tall lights. This did not bring back good memories.

They had rearranged her own real furniture, and the Boca do Lobo sofa was now populated with sequined, cerulean-blue throw cushions. There were many flameless floor candles (Pottery Barn, she assumed). At the forefront of this mise-en-scène was a strange setup that she imagined was intended to be a reflection of her.

This is how the world sees me.

There was a tacky chair, not hers, one they had brought with them, which resembled a throne. It was elevated on a riser. On the small table beside it, also an import from the set decorator, there was a tragic still life of *Sabrina*-ness.

The objects included a folded tabloid with a garish cover and title reading COUNTESS CALLS IT QUITS, a tiara, and a coffee-table book on famous families of New York. On a coaster sat a Nick and Nora glass filled with a pale blush cocktail with a small rose as a garnish.

It was the cocktail created for her by the members-only club, Raffles London in Chelsea. Pink gin, Lillet Rosé, fresh

27

lemon oil, and a small touch of vanilla bean-infused Campari. The recipe was included in an article in *Vogue*. It's called—you guessed it—"The Sabrina."

"This is all a bit me-obsessive, isn't it?" she asked Zoe, who was walking her through the setup as the set-decorator peered through a camera lens at his creation and then made small tweaks to the positioning of it all, with almost no regard for Sabrina or her presence there.

"Don't think of it that way. It's a small touchstone for the viewers. It's a reflection of you. It only seems like it's obsessive because you're like," she dropped her voice, "*normal*. You've got to remember: these people are watching because they're rooting for you. And the team *wants* them to like you. Take it from me, they're going to love you."

Because they hate me now?

"This is meant to be all in good fun. Be yourself. You're cool, and together, and the world wants to see the real you," Zoe continued. "They got all sucked into the bullshit with your ex. No offense."

Her *ex*. No one referred to the great Earl Stanhope as her *ex*. No ownership was ever given to Sabrina.

Sabrina searched Zoe's face for any sign of dishonesty. She couldn't trust her yet, but she saw nothing to fear. She had clear, brown eyes and an earnest expression.

Could she have found an unexpected ally in Zoe? Sabrina didn't feel like she could be disappointed by another person.

"I still think it makes me look like I define myself by all this," she picked up the tiara and set it down, "stuff. A tiara?"

"Part of it is your character. Like it or not, this is who you are to the people who didn't follow your career before the marriage," she said. "I know it's not who you are, and they will too by the time you're done with them. You're a powerhouse. You got this. If you really want me to swap it out with something else, I will. But I worry that putting something in the place of it will make you seem like you can't accept who you have been, which is *not* who you are.

You're the one who tore that asshole a new one and have *no* fear. Not the one who wants to hide what everyone already saw."

Sabrina gnawed on the inside of her lip and let out a sigh. "I suppose it's … you think that's the inference?"

"Absolutely. But again, if you want to swap something out, let's do it. I'll go to battle for you. I think of these as little tokens to the person you used to be. At least yours is glamorous. You should see some of the others."

"Hmm?"

Zoe looked around. "I shouldn't tell you this, but you know Lexi?"

"She's the one with the Instagram account," Sabrina puffed her lips out.

"Yes. She's … a lot. She's got quite a past. She was kind of an, um, dancer?"

Sabrina's eyebrow raised of its own volition. "Radio City, or elsewhere?"

"Elsewhere, definitely."

Getting her drift, Sabrina nodded. "I see. And her little side table?"

"It was sort of an inside joke with the crew. They found these vintage glasses from Fishs Eddy, you know the dish place off 5th Avenue? They got these Collins glasses with sweet little illustrations of strippers on them."

"Won't she notice and get upset?"

"I'm hoping she's too dumb."

Sabrina laughed at the unexpected candor. "Is anyone?"

"You met her."

Sabrina nodded. "What if she isn't too dumb?"

"We'll say we thought it was cute for her drink, the Lex Island Iced Tea, which she always calls the LIIT. I swear she picked that cocktail to get a partnership with every kind of liquor. We'll pacify her."

"That's not what you're doing here?"

Rather than look horrified, Zoe laughed. "Show me your stripper glass. You've got a drink named after you from a posh London club not a college freshman pregame. That and a book with your family in it loaded with cool-ass Manhattan history."

"The magazine? The tiara?"

"What say we lose the magazine? I thought it was tacky anyway."

"The tiara?"

"I don't think we're going to win on the tiara. It's too much of the image. I know it's annoying. But it's only a prop."

Sabrina felt too tired to debate. She wanted to call someone and ask their opinion, but who would that be? She'd long ago lost touch with her Upper East Side friends and classmates; she never had any Hollywood friends; her team (the agent, the publicist, the manager) disappeared when they were snubbed from the wedding to demarcate the new season Sabrina *the former actress* was entering; and after the scandal broke her few remaining London girlfriends had distanced themselves from any and all contact with her. There was Budgie, but Sabrina already knew that she'd have some brutally honest observation like, "*Honey, you did marry an aristo-cat. You sort of elevated the odds of being fodder for cocktail parties.*"

"Alright. Let's lose the magazine."

"Perfect. See, we're working together." Zoe said kindly.

The Verroye households Budgie and Sabrina grew up in were built around *the old days.* The homes were not modern. No sleek, empty shelves with succulents and design books. They had elaborate curtain hangings, expensive rugs, uncomfortable couches, and chairs with beautiful lines. They stopped short of dressing formally for dinner every night—though they did always sit together, and none of them owned a T-shirt.

That being the case, Sabrina—and her skull—was conditioned to tugging, untangling, and the occasional burning. It was not unfamiliar to her to sit in a chair and have multiple people pulling at sections of her hair, to have a makeup artist pressing about too hard on her eyelids with their hundred-dollar brushes, and to have someone else cutting away cuticles and applying polish to her ever-brittle fingernails. There had even been times along the way where the dolling-up of Sabrina had been for a formal portrait sitting—like they were the Romanovs or something.

Sometimes there was a photographer or cameraman in the room, depending if anyone in the family had recently inked a deal—a book deal, magazine article, maybe a documentary. This was how Sabrina understood that the behind-the-scenes footage Aleksandr was getting was being filmed on the basis of the intense hope that there would be enough scandal to warrant the unpolished moments. Sabrina knew better than anyone how to put up with constant peripheral chaos.

When she had transitioned into her stint in the British aristocracy, life wasn't all that different. She had been resignedly confident in the fact that her life was now set by these ridged rules and boundaries, and that it would never change. In fact, many in her former circle would be appalled that she'd had the nerve to be weary.

For whatever reason, it struck her as the show's team began her makeup that she might be in some of the last days of this kind of life. After all she had gone from an estate in Europe to a bathroom in Manhattan. Granted, said bathroom was big enough that you could roller-skate in it, and in a penthouse that overlooked Central Park. Life after the scandal was a slippery slope, and she seemed to be in freshly waxed skis on the highest hill.

The Verroyes would always be rich. But *she* was disgraced, old news, and it was unclear how much her family would suffer for her embarrassment. They weren't that medieval, but what if their name, the Verroye name, started to connote all this ugliness? They would never hate her, never hold it over her head (on purpose). But any further bad press could ruin them in society.

Best she could do was remind the world she was human. Laugh at herself, own her mistakes, and be the relatable one. The comeback story for a generation. Anything besides go into hiding.

This show *had* to work.

The beautifiers around her, not her usual crew but a group hired by production to devise her *glam* interview look, kept talking about how gorgeous and perfect she was, as if she was not sitting there. They kept talking about her different "looks."

"Oh my god, girl, I'm still crying over her wedding dress. I die. I'm legit dying. I'm dead. All those sparkles. Were those crystals?"

"The dress was forty thousand Swarovski crystals, twenty thousand mother of pearl tear drops, and the train was thirty feet long. Sorry, am I right?" the other young woman asked Sabrina.

"That sounds right, I don't know exactly."

"It took like twenty-five seamstresses to make, and ten to get her into it that day. And your waist, like how is it so small? It blows my mind it's like Barbie."

That part was true. Nothing could have more completely proven to Sabrina how locked in she was about to feel. Countless clasps and sharp, rigid whalebones pressing against her own.

"What about that dress she wore when they went to that party in Cannes?"

"It was Givenchy, right? It had the same lines as the dress, oh my god, why am I blanking on the movie? Audrey Hepburn."

"Was it *Roman Holiday*?"

"Maybe it was. Was it?"

"The movie was *Sabrina*," said Sabrina, interrupting the conversation going on above and around her.

They both went silent.

"That makes sense, doesn't it?"

"We are legit beyond dumb."

"How did we miss that?"

This went on for the rest of the hour it took to finish her hair and makeup, and Sabrina tuned in and out. Zoe came in and said to hurry up, they needed to get Sabrina dressed.

Soon, she followed someone into her own dressing room and unlocked the jewelry case, where a couple of unimpressed twenty-two-year-olds picked out what she ought to wear. They selected two Harry Winston bracelets and a pair of forget-me-not two carat earrings Sabrina had honestly forgotten. When she said this, they looked like they hated her, and she understood it, but couldn't take it back.

They asked to see the looks she was *hoping* to wear for her interview, indicating the final decision would not be her own. Then they took the outfits into another room and got on FaceTime with some offsite producer who gave the go-ahead on an Oscar de la Renta with off-shoulder sleeves. Sabrina put it on, they photographed her, more FaceTime with the decision she needed a redder lip and was missing some "extra sparkle." They gave her one of her own diamond necklaces and moved in to pump up her lip color.

"It's too much, I can't wear these many diamonds, I look like a caricature," she managed to say when the makeup girl paused to reload her lip brush.

"Are you kidding? You look fabulous." Zoe said. The one filling in her lips nodded in agreement. "Every carat is a *fuck you* to that scumbag."

That made Sabrina smile, and yet she still wasn't sure. There was no time to wonder, however, as she was ushered to her seat up on her wooden pedestal, beside the little decorated side table. The magazine was gone. The tiara had stayed. There was a glass, one of her glasses, with sparkling water, a lime wedge, and a straw, positioned out of camera view beside one of the legs of the throne. Zoe saw her glance down at it and caught her eye to mouth "for you" punctuated with an awkward wink. She blinked a few times to adjust to the stadium-bright lighting as her hair was combed, sprayed, and sprayed a bit more.

There was further adjusting of the set behind her, she was mic'd up, rolled for lint, and there was a sound check with a realization that the bracelets made a subtle but interfering noise, so they'd have to be taped together. During this time, Zoe was in deep discussions with a new face, an attractive young man who was drinking coffee from a can and nodding in understanding at what Zoe was instructing.

Zoe, iPad in hand, made an announcement to no one in particular, as the makeup girl took a burst of close-up photos of Sabrina with her phone.

"We're ready. Let's get going. Quiet in the kitchen please." The last comment was directed at Sabrina's housekeeper who was working away, unsure if she should stop altogether. Then to Sabrina, "Relax and be your wonderful self. If you need to stop for a bathroom break that's all good."

Zoe backed herself out of the way of the camera onto a nearby waiting chair, rotated her iPad, clipped in her keyboard, and began to transcribe.

"Sabrina," the young man with the questions and the cold brew began, "I'm Drew and I'm going to be asking you all about yourself."

He said the word *all* in a way that implied Sabrina was one of those women who loved nothing more than to talk about herself. Sabrina realized how nervous she was and reached to her feet to take a sip of the bubbly lime water. She was surprised to taste the vodka Zoe had introduced to the mix but felt it somehow appropriate not to let on she hadn't anticipated this. She had to give the girl credit, she knew *The Sabrina* wasn't Sabrina's real drink, and the vodka, soda, lime ratio was spot on the way she liked it: three lime sections squeezed, one left in. Someone had done their research. She took a long sip, cleared her throat, waited for makeup *coming in* to touch up her lips, smiled her most pleasant smile, and answered, "Hello Drew."

"I need you to answer my questions in full sentences back to me because of course I'll be edited out of all this. If I ask, 'What's your favorite flavor ice cream,' don't answer 'Chocolate.' Instead, we need you to say, 'My favorite flavor of ice cream is chocolate because....' It'll be frustrating for a minute till you get the hang of it. I'm sure you'll be a pro."

She nodded in understanding, thinking about the last time she had chocolate gelato in Rome with her daughter. Aubrey had watched through the glass storefront for more than a half hour, mesmerized as the owners and their children made the gelato, laughing and interacting with each other, showing great affection. She was twelve at the time, and Sabrina knew what had captivated the girl was not the process of how the dessert was made but rather a family dynamic entirely foreign to her.

"Tell us a little bit about yourself?"

Her heart was in her throat. "Unfortunately, I am afraid ... people know who I am. Do I need to say it? Do I need to acknowledge what my husband—my ex-husband did? I already tried to talk about that, and we see how well that went."

"Everyone's got to do a little intro. It's a brief thing."

Sabrina gathered as much poise as she could and thought about how to describe herself. All her identity was wrapped in wealth and other people. She had spent her adult life either falling for or connected to someone or something she didn't want to be hers anymore.

"My name is Sabrina Verroye, and for several years, I was the Countess of Edingale. Before that, I was an actress."

"And what do you think about your acting career?" asked Drew. The crew stared at her.

"A lot of people felt very strongly about my acting career. I was not one of them."

Then he had her go through every single in and out that she could remember about her career, in particular the scandal surrounding *Lily of the Alley*. They were thirty minutes into it when he switched gears.

"Tell us a little about your cousin Budgie."

"My cousin Budgie is someone who puts her mind to something and accomplishes it. It was no surprise when she succeeded as she did."

"Were you two always close?"

"Close?" She stopped to think for a moment, picked up on a look on the interviewer's face, and recalled the full sentence instruction. "Budgie and I were always close. I was often somewhat jealous of her. She had a way with things that I didn't. She could make people like her. Even if they didn't want to." Sabrina laughed. "If we were to get in trouble, she was always able to talk her way out of it."

"Got it. Okay."

Sabrina was loosening up; Zoe swapped out the now-finished cocktail with a fresh one, without missing a beat. Sabrina sipped while makeup went in yet again to re-gloss the lips and pat down the hair. Then she shared her best Budgie stories. She explained how when they were kids, she was always in her cousin's shadow. They were both only children, and their mothers were sisters and best friends. Every family trip was the six of them. The moms, the dads, and *the girls*.

She recalled how, even as a kid, Budgie was funny. Loud, but knew when to shut it. She mimicked the grown-ups, using their expressions as her own little jokes.

"It was always like that," Sabrina mused. "She made friends at the pool on our family trips, roping kids of all ages into pretend games that, as we got older, became elaborate plays that she would write and direct, and only sometimes, star in."

"When Budgie went to school for theatre, and emerged with not only a degree, but a rolodex's worth of connections, no one was surprised. She was a success right away. She had Broadway's biggest show of the year and directed a few *longest-running* shows all by thirty years old. By forty, she had three Tony awards and her ego had still managed to remain only a little above the pull of gravity."

When Sabrina changed her major three times before following in Budgie's footsteps but on the acting side of things, her family expressed cautious support, encouraging a backup plan—maybe a double major in business?—and always insisting that it was not a lack of confidence in her but more a fear of how harsh that industry can be.

Sabrina had wanted to be angry at her parents, to resent them, but she couldn't be, in her heart of hearts. Because she knew what her parents didn't want to say, which was that Budgie had what it takes to win at showbusiness: *chutzpah, alligator skin, fortitude, oomph, a good head on her shoulders*, and every other expression for girls like her.

By the world's standards Sabrina was a success. She realized no one would feel sorry for her because she hadn't failed; she was simply a miserable product of many poor choices. Drew's next question jarred her out of her mental trip down memory lane.

"Moving on. What about your daughter?"

Sabrina cleared her throat, "My daughter is Aubrey. She's almost eighteen."

"And what would you like to tell us about Aubrey, Sabrina?"

"Aubrey is at school in England." Sabrina wasn't certain but suspected where this was headed and had now become very guarded; her posture changed from relaxed and chatty to erect and cool.

Sabrina never discussed Aubrey with anyone, rarely even with Budgie. She never referenced the ache she felt at leaving her. It wasn't a hurt—laser facials hurt, feet hurt in heels at the end of the night. Walking away from the best thing you'd done in your life *ached*. Relentlessly. Daily. There was no cocktail, no medication that could numb the throbbing. Sabrina was given time with Aubrey, but the visits were formal and arranged, which was almost worse than not seeing her at all. And Aubrey never tried to conceal the resentment she felt toward her mother. The years skidded by, opportunity for time together had vanished not ever to be recovered.

"Okay … what makes you angry?"

"I suppose … injustice?"

"Please answer in a complete sentence." He prompted her to start with, "Injustice makes me angry."

She took in a deep breath. "Injustice makes me angry. I can't stand seeing the wrong people get ahead, and the right people get stepped on."

"Perfect." He made a tap on his iPad and then asked, "what makes you upset or sad?"

"The same thing."

"Well, what else, then?"

Sabrina shrugged and was silent.

Drew looked to Zoe who caught the cue and leaned forward. "If I can say something about myself, I've had a lot of girlfriends turn out to be pretty awful. People I thought I knew, people I thought knew me, ended up stabbing me in the back. Anything like that ever happen to you?"

Sabrina breathed in. "Yes."

"Full sentences, don't forget," said Drew.

Sabrina hesitated. More silence.

Zoe stood up and looked at the rest of the crew. "Can we take a break here for a sec guys? Clear the room please."

7
Zoe

Despite what she had been taught in school about ethics and the production process, Zoe believed successful reality talent producers were grifters with an ability to read a mark and gain their trust to get what they needed from them. This was her chance, and she could feel it.

Drew and the rest of the crew looked at her like she had lost it. She could practically taste their hesitance. She gave them a small nod. *Trust me.*

Leaving all their equipment in place, they complied, shuffling out of the foyer and into Sabrina's enormous kitchen.

Fuck yes.

Also, *fuck*, now she needed to make something happen.

Zoe looked at Sabrina. *Yeah.* She could do this.

Once the door swung shut, she looked at the camera to make sure it was still running.

"Let me make sure this camera is..." she said, hoping Sabrina would assume that meant it was off. Judging by the deep breath and relaxing of her posture, that's what she thought. The whole "red light" thing was a myth, at least on these cameras. How else were you supposed to capture the best moments? But Zoe was after something more useful here, a good juicy sound bite she could cherry pick and frankenbite into another context in the edit.

"This apartment is crazy," said Zoe. "You should see where I live. It's, I would say, about the size of this hallway. I'm about one amenity away from a shoilet."

Sabrina smiled. "At least it's yours."

"Is this not yours?"

"This home is still, technically, my ex-husband's. Everything is. I don't own much of anything, it seems. I'm not sure how that happened."

"Now *that* part sounds like my life."

"You? You look too young to have been married."

Zoe gave a laugh. "I was, I guess that was part of the problem. Anyway, my crappy situation is nothing compared to what you've dealt with. I mean, what a nightmare."

"It has not been easy."

Sabrina shut down as Sabrina The Well Bred took over, diplomatic in her responses. Zoe was going to have to crack her open and get her to bleed the petty, bitchy blood she knew was in there. Everyone whose life takes a hairpin turn in the wrong direction feels ripped off at some level. Sabrina genuinely was. How was Zoe going to get her to blow? Getting her to blow a .8 might be the answer.

"Did you think Rob had this in him? My ex was like ... basically bipolar. I didn't know. Was it like that for you?"

"Do I think my husband was bipolar?"

Ding.

"I mean, what was wrong with the guy? He's a monster. I know he's got a title and all, but what he did to those women. You think he did it, right? That wasn't..."

Sabrina stiffened. "Wasn't what?"

Keep it together, don't push her away. "You saw what the media did. They painted you like an opportunist who took advantage of a real problem, like the rest of the women."

"None of those women were lying," said Sabrina, serious as a heart attack.

Ding. Ding.

"Did he ever do anything like that to you?"

Her hesitation said everything. But she said no more.

"I would rather not discuss my marriage and its dissolution. This is supposed to be my transition away from all of that."

"Oh, I totally get that. Can I be candid with you? We're going to spend a lot of time together. I want you to know I'm here for you, and I want you to feel like you know me too."

"Of course."

Deep breath. Spin the web.

"My husband that I talked about ... he raped my best friend. She was too afraid to tell me for a long time. And once she did, I believed her, and I felt terrible, then I realized that I had blocked out some of the times he had...." Zoe hesitated, lowered her head, and bit her tongue hard to make her eyes water. "He had been forceful with me. But he was my husband so I didn't see that he had done anything wrong until I knew about my friend."

"I'm sorry to hear that."

There was silence and then, "I've experienced something similar." When Zoe didn't prod, Sabrina went on, taking a big sip of her drink. "When I first met my husband, he took me to Ravello. He was drunk the entire time. He says he doesn't remember, but we were in the lobby of this hotel, and he ... he sort of..."

Come on. Come on.

"I think it was meant to be passion."

Zoe put on her best listening face. Not too eager. Trustworthy. Calm. Calming.

"Anyway. I don't want to talk about that."

Damn.

"Are you saying he hurt you?"

"He wasn't gentle. It sounded like the stories of some of the women who came forward, and I recognized small details..."

She faded away but said no more.

She wasn't going to keep going.

"Was there any part of you that found it strange to be caught in a scandal about sexual abuse after the movie that launched your career, and all the scandal surrounding that? Or, I guess, nearly launched your career."

Sabrina's nostrils flared. *Yessss.*

"Why do you ask that?"

"Because that was pretty controversial. Your age, and all. Weren't you close to the same age as your daughter Aubrey is now?"

Sabrina stood up, unclipped her microphone, and reached around to disconnect it from the transmitter pack. She stepped down off the riser.

Zoe jumped up. "You alright?"

Sabrina strode past her and into the next room, vanishing out onto one of the balconies that overlooked some of the coveted lushness of the city.

Zoe followed her. "What's going on?"

"Next time you want me to play along, ask."

"I don't know what you mean."

"Obviously, you have an angle. I was an actress and can take direction very well. All I want now is a little control, which is why I'm doing the show. My cousin convinced me it was a good next step for me. If you disagree, then I have no reason to continue."

The garden of possibility had decomposed, but now fresh ideas were sprouting again in Zoe's mind.

If Sabrina wanted control, let her have it.

Or like in any good hustle, let her think she's got it.

8
Dahlia

I'd only met the others a week earlier and was still trying to convince myself it would be believable to viewers that these women would be my friend group. Hoping the meet and greet had broken the ice, here we were ready to film the first *all-cast* event. Fiona had explained that shooting would be broken down into three parts: the interviews, the one on one's or partial cast outings, and the all-cast events—the big parties and dinners where all the film crews and all production were on deck.

Mick watched while I tightlined my eyeliner, and I tried to forget there were two strangers and a camera in the bathroom with me.

"You look good, babe." He kissed me on the top of the head, and I tried not to react to the fact that he had called me "babe." We made fun of the "babe" people. Knowing Mick, it was one of those jokes he was putting in for us.

I pretended to touch up the rest of my makeup, purely for show since I had hair and makeup done professionally before the crew arrived at our place. But when Zoe was setting up the scene, she asked if I could toss a Velcro roller in my hair and do some *finishing my makeup* actions.

She told me to be myself and act like they weren't there, which cracked me up as soon as she said it. It's not in my nature to ignore being filmed. How many seasons of *Big Brother* had Mick and I watched, and how many times had I punctuated it with exclamations like, "I could never forget all the cameras."

Most of the exclamations came after a housemate made some embarrassing biological emissions or said something sexist or otherwise worthy of a Twitter persecution.

And now I was being tested.

Zoe assured me that most of what they filmed at home would be edited together to illustrate the *getting ready*, the *journey to the party*, etc. Establishing shots.

She removed Mick from the bathroom and suggested I take out the roller, finger comb my hair, and do something with lip gloss. Filming was like one giant staging effort when you're showing and selling your home, which meant I didn't recognize my own bathroom or bedroom. No clutter, no wrinkles on the bedspread, no branded names unless they were already on board as sponsors, and all artwork had to be cleared for artist copyright or removed from the walls. We didn't have expensive pieces; for the most part it was all mass-produced commercial stuff, making it impossible to get in touch with the artist. I was thankful for the two paintings we had picked up at Art Basel last fall because they came with a legit artist to contact for release. I wondered for a second, as a PA walked away with my giant black and white Zebra lithograph from Z Gallerie, who Sabrina Verroye would have to contact for her art? Was someone trying to get Jeff Koons on the phone for approval?

For the next shot, I had to walk out of the bedroom to greet my adoring, loving, heart-eyed husband who would be waiting by the front door like Freddie Prinze Jr. in *She's All That*. The implication was that I had undergone some massive change. Nerd to It Girl. But instead, it was a Thursday, and the only difference was that I had more camera-worthy layers of makeup on than I ever would in "real life."

The truth? I was loving this. I hadn't been *social* in ages. After a lifetime of being in the company of others—even when I didn't *feel* like it—I had been alone for months. It was my own doing. When Mick got traded two years ago, we left our beachside community filled with our family, friends, and memories and moved to a fly-over state, to a town filled with chain restaurants and strip malls. I was parked in a cookie-cutter McMansion, in a neighborhood that tried desperately to mimic adulthood with talk of preschools and upcoming block parties. Mick was rarely home. I was alone in a soulless place, encouraged to spend time with the other player's wives, but I struggled with their established cliques and social functions, like all-wives sleepovers. They weren't my people, and I didn't want to put in the effort. I had always recharged by being alone, and making friends as an adult was tough for me.

When Mick was home, I wanted attention. He needed to master the new playbook or watch film of last week's game. We pitched a hundred ideas around and landed on moving me into a *pied-a-terre* in New York since both his agent and publicist were based there. Mick promised that he would make best efforts to see me more often, and we thought we could have fun with it, banking on the energy of the city. That's how I became my husband's sidepiece. Willingly. My idea even. *Sidepiece* might be strong. I don't know how to describe it except to say that we weren't who or how we used to be together or apart. Our spark was missing, and it's not that either of us lost interest, we couldn't … find the flint.

The news from this new place wasn't much better. I'd gotten on top of my classic literature list, my AFI watch list, my experiment-with-veganism era (*big* failure). I'd posted a hundred videos on Instagram trying to make the most of my lonely days, pretending life was all "woke up to this view," making sangria (for one, though the internet didn't know that), working out, mastering meal-prep, and watching and commenting on bad reality TV.

Now, life always being such a full-circle, I was becoming the reality TV.

And I was excited to feel glamorous, to pretend life was glitz, to spend time with Mick, who during this off-season had finally taken the time to be here with me.

I'm not an idiot. I knew to worry. I knew that soon, I'd have to ask *why the show, but not me*, was enough to bring him here.

But for this now, a little bit of fun, right?

I have always been a happy person. Lately, I'd been sick to death of myself, moping around, crying at a misinterpreted text, and waiting for *my man* to return.

I flung open the double doors to the bedroom, half-laughing the whole time, not only at the ridiculous direction we were being given, but at the idea that I would wear a brand-new designer dress, full hair, and makeup for drinks on a Thursday night. It was silly, but I also sort of wished life was like that. A wife getting glam, having her hair done, putting on a sexy dress, and heading off with her husband to an epic week-night party full of champagne and Instagram-worthy scenarios.

I got to the hall and kissed Mick. I always nit-picked people kissing on screen—either too prudish or too wet, prodding and tongued. I tried to give enough to make it camera worthy but didn't drag it out to look awkward.

"Great, *beautiful*, I'm not supposed to say this, but you guys are the most gorgeous couple here. You are both *amazing*."

"Thanks, Zoe," I said, with a laugh.

"Let's go on downstairs to the lobby and set up there, we'll radio you two down, then you can make your entrance to the limo. Sound good?"

"Sounds good," I said.

Mick gave a thumbs-up.

For the next not-even-five minutes, the crew collected their stuff and headed down in the elevator.

"Jeez, talk about professionals," said Mick.

"This is strange, right? Do you think all the shooting is going to feel this stilted?"

"I have no idea. It is odd, though," he looked behind him at the young, *young* looking guy left behind with a two-way radio transceiver, our escort downstairs.

Mick and I exchanged a look—the one that means *we're going to talk long into the night about this once we're alone.*

We got the go-ahead, and the boy, Mick, and I got into the elevator. The two of us caught eyes again and stifled our laughs. I squeezed his hand, and he squeezed mine back. For the first time in months I was having fun with him. We were acting like we remembered who we had been, and instead of dwelling on the fact that it *did* still exist somewhere between us but for whatever reason we couldn't access it, I decided to enjoy the night.

The doors opened, the escort hid in the corner, and we were faced with the big open mouths of hungry camera lenses. I lifted my chin and put on what I hoped was a satisfactory TV-face, and we walked hand in hand out of the elevator.

The SUV limo was waiting outside. Did anyone even think of limos as glamorous anymore? Now that anyone could order an Uber, who cared?

The boom and cameraman covered our limo entry, and once inside, we discovered there were two ride-alongs already positioned in the back (sound and camera) seated facing us on jump seats. Zoe hopped in the back as well, scrunched on the floor, between the two other crew, her headset resting on her shoulders and typing into her phone. The windows were getting foggy from all the passengers.

Once underway, the fish-eyed crew pointed their everything at us, and Zoe again instructed us to act natural. "Dahlia do you think you'll get anything done tonight?"

"I'm sorry?"

"It's a procedure party, right? Have you ever had any work done?"

"Um—"

Mick nudged me. "Own it, baby,"

I looked at him. What was he doing? "Um, I've had my lips done, and I've had Botox because whenever I concentrate, I look a bit mean. These little lines here?" I said, pointing between my eyebrows, "Well, it's one thing to have resting bitch face, but once you pass like fifty, you're likely to look like a mean old cow."

Zoe glanced at the cameraman before she asked, "So it's preventative?"

"Yes, it's preventative." Trying to sound funny I added, "I don't want to look like that woman on the news who tanned religiously and now looks like a shar pei!"

Before Mick could say anything, Zoe held up a finger, "would you mind—I'm sorry, I know it's annoying, but there was some sound interference from outside—can you repeat the end of that whole thing? Something like, *no, I don't want to look like her, she looks like a shar pei.*"

I repeated, "I don't want to look like her. She looks like a shar pei."

"Perfect."

Mick kissed me on the cheek, distracting me from answering another question.

The constant distance between us had made me both crazier for him and feel less like I even knew him.

He felt all new, but familiar too.

We pulled up to a brownstone on the Upper East Side—our place was near Gramercy, which seemed a little more down to earth, less sterilized to me. Once there, I expected to get out. Instead, Zoe hopped out, and the rest of us stayed trapped in the limo for nearly forty-five minutes while the entrances of the other ladies were filmed, filmed again, and filmed once more for good measure. We drove around the block, I counted, five times, which made me think maybe we could have been given a later call time, rather than being on a cyclical hell-loop of New York City traffic.

When our turn came, they checked our mics, which had been running the entire time we drove in circles.

The remaining crew got out of the car, asking us to *hold in place*, and entered into serious discussions with Zoe, who was making large hand gestures like a traffic cop. Alone in the car with the driver and Mick, I downed the last of my bubbly (they'd loaded the limo with Perrier-Jouet) and took a sec to reapply my lip gloss.

"Whose party is this again?" Mick asked.

"It's Budgie's. Budgie Verroye. She's the one who singlehandedly runs all of Broadway."

"She's the one you said you thought you liked, right?"

"Right. Well. I said I thought she seemed sort of fun. I think I like her, I'm taking everything with a grain of salt either way."

"Which one did you say you didn't like?"

"Did I say I didn't like someone? Oh, Lexi seemed a bit much." I screwed up my face and regretted my words.

Ever since I was a teenager, my mother told me to be careful what I put in writing and what I said to those likely *or unlikely* to repeat it. Anything I said out loud or wrote down better be something I'd be okay with the world hearing. I'd avoid getting in a lot of trouble that way.

This time the slip up was Mick's fault! He was over here talking like it was only us in the car. He should have known better; he'd done bits on *Mic'd Up* and *Locker Room Sound* and was used to being filmed, watched, and listened to, wearing a mic. We weren't even at the party yet, and my hot mic moment had me bashing my newly minted friends.

Eventually, we got out and were permitted to climb the steep steps of the townhouse.

The building was a big, old, dark iron-colored place, but through the mullioned window I saw lots of motion and heard piano music.

Inside everything was gorgeous. The entry was like a feature from *Architectural Digest*: a floor with geometric-shaped slabs of black and white marble, an abstract sculpture on a pedestal, and a regal iron and gold-railed curved stairway with a backdrop of expensive-looking fabric wallpaper depicting a grayscale countryside landscape. Two cushioned chairs flanking an ornate granite console, which held a small framed modern painting of a blue triangle, were taped off with masking tape x-es and had paper signs that read DO NOT SIT/DO NOT USE. The cameras followed as we were instructed to make our way to the cramped space of the antique packed living room where we were offered stuffed snow peas, tiny blinis dotted with caviar, and tuna tartare bites. There were silver trays crowded with champagne coupes. The waters were small glass bottles of Evian with paper straws.

This event was a far, far cry from the parties of pre-Mick. Female soccer players, like I used to be, make enough to get by but not much more than that. Some of my teammates in Europe even had second jobs. I spent my earnings on things that went away: circumstantial friends, cute boots, spa treatments. Because I believed I deserved whatever I wasted my money on, I had no savings. Mick's wealth was *not* part of the equation. It *was* however cool as hell to go from manage-to-get-by to using a crack-a-tooth heavy AMEX for whatever I wanted whenever I wanted it. I loved my husband, and I was grateful.

The staff at the party all looked the same, like they'd come from one village of servers. All brunettes, no male or female above five and a half feet. Did they all even have blue eyes?

Knowing, and yet not knowing, Budgie, I imagined this was no mistake. Possibly another casting opportunity.

Not long after our arrival, before I even had a chance to greet my co-stars, Budgie stood in front of the gentleman seated at the grand piano, had him play a flourish, and got everyone's attention, looking as confident facing a crowd as anyone could be.

"Hey folks, thanks for coming to the party! As most of you know—because you're not here if you didn't sign that NDA—this is also the cherry poppin' for the new show!"

She paused for applause, while fluffing the air upward so subtly one might not even notice that she was encouraging an ovation.

"Now, most of you have been around for the *stage* productions in my life, but this is something different. A show with real people, no scripts, and real feelings. While I adore the stage and the energy that bursts forth the second the lights are on and the curtain is peeled back, I am excited to see what this unrehearsed improvisio will bring!"

More clapping. I patted my fingertips together, always feeling a little ridiculous when participating in mandatory applause.

Then she held her glass in the air and told us to *drink up!*

"Alright, if you could follow me, Dahlia?" Zoe said, "I need the cast in the library. Mick, you too if you don't mind."

Zoe spoke into her radio mic, saying she had us.

In we went, to a room adjacent to the living room. Mariana, Lexi, and the others were also coming in and being assigned specific positions. The doors shut behind us as Zoe guided Mick and me to our mark. Before she left us, Zoe asked us not to speak to the other participants. I smiled *hello* to Sabrina as the camera and boom operators were setting up around us. Most of them were young men with scruffy beards who either looked bored or itching to leave. I had done plays in high school. They reminded me of the tech kids.

But beyond this new and unusual scene was something far more disturbing. A woman was led from behind a curtained area and helped onto what resembled a hospital bed. Draped all over it were fluffy, feathery, or cushy white pillows and blankets. She was in a plain white dress and seemed drugged out of her mind.

The whole setup would have looked right for a drag queen getting married from the ICU.

The door opened, and suddenly I felt extremely sober, and realized that my fingernails were close to cracking in Mick's forearm. I looked up at him to see that even he—who had seen femurs crack in half on the field—appeared to be freaked out.

Aleksandr walked in smiling a crocodile grin.

"Hands up," he said, "I am thrilled to have you all here, under the watchful eyes of our kind cameras, ready to reinvent the meaning of storytelling." Taking a leaf out of Budgie's book, he clapped so we would follow along. "Tonight, with our first group event, we begin filming in earnest."

The woman on the bed moved, her head lolling from left to right. Mick nudged me, and I looked back to Aleksandr.

"I want you to be yourselves. I want you to be honest. I want you to live without fear when the crew is here. We all want this to be something special, is that true?"

When no one responded, he leaned in.

What was this, a fifth-grade assembly?

Sabrina was staring at the glass of champagne in my hand and looked away when I caught her. She did not have a drink. She looked more collected than last time we met and far more bothered.

Lexi was standing at the end of the woman's bed, looking nonplussed. She wore a tight long braid that grazed her perky backside.

Nicole was there, too, though at first I hadn't noticed her. She had gotten her blonde fixed and seemed to have undergone a skin treatment. Her whole face looked glowier, if not also a bit swollen.

Mariana was pursing her lips and nodding with her eyes closed and clapping with her fingertips separated around the stem of her champagne glass, looking as devout as a virgin at a southern Baptist church.

We hadn't even interacted as new friends yet, and it was odd being thrown into a scene with them like we all did this all the time. Whatever *this* even was. Mick was the only husband in the room, and it struck me that maybe that was intentional. Maybe the others were outside with the other party guests?

"I invite you all to look on with truth." And Aleksandr stepped aside like a ringleader exposing the next act.

Budgie was standing beside the bed, and her makeup guy was finishing a touch-up of something with a floofy brush before he vanished into the curtained backdrop.

On Budgie's cue, a man in a pitch-black suit with a thin tie—bordering on a bolo—stepped forward.

"This miracle-worker here is Dr. Benjamin Sampson, he is the *best* in the country."

"What in the hell are we about to watch?" I asked in Mick's ear.

He made a slow, cringing face and shook his head to say he hadn't the slightest idea.

Sabrina was next to me now. I glanced at her, but she didn't look over.

"Let me introduce our lovely and willing volunteer, Jenna," said Budgie.

"Jenna is a beautiful woman who is looking for a refresh and rejuvenation without the downtime," said Dr. Ben.

The whole scene had the weird, creepy rehearsed meter of a well-practiced joke told so often it's no longer funny. I could only guess that our role was to scream and squeal like squeamish eighth grade girls, as dependable as the shrieks from the top of a rollercoaster that permeate the air of the theme park every five minutes.

"I will be performing a thread lift here today."

At this, Aleksandr grinned, looking at us like we were absolutely delicious, and he'd been starving for weeks.

The needle in the doctor's hand looked like the one I bought off Amazon this year when I tried to stuff and stitch my own Thanksgiving turkey. After it made contact with the woman's skin, I grabbed two glasses of champagne from a passing tray nearby and handed one to Sabrina.

She hesitated, but then accepted it with a grateful, reluctant look, and took a sip.

9
Sabrina

Her cousin Budgie had always loved drama, but this was … unexpected. Fiona had sold the evening to Sabrina as a wellness event intended to introduce and promote some new cosmetic creams. And Budgie had confirmed the party would be "something like that" when they had spoken earlier that day. She could have warned her of the spectacle she was staging.

Sabrina took the champagne Dahlia handed her, even though she knew she shouldn't. Budgie *had* warned her not to drink too much, in fact to drink nothing if possible although complete abstinence was impractical. Sabrina understood Budgie's words to be cautionary advice. "One glass is like a bottle," she'd said. "You'll find yourself saying things you hadn't anticipated. Be sure to keep control of yourself, rather than giving it away."

Budgie used to give her similar warnings about lending her credibility to flights of fancy when she was young and plastered all over the tabloids in skimpy, silky dresses, holding hands with whatever It Guy. Sabrina hadn't listened then, and look where it got her.

And yet she'd abstained only a few minutes into the first real scene.

Not that seeing a live surgery at a party in a townhouse uptown was *not* a reasonable reason to accept a drink.

She hazarded a glance at Dahlia's husband.

He leaned down to Dahlia's ear and said, loud enough that Sabrina could hear, "Do you remember the goat in *Jurassic Park* in the velociraptor cage? That's this."

Dahlia laughed and smacked him on the chest.

Were they in love? Did they fake it well? Were they merely best friends, or was there some, any romance there?

Something seemed off about him, and she could not get close to putting her finger on what that was.

Playing this game was something she did when she found herself around a couple after her own divorce. There were many interesting subtleties to untangle. In Sabrina's own marriage, Rob had changed almost completely from who he was when they first met. But the closer she examined his dynamics, the more it became apparent he was reacting to situations according to his personality. Change involves effort and time after a conscious decision. Rob was always a narcissist. Over the years he became lazy with his charm. The cycle of emotional high highs and low lows was both exhausting and addictive. He withheld attention and even sex, because that gave him the control and power. He needed to make Sabrina feel not good enough.

Sabrina knew she had been seen and questioned in her marriage to Robbie. What no one got right was that she had once loved him, deeply, rockingly, and that she discovered an altruism in herself after the accusations that she had never known she possessed. In the same way as thinking you might be alright in an emergency, not the best, then unexpectedly being able to disengage a bomb.

She hadn't read up on any of the ladies, but Sabrina had heard of sports star Mick Irvine. If she had to guess, neither he nor Dahlia had been born into the lavish lifestyle, but they were adapting well. His suit was custom-fit and looked beautiful on him. Her dress was tasteful and not blatantly revealing. Sabrina couldn't quite determine who designed it, but the plunging neckline, bare back, and clingy fabric suggested her wardrobe choices were driven by a need to remind her husband what a catch she was. Her evening bag was Chanel. The jewelry she wore was all Tiffany. A telltale sign of a girl who had been raised wishing she was Blair Waldorf and, once given enough money, went to the places she could connect with for more than vapidity.

Dahlia was also in heels that had been featured on celebrities and fashion influencers around social media. In her wealth, all Dahlia knew how to do was imitate.

When people say *new money*, that's what they mean. Sabrina came from money so old it was ancient-ghost money. The people she'd grown up with and socialized with of her own class were often horrible about people of new money.

She had a pang of desire to help guide Dahlia and then immediately felt a squashing of the urge. The squashing had become Sabrina's second nature.

If Sabrina could feel anything at all these days, she imagined she would be quite horrified, watching the flesh yield to the whim of the doctor and his sharp tools, and worse than that, for an audience.

The face bleeds more than anywhere else on the body, it seemed.

Sabrina had gotten pregnant with Aubrey almost as soon as Robbie and she met, which was an explanation for the quick wedding. The baby had arrived a few weeks early, with a low birth weight. Robbie had said how *good for us* that was, because they could get away with hiding the child for a little longer. Those were some of his first words as a father.

"What I'm doing is threading a dissolvable material down the side of Jenna's face," said the party doctor.

Aubrey had been a little tomboy who got nicks and scrapes multiple times a day—always unafraid to climb the highest point on the playground, with Sabrina running around trying to implore her to come down. She was often covered in bruises and had a particular skill for losing her balance. Tripping over a footstool at Robbie's parents' residence, Aubrey had sliced open her lower lip that bled profusely and would not clot. It took hours to stop. That was all Sabrina could think of watching Jenna, whose face was not bleeding. What had he injected her with that could stop the blood? Only a few droplets came off on the dabbing cotton he used.

The other cast members in the room were laughing and gasping. The presentation may as well have been a contortionist—hard to look at, hard to look away, but ultimately not harrowing.

"Now, see this knot here, I can tighten it in order to lift the skin as much as needed." The party doctor pulled and let go to show the slack versus taut.

Jenna smiled a drugged, somewhat frightening smile, and her eyes shut and then opened again like one of those baby dolls with moving eyelids.

The doctor landed on a level of tension. "Here we are, and I'd like to note there will be minimal bruising. The patient can return to work within a few days. And this thread will dissolve within a few weeks." He smiled, and Sabrina wondered if he'd had any work done. "I'll post some follow up pictures on my Instagram. It's Doctor Benny dot com," the doctor is spelled out, "you'll see how well she heals. It's remarkable."

Dahlia looked horrified and a little nauseous. Mariana appeared beside her with a camera. Dahlia didn't quite wipe away the disgusted look on her face before noticing that she was being filmed.

Mariana's reactions would have given William Shatner a run for his money. She was cringing and grimacing and holding her head, pretending not to look. The worst of it was over, and still she was acting like it was an adult circumcision.

"This is such a messed-up party, isn't it?" she asked in a stage whisper. "Budgie's theatrical I get it, but this is some dark stuff, don't you think?"

Dahlia laughed, seeming to scramble for an answer. "I've never had plastic surgery, so it seems gruesome. I guess."

"You haven't had anything done?" Mariana raised the part of her eyebrow that moved.

A tinge appeared in Dahlia's cheeks. "No, I said I've never had surgery. I mean yes, Botox and a little filler. But this is next level."

"Do you think Budgie's trying to prove something? Perhaps trying to show off how macabre she can be." Mariana said.

Another cameraman had appeared focusing his lens on Sabrina.

Mariana looked to her, as though waiting for Sabrina to deliver her line in the script.

"Budgie has always been grandiose in the best possible way. She likes to surprise people," Sabrina said.

"Jenna is all done, let's get a round of applause for her!" The small group obliged. The party doctor held up a hand and added, "not because it's a difficult procedure but because she made a choice for herself that she's going to feel great about!"

More applause and even a *woo!*

"I have some injectables, filler, and Botox here tonight as well. If anyone wants to get anything done, it's on your lovely host! So, step right up!"

Lexi, the little one with a big Instagram following, shot an arm into the air. "I've always wanted my lips done, but never had the guts to do it!"

"There's no way that's true," said Mariana, leaning in toward Dahlia again. "She looks like she got stung by the entire beehive already! This ought to be good."

As the doctor conferred with Lexi, Zoe began ushering the others out of the room, telling them to please not speak to each other.

Budgie found Sabrina's side and ignoring Zoe's instruction said, "That was something, wasn't it? The bee's knees of party tricks."

"Might have been a bit much, Budgie."

"Please, it's all in good fun!"

Sabrina stopped, pulling her aside from everyone who might be listening, forgetting she was mic'd and that *everyone* was listening on the headsets.

"They're going to paint you however they want, are you sure this is the sort of material you want to give them?"

"Bri, it's like I told you, it's an acting job. This is all for fun! I'll be the loudmouth with the controversial party, I can handle it. Now you need to remember what we talked about and perk up.

You're supposed to be reclaiming your narrative here. Or at least changing the arc. Remember ... the goal?"

Sabrina's arc had been more of a flash after the separation. It wasn't supposed to have happened this way. The offer after the first round of negotiations, to reside on the estate in Barnwell with Aubrey, Robbie, and his parents, was a prison sentence she could not contemplate. At fourteen, Aubrey had been angry and blamed Sabrina for everything that transpired. There were no allies in this war. Sabrina was making hasty decisions, and with the pressure from the tabloid press "Sabrina's Sabatoge", his parents' position "more than ever Aubrey needs structure and continuity, in a stable, secure and consistent home", the school's opinion, "Year 9 is a transitional year and any upheaval could prove damaging", and the protection officer's unnerving note-taking, she had thought going home to America was the only option to spare her own mental stability. She'd reset, hire the best law team, and go back for her daughter. That was four years ago. Fighting this battle was costly in many ways, and they owned the battlefield.

Sabrina bit the tip of her tongue and wondered if her rewrite was even possible.

10
Dahlia

They gathered us together, repeatedly reminding us not to interact, because they wanted everything on camera, and there were two PAs policing us to ensure this direction was followed. Zoe was talking to Nicole near a bar area across the room. From the gestures she was giving, she was telling her to do more. To speak up. Zoe smiled at her, and handed her a shot, taking one herself.

Nicole gasped at the power of the shot. As an avid reader of too many trashy news sources, she was no stranger to booze. I couldn't help but think that I could only see a seasoned drinker reacting in such a way to a shot of something like grain alcohol. Everclear. Ninety something percent. I'd had one—*one*—shot in college and it burned my esophagus to the point of gasping.

And that's what Nicole was doing now.

And Zoe was gone. Not gasping. Not reacting.

Had she done the old water shot trick? The Melted Snowman? Having a shot of water while the other drinker has a real alcoholic shot. Hadn't I read that Nicole stopped drinking? If she had, and if I was right that the shot was Everclear, she would be messed up, like downing three shots of vodka in a row. And judging by how thin she was, she didn't eat much.

"We're headed up to the fourth floor where Budgie's going to invite you all out onto the balcony. You can all talk among yourselves out there." Zoe nodded at us after these instructions, and then spoke into her earpiece.

We ascended the winding stairs, single file, past two levels to the top floor, which Budgie told us was her party room. The space had spectacular wood floors with an intricate design fanning around the built-in cocktail bar made of wood and thick turquoise stone. The area was already populated with a few of the party guests I recognized from earlier downstairs.

When given the go-ahead by Zoe, Budgie said with all the ease of a well-practiced actress, "Ladies, come join me outside on my terrace. It's a beautiful night in the city, let's go, hop to!"

Lexi said, "Oh my *god* yes!"

Mariana did a little dance, "Let's do it!"

Nicole looked wobbly on her feet and got pulled to the side once again by Zoe.

She was handed a drink and shook her head *yes* in understanding before heading out. Sabrina was at her cousin's side, playing her role well.

As I started outside, I looked behind me for Mick but saw he was detained indoors, being filmed while talking to a couple of girls and women half his height, desperate for his attention. I was used to this kind of fandom at social events.

Mick and me. Mick and Dahlia. Things had been hard lately, but how had I ever doubted that we were the same us. Even in this weird new environment, all we needed was to be around each other.

He held up his hand to show off his Super Bowl ring. I smiled thinking I'd tell him what a loser he was later.

Fiona saw my hesitation and whisked me along, "We're going to film with only the ladies to start. If I can have you with the others on the terrace?"

Outside the rooftop garden twinkled with tiny white lights. It was lushly decorated with several hibiscus and boxwood topiary trees positioned at intervals around the perimeter, with ivy cascading down their square planters. An exotic looking maple tree occupied the corner space, and at the other end there was a fountain in front of a mirror, guarded by two large stone lions. The floor was some sort of polished stone with an inlay in the center that suggested an outdoor dining table occupied the space but had been removed for tonight. There were high red brick walls that surrounded all sides and had arched cutouts filled with wrought iron. We could have been in Florence instead of a few blocks from Fifth avenue.

Once gathered and positioned in a circle (standing because there was no furniture), once the sound was cleared as acceptable, the fountain shut off because the noise interfered, we were permitted to chat.

I was feeling tipsy, and everyone was a little looser now. Nicole, after god-knows what shot she'd had, was glowing a little, and laughing louder. Poor thing. She might be one of the types who are only fun when she drinks.

"Everyone talk about the thread lift, say whatever comes to mind." Zoe instructed.

"Fine, I'll say it," said Mariana. "It's messed up you had that happen at your party. What do you think we are, *animals*? We don't want to see that!"

Budgie laughed before I could feel defensive on her behalf. "Please, who hasn't had work done here before? It's fascinating! Interesting to watch, a different perspective from above than under the knife, isn't it?"

"Are you implying that I've had work done?"

When I laughed, Mariana's nasty gaze landed on me. Embarrassed for my reaction, I covered my mouth. "I'm sorry. I thought you were joking."

That made it worse. That *definitely* made it worse.

"No offense!" I said. "It looks great, I'm not saying that, I-I mean, you have, right?"

"Wow," said Mariana.

"I get it," said Budgie, "you're fine with eating the chorizo, but you don't want to see how it's made, huh?"

"This is *incredibly* offensive. If I'd had anything done, I would *never* have trouble admitting it, but I haven't, so you're actually attacking me." Mariana insisted.

"I'm attacking you?" asked Budgie, amused.

Lexi was holding an ice pack to her swollen lips. "I don't see what's wrong with getting anything done anyway."

"Neither do I, Lexi, I would *own* it." Mariana said, then looked to me.

Pressured by the eye contact, I stammered, "I-I'm sorry, Mariana it seems, like, sort of obvious."

And it *did*! She had all the telltale signs of work done! Immovable forehead with lifted brows. Deer-in-headlights eyes. The stone-cut nose. Swollen cheekbones you don't see that often in the untouched. And her lips—well her lips were the worst part, the top lip stuck out like she'd been drawn by the Simpsons illustrators.

Not that I would say any of that. To Mick, maybe. Yes definitely. I always told him everything. At least I used to.

"You are unbelievable," said Mariana. "How dare you?"

When I played soccer, I was super-competitive, resilient, and unafraid—it was my game face. Any opponent who was too aggressive, tried to mouth off, play dirty, I was used to it; I had a persona for that. And that's where I found myself now.

"Look, I told you what *I* had done, it's not a big deal. I'm sorry if I'm mistaken." I laughed, involuntarily. "Lucky you, right?"

Without warning, Nicole dropped her glass on the stone surface. Attention redirected to her.

"Are you okay?" I asked.

"Oh yeah, sorry, I—yeah." She stumbled into one of the topiaries. Whoa. She was messed up.

"Oh my god, Dahlia, you're bleeding!" squealed Lexi, her *bs* all puffy through her swollen lips.

I looked down at my leg, and a piece seemed to have sliced me. "Oh, what do you know, I am bleeding."

Zoe asked off camera, "Dahlia are you okay?"

"Yeah, the glass cut me."

"Say it again?" she took off her headset, to hear me better.

"The glass cut me, I'm bleeding. It's not a big deal."

"Where?"

"My leg. It's my leg, it's fine."

"Do you need a medic?"

I *hated* being fussed over. "No, it's fine. It's a cut. It's fine. I cut my legs shaving worse. Truly. Could I grab a napkin?"

"A napkin?"

Okay, was I speaking in code? "For my leg? Which is bleeding?" Like I had perhaps mentioned? I laughed again, feeling like this was hilariously excessive as a reaction.

"How did that happen?" asked Mariana, as I dabbed at it with a beverage napkin.

"It's—Nicole's broken glass cut me, it's nothing. Carry on."

Nicole had already been handed another cocktail.

"Sorry," she said.

I laughed. Partially because it was Nicole Trace, of the-first-CD-I-ever-bought fame, apologizing to me, but also because when people make a whole big thing out of an accident, it's embarrassing.

"Mariana, are you still mad about what Dahlia said?" prompted Zoe.

"I'm furious, it's honestly offensive that you could look me in the face and accuse me of not being *honest* about something like that."

"Okay, fine," I shrugged. "I was wrong, what do you want me to say?"

"Who the hell even are you?" scathed Mariana.

"Dahlia. I'm the one who took flying shrapnel in the leg." I smiled at Nicole, hoping to indicate it was a joke, but she made a shocked face. "That was a joke, Nicole."

I shook my head. Until now, I had thought I was the Jim Halpert of the show, dealing with some insanity that everyone in a "normal" world might understand, but suddenly I was starting to feel like I was the one who was wrong.

"Sincerely, Mariana, I'm sorry if I hurt your feelings."

But I thought, *I've watched too much* "good reality TV" *to think they'll include my on-the-spot apology.*

Maybe experiment with honesty.

"This is ridiculous, I apologized for something I thought you would admit to, *not* that I give a crap whether or not you've had anything done. This is a mountain out of a molehill. Can we talk about something else and I'll vent to my husband about this later. You don't need to forgive me for something so stupid."

I took a deep breath. Dammit. This was the bad part of me. Of my wall. Of my guard-up persona. The sides of my vision blur, everything starts to feel surreal, and I get mad. Mick tells me it's my warrior athlete temper, and I tell him that's not a thing, then we laugh. But that was not going to happen here. All I felt was frustrated.

Frustration has always been my worst enemy. If I can't get a computer to work, I get *furious*. When I feel unheard, it's the same—I know I can't do anything about it, and I get unduly angry.

"You're going to go talk to your husband?" asked Mariana. "You mean the guy in there surrounded by women, ignoring you?"

And now I'm seeing red.

I opened my mouth, aware I couldn't say, *you know full well they told us to come out here and to leave the husband inside.* I took a deep breath. "He's always surrounded by women. He's Mick Irvine."

"What is that supposed to mean?" asked Lexi, still bleeding onto her ice pack.

"He was barely edged out last year for Sexiest Man Alive in *People* magazine. Yeah, women always want to talk to him. It's not a big deal."

Mariana and Lexi exchanged a judgey look.

"He's a gorgeous man, that's for sure," said Budgie, trying to help.

"There's something gross about a woman talking about how *every* woman wants her husband, you know?" Mariana directed her question to Sabrina.

Something plunged in me, thinking about Sabrina's past with Robbie and the accusations.

Sabrina breathed deeply through her nose and said, "What is your implication, Mariana?"

"You were married to a man every woman wanted. That was your position, right? That all those women he supposedly assaulted, you insisted they *all* wanted him *so* badly, right?"

"No, I did not. I did not say anything remotely like that, Mariana."

"Which is it, did he assault unwilling women, or was he a cheating husband with women obsessed to the point that they'd do anything?"

Sabrina's face went pale.

Lexi's eyes were wide as saucers now, and not simply from well-applied makeup.

"All I'm saying," continued Mariana. "Is that you went on the record saying how shocked you were that he assaulted *all* those women. Some people believed you knew about his antics the whole time and only feigned outrage once the press found out."

"That is a very ugly accusation." Sabrina said.

"My point is, Dahlia's over here saying how every woman wants her husband. Does it make you wonder what she's covering up for him or herself?"

Sabrina looked at me. I wondered if she was as lost as I felt, but she was more composed than me.

"I did *not* say everybody wants my husband, oh my god, I'm saying I'm not threatened because a few dumb girls want his attention! I'm his wife!"

"Whoa, those are Budgie's guests," said Lexi. "That's like, super rude."

"Oh my god." I had wanted to scream but exercised self-control such that it came out a whisper.

"I wouldn't blame him for trying to find someone who notices him," tossed in Nicole. The ice jingled as she downed the last of her drink.

"Dahlia loves her husband, and she feels comfortable with him talking to anyone, because she trusts him," said Sabrina.

I appreciated her saying it, but again, I doubted the edit would include someone coming to my defense here.

"Honey, as the founder and CEO of a sex toy line, I can guaran-god-damn-tee you that neither of them feel satisfied. When you've done it as long as I have, you can tell. It's like another sense. Looking at this one here, she looks as sexually frustrated as an ugly teenage boy. And that one in there?" she pointed at Mick. "He looks like the devil gave him the world's best dick, and god told him he couldn't use it."

"Are you freaking kidding me?" I said, blown away.

The glass door slid open behind us, and Mick came out onto the balcony looking confused. He was with one of the PAs. Someone had gone inside to get him, and I'd been too distracted to notice.

My relief to see him, someone always on my side, was eclipsed by my desire to leave him out of it. Things were good right now between us, but since we'd seen very little of each other, it felt precarious.

I hated feeling like that.

"Hey," I said, trying to shoot him a look that told him *if this becomes an ugly conversation, I'll explain later.*

He used to understand those looks, but now he gave a small shake of the head asking me *what?*

"How are your girlfriends inside, Mick?" asked Budgie in high spirits, trying to make a joke of a whole thing.

He smiled and put an arm around me. "You have a surprising number of football fans in there, Ms. Budgie."

"Oh, please, love, they're mostly theater people who adore any good show."

He brought me close and kissed me on the top of the head. "How are things out here?"

Mariana made a face, and Lexi copied her.

"We're good." I said before anyone else could answer.

"Word on the street is that you're a bit of a Casanova," said Nicole, leaning forward with a low-rent laugh I would picture from a coked-out hooker trying to pick someone up off the strip in Vegas.

"Am I?" he asked, looking at me.

I shook my head, at a loss.

When silence ensued, they wrapped, and we were told we could leave. They directed Mick and me to leave first. We took the elevator down to the main floor where we were unmic'd and dismissed for the night. I didn't say anything and avoided eye contact with Mick to prevent engaging him. Once in the car alone with the driver, he was the first to speak.

"That was intense." he said

"That's one word for it. You should have seen Mariana come for me when we were outside. It was full on."

He looked surprised. "I was talking about the surgery. I'm sure the others were being dramatic for the cameras, Dahl. You know, trying to be memorable."

His statement was intended to be comforting.

"No. No, Mick that's not what they were doing. They directed their confrontation toward me. The easy target. I'm the only one here who isn't someone in her own right. Budgie, Sabrina, even Lexi. They're all somebodies and I'm Dahlia, *wife* of somebody. I guess I'm the nobody outsider they're going to go after."

He had no response.

"And I don't like being the first to go," I continued. "That's not a good thing. Do you think they kept filming after we left?"

He shrugged, "You know I don't know, right?"

He didn't seem as concerned as I was with the evening, and his indifference calmed me down. I undid my seatbelt and slid over to him, leaning in, and burying my face in his shoulder. He pulled me close and rubbed my back.

"This was supposed to be fun and it's not," I said in my funny voice.
He didn't laugh. He didn't answer. I could tell he was tired.

"You think I'm reading too much into this?" I asked.

He sighed and nodded, hugging me tighter.

I *had* been overthinking lately, maybe the night wasn't all about
me. I mean, when this aired, Budgie would get roasted for hosting
such a gross party. And Lexi got her lips done, *on camera in someone's
den*? There *was* a lot else going on. But as the car headed South on
Park Avenue past Grand Central, I couldn't help but worry that
I was the team player who found themselves without a team.

11

Zoe

This was gold. This was reality TV gold, thought Zoe.

Mariana was a godsend. Who knew she was such a good shit-stirrer? She wasn't meant to be the zero-fucks lead; she was meant to be brassy and crass, the butt of the joke. She got all the money for her business from her husband, who did something boring in publishing and refused to be fully part of the show. This was not the first business she had tried.

Nicole was sloppy, but necessary. She could be managed, and she seemed keen to do Zoe's bidding. She executed the glass drop as directed, and her interactions were the right amount of subtle—crucial for the edit.

Sabrina needed to remove the giant pickle from her ass. Fiona could work on that. Maybe have Budgie talk to her as well. Budgie was performing as expected, self-involved and nonpartisan—so far. And Lexi made for a great sidekick to Mariana. That was a surprising alliance. They'd have to film something with Lexi and Mariana rehashing the night and hating on Dahlia. Zoe made a note on her iPad to get that beat.

When they started planning the show, and once they realized they had a shot at Mick Irvine's wife, Zoe had done some deep research. Zoe was pretty sure she could have been a detective or something. Dahlia was a normal girl. She was plucked from nothingness by a hot somebody, and Dahlia didn't keep up that well. She had her comments turned off on her Insta posts and stories, but she still posted. Read—she wanted attention, but she couldn't deal with the negatives. It made sense. Normal people didn't have to face constant backlash for merely existing, but that's what happens the second you're in the spotlight.

And worse than that, Zoe had gleaned from the psych evaluation that Dahlia was lonely as *hell*. That loneliness had probably gone on long before she met the big football star. Dahlia must have thought marrying him would solve all her problems but had too much hope to foresee that the lifestyle might make everything worse.

Zoe's hot pursuit of Dahlia took place shortly after she bumped into Mick Irvine's publicist, Regan Whitmore, when grabbing a salad at Sweet Green on Bleeker in the Village, months before production. She recognized Regan from a bunch of first-year media courses they'd taken together at NYU, and in turn Regan did a bad job recalling Zoe from eight years ago. But the "so what are you up to these days" that followed led to Regan's suggestion they meet for drinks "and a casting sesh." Because, as Regan, the young woman who must have had contacts that read like a seating chart for the ESPY's had put it, "I could come up with loads of player's wives who would kill to be on a show like that."

Out of all the missus, Zoe wanted Dahlia for the show. It started with her look. Dahlia was striking. She was unusual looking—not like weird, or worked on, but not ordinary. She was way more than simply a pretty girl. Pretty girls sometimes got a modicum of empathy from the outset. Some people look at a pretty girl and think she looks sweet, or think, *aw, I bet people don't give her a fair chance.*

But girls like Dahlia, the ones with all the smarts, wit, and dynamics of a homely girl who *also* have a great body and a beautiful face? No, they never stand a chance. People hate them. How does a girl get to be *cool, fun,* and *also* hot?

In another life, Zoe thought she might be friends with someone like Dahlia. Among the women, she seemed like she might be the most normal.

Pity. That was the easiest kind.

12
Dahlia

I woke up at eight, to the sunlight that I loved so much that came through the windows in the bedroom at the New York place. Our other house in the gated community of America's heartland was surrounded by big, tall, hideous trees void of any natural light. I would never have agreed to a dark and gloomy house like that if I'd been involved in choosing, but when we—when Mick—made the purchase, I was told it was a place to land. Soon after I found out we were going to have to live there. Build a life there. Exist there.

I could sleep until the early afternoon in that house, nothing to do, no one to see. But here in the city, I always woke up to the sun and delighted in going to the big bright, open kitchen where I could slice open a grapefruit, make a coffee, and use all my little *things* to have a morning ritual. A glass beaker for the steamed milk, a cute sugar bowl, pretty silverware, a view to look out on, music on the speakers. I was pretending, a little, that life was like that, every time.

But since I was going through the motions, didn't that make it real?

This morning, the day after the party at Budgie's, I was in a good mood—hangover avoided with Evian and a few pricey preventative vitamins. Plus, Mick was home. When I knew he was home, I always knew I'd find him out in the dining room, lit by that thirsty pale morning sunshine where he'd be reading on his iPad, already a few hours past his early morning workout. He always waited to shower—he said in case we had sex. Something about him in the morning, hot and sometimes still a trace of his good-smelling sweat, meant that he was often right to wait.

To my disappointing surprise, he was not alone when I came out. He was fully dressed and showered and his publicist, Regan, was over.

Regan, by the way, is super attractive with the kind of good looks that I hate the most. She can make a hideous face, and instead of looking like Kristen Wiig doing a character, like I do, she still looks cute. She's smart, she's funny, she comes from money, and she can do more for my husband than I can in the ways I sometimes fear matter to him more than anything. She has no boyfriend and is in no hurry. We talked once at the horse races, when she came along in a big group with us, and she said that she didn't expect to get married, but that if she did one day, then sure. Raspy voice. Unbothered. She was dripping with real cool. She didn't have an ounce of desperation. Not a degree of need.

Whatever they were discussing they stopped talking when I walked in the kitchen.

"Everything okay?" I asked.

"Hey you, good morning. I wanted to let you sleep," Mick said. "We're sorting out my schedule and stuff while I'm here. I'm going to have to fly back tomorrow for a few days." He came over to me, kissing me briefly and putting a hand on my waist.

"Oh, okay. Sure." I nodded. "Hey Regan."

As I stood there in my pajamas, I realized there would be no further analysis of last night's party. We'd barely had a chance to talk in the car, and Mick had fallen asleep fast once we got home. Not that I wasn't accustomed to living in the company of Mick's business team. There was always a manager, an agent, a stylist, a lawyer, a watch dealer, a shoe rep, a photographer, a nutritionist, a travel agent around, in the car with us, on the plane with us, in our home; sharing my space and Mick's attention were part of the deal, what I signed up for. But he had, at one time, been sweet at carving out *us* time, and I was hoping to have a chance to dissect the party in great detail with him today.

"Dahlia, I love that pj set," Regan enthused. "They look super luxe. So, *so* good on you."

"Thanks," I answered. "They were a freebie from that photo shoot Mick and I did last year. I think they retail for something crazy like around seven hundred dollars, but I'm sure they'd gift you a pair if you asked. I mean you set the whole thing up."

"Oh I'm good. I sleep in the nude," she deadpanned. "I read somewhere that sleeping naked helps you fall asleep fast and reduces stress."

Not knowing what to say or how to respond, Mick and I both nodded, and he kissed me again on the cheek.

"Mick, we have to go." Regan stood up, "We're already running late for the meeting."

"What meeting?" I asked.

"The new accountant," Mick explained, now competing with the low hum of our Nespresso. Caffeine was going to be critical today. "Apparently, I missed some signatures, and I said we'd go there rather than ask him to come over here."

"After which he has a podcast at the Sirius studios midtown, a promo for the Boys and Girls Club and if we can squeeze it in, an interview for *Men's Health*."

"Haven't been around the city in a while you know. You're right, I do miss the energy. What time's your thing today?" he said as he downed the last of his juice.

"Two."

"Let me know when you're wrapping up. I have a full day but maybe we can grab a bite later or something." He hugged me and I let out a groan.

"You'll be great. You're Dahlia. You'll be awe-some."

Nothing was wrong. We were out of synch. I didn't need to worry.

He grabbed an apple out of the silver bowl on the counter as Regan gathered up her things and after he kissed me again, longer and on the lips this time, they boarded the elevator together and left.

Standing alone in our apartment, I felt a little like a psycho girlfriend. Okay, things were a little different right now. But he was still being cute and sweet; he was still him. We made plans for later. He kissed me.

And why was I upset? Because I didn't get a chance to complain more about the night before? We'd talk at dinner.

God, why was I dismantling him like he was a new boyfriend and I wasn't sure he was into me? He was my husband. We'd made vows. We'd made promises. And I had no reason to think he'd broken any of them.

The truth was that I was nervous about today. We were filming Mariana and me meeting up for a drink at a rooftop wine bar. I was not one to doubt myself, but last night I'd fallen far away from where I ever thought I'd be once being filmed. I always assumed I'd be myself, that I'd be comfortable, funny, charming, all the things I can pull out even at the hardest times.

Uncertain how on earth I was supposed to come off as likable today, I determined I would have to perform better.

There was no space for my own resentments—like how Mariana had been the *actual* jerk. Worse to Sabrina than to me. And yet she'd kept her cool.

Two and a half hours after my shower, I was ready. Perhaps doing my own glam was a bad idea; the beauty gods were punishing me with a bad hair *and* face day which was unfair; they're not supposed to align at the same time.

When fishing in my makeup drawer, I'd had a terrifying moment where I thought I'd chipped my nail polish. When I gasped and looked at my hand in fear and then felt enormous relief, I wondered how much worse this was all going to get. I never cared about a chipped nail. I never took that long to get ready to go out.

I was more of a concealer, mascara and lip gloss kind of girl. Not like this version of myself, for the second day in a row made up like it was my wedding.

***

The bar was almost empty downstairs, and the rooftop upstairs had a few people who looked conscious of the cameras.

Production had me arrive first, and they served me an extra full glass of wine. I tried to sip some to bring the level down to normal, so I didn't look like a total lush.

After half an hour, once my rosé may as well have been microwaved, Mariana walked up in a bright yellow jumpsuit and big silver earrings, bright pink pumps, with a large white wicker tote, and white sunglasses with pink lenses.

I was *very* proud of myself for managing not to say, *holy*—

The thing is, if she was my *actual* friend, I would have teased her for being that bold with her style and would have meant I was impressed. But with her, I was going to have to act like this was normal. I was in an Isabel Marant dress, Stuart Weitzman sandals, Ray-Bans I'd had since college, and carrying my Saint Laurent shoulder bag. Loud as her outfit was, I felt like I was dressed as a before picture.

Usually, I loved this outfit. Felt like myself in it, confident, even.

She gave me a big smile and showed a grand wingspan as the beginning of an unexpected hug. She kissed me on both cheeks, then said how *cute* I looked.

"Thank you, I love this," I said. "You're—" She's what? Like a bird of paradise? "Stunning! So summery."

"You're sweet, you know I got this straight off the Mugler runway in Paris a few months ago, this was my first chance to wear it."

"Ah, well, I'm honored."

"After this I'm going to a friend's bridal shower."

She turned to order, and I took a deep breath in. I get it, *you didn't dress up for me.*

"I'll have a Pellegrino, with a lime? Thank you."

"No wine for you?"

"Oh, no," she shook her head like she never touched the stuff. She was good.

She was really good.

A breeze blew and I smoothed my hair down before continuing. "I wanted to apologize for anything I said last night."

"Please, honey, don't worry. We've all been there. You had a few too many, no big deal! No hard feelings."

"I didn't have a few too many, it's more like I came off wrong. I joke around a lot. I'm not a judgmental person."

"Okay, now when you say that, I feel like you're still trying to say the same thing except," she laughed and held a hand up to the sky, "under the sun, instead of the moon!"

"No, I'm not." I respond, with ungrittd teeth. "I was wrong, I shouldn't have said anything. I'm sorry if what I said hurt your feelings."

"You know," she said as she shook her head, paused, taking her time, then spaced out her words as though they were brilliantly thoughtful, "there's something insincere about apologizing to someone *if it hurt their feelings*. You're apologizing for *me* that I allowed that to happen to myself."

She looked at me like I didn't understand basic addition.

I took a sip of wine, trying to cool the magma that was already threatening to boil over. "I actually agree with that point of view, and that's not—"

"Oh, thank you so much," she said, taking her water.

"That's not what I'm doing."

"Look, I don't know what your issue is with me, Dahlia, but I promise you, I want to be your friend. It's dead and buried. I've moved on if that's what you need to hear." She gave a shrug and wrapped her swollen lips around her straw before setting her glass down.

"Mariana, I want things to be good between us."

Ooh, that took everything for me to say.

"Understood, truly, I don't know why you're this stressed."

What a saint.

"Okay, then, we're good?"

"We're good. Like I said, you had a little too much to drink. Happens to the best of us." She gestured at my wine.

I smiled the smile I only muster when I consider homicide. "Mariana, you need to stop implying that I was intoxicated, and that alcohol was the problem."

"You're right," she said, with a sweet smile back. "Maybe that's who you are." She shrugged again.

"It's not who I am."

"So you admit it was completely out of line? I'm confused. Are you contending that it was intentional, and you were sober and rude, or ... what?"

She squinted her eyes and cocked her head at me.

I wanted to point out that I hadn't *even* been the one to initially make the outlandish and true accusation, Budgie did. But I had been raised never to bring other people into my own disputes.

"I'm saying I misspoke."

She made a puzzled face. "Alright, Dahlia. Apology accepted." She scrunched her sculpted nose and squeezed my leg a little too hard. "You're forgiven."

"I—"

"Oh, and you know what, I brought you a little something."

She pulled a bright red and white polka dot package out of her bag. The box had a giant black bow.

I looked at the gift like it might be a bomb, and then looked to her.

"It won't bite. But you might!"

She laughed.

"You want me to open this ... now?"

"Sure, please, yes!"

She took another big sip of her water, and I cautiously pulled on the ribbon.

Inside the box, and beneath a wad of tissue was an assortment of … things. I thought I was looking at hand lotion, but I read the label on the tube—*vegan personal lube.* There was also a purple vibrator that looked like a cactus, a large green silicone ring, and two additional velvet pouches. Not wanting to give camera time nor risk my reaction to the other items, I stopped there.

I knew my expression was a grimace, not a smile, as I looked at her and said, "Hey, what is all this?"

"It's my company! Come Get Some! We're vegan and sustainable and have options for everyone."

"Um." A moment passed. "Nope, I don't have words."

"Oh sweetie, don't tell me you're a prude. You're too young to be a prude!"

"It's not that, it's … why are you giving me this?" I wanted to add "since you don't *know me?*"

"Like I said, you and your man seemed like maybe you could use a little *sparking up.* So there you go!"

"That's such a weird thing to say or do. My husband and I are *great.*"

"I'm sure you are, sure, sure." She laughed to herself. "But everyone needs a little fun to mix things up in the bedroom. Trust me if that doesn't do the trick, we've got plenty more that will. We've got outfits, jiggle balls, bondage gear, everything! Whatever you fancy!"

I was not going to come off as likeable if I didn't loosen up a little.

"Well, hey. I'm excited to try out your … wares, Mariana."

"Mmhm! Anytime, love. And no hard feelings about last night, you're *fine.*" And she winked her ridiculous, long fake eyelash at me.

I know I'm fine. I'm going to kill her, but I'm *fine.*

"Anyway, I've got to scoot, but it was lovely meeting up. You drink your wine, and I'll see you soon, okay?"

She stood up, gave me another hug and double kiss, then waved goodbye and left like a self-righteous banana on too-high heels.

Once she left the rooftop, and going off an instinct and a small whiff I thought I might have gotten, I picked up her glass and sniffed the contents before taking a sip.

"Oh my god," I said. "There's tequila in this!"

But no one reacted, no one cared. Zoe had disappeared down the stairs after her, and the cameraman was fiddling with his gear. There was no one to commiserate with.

I had a nauseating feeling that my husband was going to wind up blowing me off tonight, and I'd have nowhere to take all this infuriation.

Going forward, I'd say as little as possible. Engage as little as they would let me and avoid any potential future misunderstandings.

But I had been a girl too long and knew myself too well to think that was ever going to happen.

13

Zoe

Zoe reappeared at the top of the patio stairs, "Alright, thank you, Dahlia, good job. Seriously, that was amazing."

"Was it, though?" she said, taking another sip of her wine.

"Oh, yeah. She looks like *such* a bitch. Are you holding up okay? This is wild."

"She is, right?"

"And that *gift*? So weird."

"Okay, then I'm not crazy."

There was a desperation in Dahlia's tone that Zoe recognized. She looked at her for a moment, taking her in.

On a transactional level, Zoe knew how to interact with Dahlia. The EQ assessment had revealed a woman with a high emotional intelligence who was seeking validation and approval. Dahlia had transitioned from performing for her soccer team to performing for her husband within their marriage. In both instances she was aiming to work for the greater good without deliberately looking to benefit herself. And now, in exchange for recognition, Dahlia was going to serve Zoe's needs. Some might have labeled Zoe's intentions "calculating and self-serving," but she didn't see herself as the least bit manipulative; rather, she felt she ought to be respected for what she considered self-awareness.

Zoe had dark, floppy hair and dark eyes, and despite the experimentation in high school, going chocolate brown or getting purple highlights or trying bronde didn't make her look anything but fake. She had bad skin with dark splotches, and makeup seemed to sit on top of her imperfections like a silk cloth laid over a pile of Lego. She wasn't overweight, nor too thin; her figure was boring. Her skinny legs lay flush against each other like a cartoon drawing. Her boobs were non-existent, but she couldn't rock the waifish, flapper look.

Jeans were always too tight in the wrong places—often the crotch and beneath the hip—and too loose in the other places—her butt. No, she wasn't a monster. But she was neither a classic delicate beauty nor an exotic. She had a pudgy nose that she self-described as a Play-Doh nose. She had full eyebrows that, no matter the waxer, could not be formed into an attractive shape. Her lips were thin, chapped, and pale. Lipstick looked stupid.

The good news was that she had learned early that no amount of work or expensive grooming could make a difference. Halfway through her teen years, she'd accepted that attractiveness wasn't in the cards for her. This enlightenment had freed her.

She never had to yearn for the right clothes to make her look good. She could wear whatever she wanted, she could do whatever she wanted, and the resignation wouldn't matter; no one would see her differently.

There was no makeover that could change the poorly built person that she was. She believed she was an unattractive girl. And by learning who she was in time, she had gained as much freedom as the pretty girl who never had to worry about makeup or no makeup, sweats, or a form-hugging dress. She could do whatever she wanted.

The problem was she wasn't a great learner, wasn't an athlete. She got meager grades. She was the kind of kid diagnosed over and over with different disorders, ADD, ADHD, red-dye allergy, even bi-polar diagnosis from one doctor. Medicine only made her worse, deader inside.

One therapist tried to convince her that she was depressed. But that wasn't accurate. Could she not be indifferent instead of obnoxiously joyful and cheery all the time?

Her parents must have been the young couple who snuggled together under the stars talking about how beautiful their kids would be. But they had stopped at one, and that one had never had her swan moment, and was not a person either of them could understand.

The one thing Zoe had in common with her parents was movies. They could talk for hours about them, and once they'd all found out they had this in common, her parents had moved mountains to get her into NYU for film.

Sometimes she felt bad for them when she remembered the enthusiasm with which they'd dropped her off in Manhattan that first weekend of freshman year. She'd sent back a box of things she didn't want when they left, including the framed picture of the three of them.

For sure her parents had felt hurt, injured that she hadn't wanted the photo. Zoe had no desire to display a picture she was in and thought she was being pragmatic.

Dahlia was easy for Zoe to understand because she was unlike her. She could look at her objectively. Dahlia needed a friend. Zoe was no friend, but she saw the need and she could use that.

Zoe didn't think that Dahlia even had much of a pal in her husband. Unfazed by any beauty in the man, Zoe saw him for what she believed he was: an athlete with an expiration date on everything good in his life and no control over the loss of any of the cachet. If Zoe was right, Dahlia was the only part of his life he could control, and she'd had a feeling she could guess what he'd do with that control.

"You are not crazy. She's awful, and what was that outfit?" Zoe asked.

"Oh, I mean … if you can rock … bright yellow, then go right ahead I guess."

Zoe shrugged. "Or if you can't."

"Wait, did you see there was booze in her water? I mean…" Dahlia grimaced.

"She is a piece of work. Anyway, you did great. Already I'd say you are the lifeblood of this show. Do you hear that a lot?"

"Hear what?"

"I bet you're sort of the, like, beating heart of everything in your life. Like when you used to play, I bet you were the MVP more than once, right?

Dahlia cocked her head, "Once or twice."

"And do you feel like if you don't keep things fun and going for your friends, that the friendships will," Zoe gestured with her hand, "vanish?"

Dahlia sipped her wine.

"Ever feel like that with Mick?" Zoe pressed.

Dahlia's eyes snapped to hers. "Mick and I are ... no, we're totally equals."

Zoe paused, briefly made a puzzled face, then patted her on the back, and gave her a hug with a tight squeeze at the end. "Ugh, I'm glad you're here. Finish your wine, I've got to do some wrap-up stuff. Oh, and one last thing. You have tomorrow free. We're shooting a dinner at Mariana's friend's Greek restaurant, but you don't have to go to that."

"Wait. I don't have to go?"

Good. She was still hungry.

"I thought you'd be ecstatic not to have to go!"

"Well, sure, but why not?"

"Mariana is hosting and being a nightmare. Besides you sort of got jumped on the other day. You being excluded like this will win you loads of support from the viewers and solidify her bitchdom. If you feel you really *need* to be there, we can brainstorm something."

That would work too. They *could* have her *unexpectedly* show up...

"No, no, it's—I don't want to go if I'm not inv—if I'm not supposed to. I'm fine with that."

"Cool. Okay, I'll see you soon. Great job, again!"

She walked away, and Dahlia seemed to consider if she wanted to finish the rosé or not; she gathered herself, left a generous tip with the bartender, and disappeared with a wave.

As soon as Dahlia was gone, Zoe went to Paul, who was working today's main camera.

"Hey, you got her taking a sip of Mariana's drink after she left, right?"

"Got it."

Zoe laughed. "Awesome. Great. Don't forget—the scene isn't over until they're gone. Great job. Perfect."

She shot Aleksandr a text and told him everything had gone even better than expected.

There was no way Aleksandr didn't take her with him when he was done with this project. No way. She was killing it. He'd have to be able to see that. He'd have to. And if he didn't yet, she'd ensure that he did.

They'd only begun.

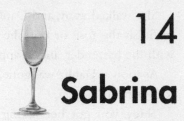

14

Sabrina

Sabrina hung up the phone. If not for the constant encouragement from Budgie, she would have ditched this bad idea already. If she even could with that ridiculous contract in place.

The next "scene" Sabrina had to film was a visit with Lexi at her house.

Something about the setup rang wrong to her. Perhaps because Sabrina had the penthouse above Central Park, and she could imagine a phone-obsessed, Kardashian knock-off would live in a tiny little upstart apartment and a one-on-one would be awkward. What did she have to talk about to a girl in her mid-twenties?

Nevertheless, and with Budgie's reassurance, she got in the black car and went. She was surprised to find that they were headed to the Financial District. Not where she would have expected.

They pulled up at an unassuming grey door in a red brick building. Sabrina knew well enough to know that looks could be deceiving across the spectrum in the city. On the one hand, someone with a fair amount of money could pull up to a glamorous façade and find themselves in an out-of-budget shoebox with a toilet in the kitchen. On the other hand, one could pull up to an old aluminum door and climb a flight and wind up in an industrial, architectural dream worthy of a college course.

The first thing Serena noticed was the film crew waiting by the door. Milo waved to the driver, approached the car, and popped into the backseat with her and the sound guy who helped her on with her mic pack as Milo spoke.

"We'd like to keep the scenes running as smooth and natural as possible. You've come to Lexi's place to get to know each other better and have some 'girl talk'." Sabrina winced mentally at that expression.

"We might have to stop and start you a few times for the entrances, but try to keep it as fresh as you can."

He left the car and disappeared inside the building. The driver got out and opened her door. The cameramen followed her as she approached the double doors. Sabrina hurried inside, smiling, trying to look as pleasant and natural as she could.

They passed the doorman and took the elevator up to the fifth level. The whole affair was a tight, overpopulated mess, with this ridiculous group of four of them (two cameramen and a boom operator) reaching Lexi's floor where the elevator door opened on Lexi, another camera, and a blessedly large space.

Sabrina stepped out of the elevator and walked toward Lexi, giving her a hug hello.

"Lexi, it's beautiful," said Sabrina, meaning it, and trying not to sound surprised.

It was a masterpiece of engineering, structure, and materials. All glass, concrete, metal, and marble. The place was black, white, and grey. No pop of color. She was trying not to be regressive, but it seemed to lack a woman's touch. Nothing sweet, nothing cute, nothing feminine, nothing soft. Not what she would have pictured for Lexi, who was all pop, but what did she know? Who knew which part of her was an act?

Or maybe it was all real. Maybe some people can be what they seem like.

Sabrina handed her a large, velum-wrapped candle, "This is for you. I wasn't sure what your taste was so I went with Feu De Bois, a favorite of mine."

Lexi smiled, "Awe, thank you. If you like it, I know I'll love it."
She took the gift and placed it on a mammoth stone island.

"This is the kitchen," she said, running a hand over the counter.
"We never use it."

We? Was Sabrina supposed to know Lexi had a *we*?

Ah, she had said something about her "man" being ... something,
when they all met on day one.

The two women were directed by Milo to make their way into
the living room, which was a two-story room at least, ceilings
soaring above them.

"Sorry for my appearance, I got a little behind today,"
Lexi said, referring, Sabrina guessed, to her Lululemons and
no-makeup-makeup.

"Oh, please. Don't worry about me."

Sabrina and Lexi turned to where the cameras were already
fixed. A man with a blonde bun and piercing blue eyes had rounded
the corner.

"Lexi, everything's wiped down upstairs."

Was that her *we*?

He had an accent; it sounded like Australian, from the one
sentence. He was shirtless, with a black cord dangling a silver Om
pendant that rested at his collarbone. He had that taut sort of build
where the six-pack verged on almost double. He was tanned, with
a tan line exposed at his low-slung athletic shorts. He was barefoot
and had a yoga mat under his arm.

What a type!

It's funny; the whole look he was going for was very fleeting
in a way. But in another way, quite timeless. He looked like all the
men she envisioned in all the romance novels she'd devoured as a
young girl—particularly the time travel romances. He looked like
he might be a cowboy, a pirate, a pioneer, anyone from a more
primal time of life.

Perhaps she always would have said that, or perhaps Sabrina was
tired of the Wall Street types, the Promising-Future types from her

youth, the Curated Bad Boy (these always have more hair product than women in their bathrooms).

The trendy types—though she had been attached to them again and again in her life, before her marriage—were tiresome; perhaps, he was tiresome since this too was a trend. But she was surprised to find that he made her cheeks burn up when she looked at him.

Wow, she thought. *I haven't felt that in years.*

That blind crush feeling was, until that instant, a forgotten feeling for Sabrina.

"Oh, thanks Leo," said Lexi.

Leo and Lexi. Cute.

"Do you need anything else from me?" he asked. "Hi, how are you, I'm Leo, pardon my manners."

"Sabrina," she shook his hand, which was strong and callused.

"Sabrina." He smiled. Good teeth. They looked real, but they also looked like the sort of teeth veneers were aiming to mimic. "Such a pretty name."

"Thank you."

He moved past them and stopped in front of a canvas rucksack near the entryway where he found a shirt that he put on as he asked, "Is it for Sabrina Antoni, by any chance?"

She was taken aback. "That's never the first guess. Yes, I think that might have been part of the inspiration."

"I'm surprised people don't guess it. One of the best ballerinas ever to dance in our world."

She nodded, and he held her gaze. She looked away, uncomfortable, and he cleared his throat. Then he stepped into some sandals.

"Sorry, Lexi, do you need anything else?"

"No, we're good, thank you though! You're the best."

He left, and pulled the elevator door shut behind him.

"Who—?" Sabrina started, but Lexi held up a finger. She looked skyward, evidently waiting for the elevator to begin its descent.

Sabrina thought this was for dramatic effect, given the entire interaction was being filmed. "Oh my god, that was some *chemistry* between you two!"

"I'm sorry?"

"You and Leo!"

"I'm not sure what you're talking about."

"Okay, first of all, he's my yoga teacher he leads me in mediations, and like, one time I made him guru me through some ayahuasca. He's *amazing*. You should hire him! As you can see, he does house visits. He's incredible, I used to do yoga. And. Did. Not. Get. The. Hype. But I was doing it wrong. I swear he has some magical knowledge of the body, he seems to know where all the tiniest muscles are and he can move you around and you feel things click, like *oh* that's why Warrior Two is a thing. He's amazing."

"It sounds like you like him."

"Oh my god, no, he's not my type."

"What's your type?"

Lexi got a devilish grin on and said, "*rich*."

"Oh ... I see."

"I know. Most people don't say it. But it's true. Like how some girls only date black guys or tall guys or funny guys or gay guys or whatever. It's not *all* I want in a man, but what's wrong with knowing what you want?"

"Right," said Sabrina.

"What? You've got this look on your face like I said the n-word or something."

Sabrina's eyebrows shot up. "No, it's ... well when I was your age—"

"Oh, thank you, Billiam."

Sabrina looked behind her to see another unexpected man. An older gentleman in what can only be described as a butler's costume. He looked straight off the casting call for a remake of *Clue*.

"You drink vodka soda, right?"

"Sure." How did she know? Zoe? Google? Both?

"That's what I thought. Mine's a LIIT. It's a long island but named for me, using a few of my favorites." Lexi looked at the camera for an instant, and then gestured at the table where Sabrina now noticed four bottles.

The butler distributed the drinks and left with a small bow.

"Did you call him … Billiam?"

"That's a nickname. He's William. It might annoy him but deep down he finds me charming."

Sabrina sipped her vodka soda.

"Anyway, you were saying, in your day?" Lexi asked.

"Yes, well, in my day, looking for a man for his money was not something you could simply say."

"Out loud? Maybe not. But yeah. I mean it's a thing. Also you're aging yourself up by saying *in my day*." Lexi put on a deep, sophisticated voice. "What are you like forty?"

"Thirty-nine."

"You carry yourself like you're creepin' up on sixty. You seriously shouldn't, you're like absolutely gorgeous, and you were *the it* girl for *evvvver*, why do you act like your life is over? Because some douchebag dumped you?"

"Technically he didn't 'dump' me, I divorced him."

"Same thing. Honestly, what you need is a guy like Leo. Like, have you had a fling since things ended with that royal lowlife?"

For the first time since filming began, and besides a time or two with Budgie, Sabrina smiled spontaneously. "No, I haven't had a fling."

"Mm!" Lexi swallowed a sip. "Please let me help you find a fling. You need one. It's magic. And sometimes you meet someone real that way, like I was with this guy Bill—not Billiam, this other guy Bill—and he was this super high-powered attorney who represents like every scumbag in the city, blah blah, and then he *dumped* me for his wife, so I said, you know what, I'm getting back out there and I'm doing it *now*, and I went out that very night," she punctuated *that very night* with a wave of her bright fingernails. "And that's when I met Tom!"

She indicated the space around her.

"Now you're with Tom, and this is his home?"

"Ew, can you call this a home? It's legit boring. But yeah he lives here."

"Do you live here with him?"

"Hell yeah, it's sick. It's not as close to the action as I'd like, but it's fun. Never thought of myself as a FiDi girl, but here we are."

Sabrina smiled again, remembering when FiDi became an expression for this previously dry area.

"Why not like a Leo for you?"

"Why not a Leo? I–I'm far older than he is."

"So the hell what? Men do it all the time, and also he's like thirty-five, that's not even that much younger. I'm telling you, you age yourself up. Wait, you have a daughter right?"

"I do."

"How old is she, like sixteen?"

She paused. "Eighteen."

"That's *why*, you had a kid when *you* were a kid, and now you think like, your life is over and it definitely isn't. Where is your daughter, why isn't she telling you to get back on that horse?"

"She's with her father."

A flicker of deeper understanding than Sabrina would have anticipated flashed through Lexi's eyes. "Okay she's being a little asshole, and she'll get over it. She's with her dad? Like after what a pig he was. Don't even worry about that, she'll see him for who he is and come around."

Her voice had lowered to something less fake, far more human for a moment.

"Let's hope," said Sabrina, saying the only thing she could think to say.

"Anyway, my thing is, you need to start dating. Or sleeping with someone, I mean please, something. Put *someone* between you and Rapey Robbie."

Sabrina choked on her drink and then burst into laughter.

Lexi reminded her of Aubrey. Not because Aubrey had ever called her father such an incendiary, accurate, and alliterative insult, but because Aubrey had a hard time watching her mouth. It was hard the whole time she was growing up because she would ask very frank questions no one in Rob's family was prepared to answer. Sabrina always had to answer in private.

It was one of the reasons she found herself stunned that Aubrey had chosen her father—and his indefensible side—over hers.

Sabrina and Aubrey had been very close. They used to snuggle up together, watching movies or playing cards, hiding from the world they both felt—once—had oppressed them.

Why? Why had Aubrey blamed her for Robbie's actions?

Sabrina pushed the thoughts from her mind. She'd asked it enough, of herself, of Aubrey, and never gotten an answer. Satisfactory or otherwise.

They chatted for another half hour, this time with more guidance from Milo. He prompted them to talk about the other women.

Sabrina tried her best to defend Dahlia, feeling that she deserved it. Lexi said Mariana was fake but that she was "obsessed" with Budgie.

Lexi's ears perked when she heard the elevator engage and sat up straighter and tried to look, Sabrina guessed, more sophisticated.

"Okay, let's cut, Tom is ready downstairs, we're going to reset," said Milo. "And for you two," he was looking at Sabrina and Lexi, "let's act surprised that Tom has shown up, and don't forget to keep things *spicy*."

Milo grinned, and Sabrina noticed that he had grand spikes of nose hair that no one had told him about.

"Sounds good!" said Lexi.

The elevator arrived, and in walked an older man that Sabrina guessed must be Tom.

He entered the living room, giving off the air of someone far too important for whatever was going on around him.

Perhaps he felt that way about reality TV, or perhaps he felt that way about everything.

Sabrina had a feeling she could guess which.

"Lexi," he said.

"Tommy, this is Sabrina. I'm sure you recognize her."

He blew over, giving a grudging handshake with his distinctly uncalloused hands.

"Can't say that I do."

His tone dripped with irritation. *Why would I recognize someone mixed up in all this?*

"Okay, you're lying, Tommy, she's an icon." Lexi looked at Sabrina like this was baffling.

"It's—I would never expect anyone to. It's lovely to meet you. Seems that we are total strangers."

He shrugged and walked over to the bar in the corner. "Sorry."

Lexi looked after him, face falling almost imperceptibly.

She whispered, "He's always grumpy after work."

Sabrina nodded.

"What are you two hens jabbering about?"

He poured himself a generous pour of Glenfiddich and then sat down with them.

"I was telling Sabrina she needs to get back out there and *date*. She's recently divorced." She squinted her eyes at him. "Which you know because I have, for sure, talked about it. She was an actress and then married that English Count guy? She was an actual countess. Like *actual* actual."

"Earl," Sabrina corrected. "My husband was an Earl."

He leaned back in his chair. "Ah, right. That Sabrina. Apologies, you look different in person."

He said it like an insult.

"That's because I don't have red font splattered across my face calling me a liar and a traitor." Sabrina meant it but said it like a joke.

He gave a small shake of the head. "If the shoe fits, right Cinderella?"

The silence plumed with sudden tension as Sabrina stared at him and Lexi looked between them like an anxious songbird.

"Sounds like you do know who I am."

"I guess I do."

"Sounds like you agree with the news."

"What other information should I have?" he swigged his smoky scotch, and its scent traveled through the angry air.

He had an ugly, ugly smile.

"I don't suppose you're expected to have other information." She almost stopped. But then she did not. "I suppose you might understand it differently than it sounds like you might."

"I think the papers have got it right. Not too fond of you, are they?"

"Not much, no."

"But neither is your daughter, correct?"

"Excuse me?"

"I think the kid staying with him sort of ruins your case, sugar." Sabrina's hackles spiked.

"You're a successful man, haven't you learned not to talk about things you don't understand? Or perhaps your success has convinced you that nothing is beyond your comprehension."

"Whatever you want to think."

Sabrina glanced at Lexi. Was it possible that this man was coming in and being this awful, as an introduction? How could it help him?

"You think," she said, hoping to push him to a point of no return, no matter the side, "that Robbie is the sole truth-teller amongst the women who say that he is abusive, a liar, and a criminal?"

"Not for me to decide. But. Yes, I think old *Robbie* got a bad rap."

"You think it's likely that those women could come forward about the same thing and varied versions there within, accusing a former playboy of exactly what made him infamous in pop culture?

And that his wife might divorce him out of … what, interest in negative press?"

"Listen, sweetheart, I don't care to know about the ins and outs of your romance with someone you thought was going to be your Prince Charming."

Anger such as she had not recalled in a long while began to reach boiling point under her skin.

"Is that what I'm asking of you? Did I start telling you about our first date, or all the love letters? Or did I ask you if you agree with the news?" Before he could answer, she went on. "Of course, perhaps I should allow for the possibility that a man of your years has made up his mind long ago about whether he'd like to make up his own mind or have it made up for him by pandering media."

He let out a booming laugh. "You want to talk about pandering media? It's women like you and all those," he did big, hairy, curling air quotes with his soft hands, "victims. Things have gotten out of control if you ask me. Believe it or not, I even had a few women start reevaluating the past and come crawling out of the woodwork asking for money once it got popular to complain about…," he sought the word.

Sabrina found it for him. "Regrets? Yes, perhaps at best the women regret their forays with men like … that."

"Women," he said, speaking to his drink.

Sabrina burst into a biting laugh of her own. "Don't you hear yourself? You're a cartoon! A caricature."

"Pot," he pointed at himself, then to her, "meet kettle."

"My god."

"*My god*," he said, mocking her.

"You're an ugly, pointless man who thinks it's okay to date a bright young girl like this, and who doesn't even mind that it's only for your money. That doesn't seem questionable at all to you?"

It didn't matter that Lexi was vapid and unreal half the time—she was bright, she was young and beautiful, and she deserved better—far better—than this.

She glanced at Lexi, who was at a loss for what to do.

Sabrina's heart was pounding, and her bones were shaking from somewhere deep within her.

She stood up, not sure where else to put her energy unless it was to crack her crystal glass over his bald head.

Sabrina pointed a finger at Lexi scolding, "This is why you don't look for money first. This is the sort of age-spotted, sexist, micro-penised buffalo you wind up with. Trust me, it isn't worth it. This," she pointed at him now, "isn't worth it. Do better."

Was she yelling at Lexi? Lexi because she was like Aubrey? Was she yelling at Aubrey? Young Sabrina? She was furious, that was all she knew.

She stormed out of the apartment onto the waiting elevator.

Milo called after her and she said, "No. We're through."

She dragged the caged door to close it, mashed the lobby button and heard Tom's deep, resonating tone say, "What the hell did you bring into my house, Lexi?"

Sabrina couldn't tell for absolute certain, but she thought she heard a weak apology from the strong girl in the big cold house. She walked with legs of jelly through the lobby, knowing the crew would be in pursuit. She flew through the second door and out onto the street.

"Hey!"

She turned and saw a breathless Lexi, not the cameras.

Sabrina walked back to her.

Lexi looked humiliated. "I'm sorry. I'll—I'll apologize more later, but here, please take this." She handed her a business card. "You don't have to do it for the show, but maybe for you."

She closed her hand over it in Sabrina's palm, and then went back inside, passing the cameras that had made their way down.

Sabrina took off her mic and handed it to Milo, ignoring everything he asked of her, and then she walked away as fast as she could.

She knew every street of New York. If they tried to follow her, she could lose them.

Her driver was probably parked nearby, but she wanted the walk.

She walked for almost twenty minutes, clutching the thick, unread business card in her hand until it was slick with sweat. She had made her way all the way to one of her favorite places to hide—a library with a bar hidden in the back behind a bookcase.

She got to the bar and ordered a vodka soda to negate the last one.

Seated, she unfurled her hand, expecting to see some frustrating card for a therapist or psychiatrist. But it wasn't.

It was a canvas white card with the Om symbol and the name Leo Michaels.

15

Dahlia

I tried to pause and take a breath, but all I ended up doing was taking another sip of wine, which we both knew wasn't helping anything. It was now close to midnight, and I could tell Mick wanted to go to bed.

"What am I supposed to do?" he asked, sitting at the kitchen island, his head in his hands.

"I don't know. I don't know. I'm not worried about her, it's not that, I get that she's your publicist and that you need her. I know she's good at her job—it's not even about her. It's…"

"It's what, Dahlia? If it's something, then talk to me about that, not about this crap."

A surge of anger I tried to ignore raced through me. "I was banking on that time alone with you. And instead you blew me off."

"I didn't blow you off. I was working, Dahlia."

"Then maybe she shouldn't be posting on her story about *work*, like she's out with her hot new boyfriend eating tacos at Mexicue."

It wasn't even what I *meant*.

He shot up and started pacing. "I don't control what Regan does. We were talking about the game plan for what I need to do next to stay relevant. I can do my best on the field, but it matters that we plan this out. Now I have the sports drink thing too, and you know I'm trying to make sure this never *ends* for us. NFL Dahlia—Not For Long. My work doesn't stop because it's off-season."

"I know that, but—"

"You know that but *what*? You know that, so let me do what I have to do. It was her idea to go there, I wanted something to eat."

"Okay, can you try to make a better effort not to ditch me, and try to make some time for me here and there? God, I mean we've spent almost no time together since I, no, we moved here, and now I want to make sure we don't lose what we have!"

"You're doing a great job of that."

A beat. "Really."

"I'm sorry. I didn't mean that. Look, I don't know what to do here, how to make this stop. I told you two hours ago I was sorry. I do want to show you I care, I'm sorry you don't think I do right now."

It had the air of opportunity for me to latch onto it, apologize, and then help this end. We never used to fight, and we didn't develop around it. Now it felt like a symptom of an incoming virus, taking us over.

But I'd spent the past week working on this show, where the women were impossible. I wanted to talk to him about everything going on and how infuriating it all was. Instead, I said, "I'm sorry too. I'm feeling a little lost and my whole life is built around you. I feel out of sorts when you aren't around, and we aren't us."

"Your life shouldn't be built around me," he said, "that's what this show is supposed to be for."

"To give me something besides you? Mick, I have immersed myself in your career. All in. It's all tied together."

He shook his head. "I don't know if that's right."

"And what, this show is a gift in case we get divorced, and I'm left with nothing?"

The few seconds of silence before his answer was enough to send my whole body ice cold. My blood froze, I felt my capillaries seize, felt the hairs all over my body stand straight up.

"No, of course not."

"You hesitated."

That was going to sound petty and small, but it was true.

He let out a heavy sigh. "No, I didn't hesitate, Dahlia. I'm exhausted."

Suddenly, I was frantic to get things back to normal. I would fake anything I had to, pretend to be *easygoing* and *chill* and *low-key* for the rest of my life if the alternative was him having meant that small hesitation.

"Okay, you know what?" I sighed and put on a smile. "This is stupid, and I'm sorry. I-I'm feeling hormonal, and this show is weird, and all I wanted to do was tell you about it. I'm sorry, honey. It's all a very strange and new feeling and I-I miss you. That's all."

He nodded, perhaps not quite believing me, but wanting to.

In that moment I remembered he was only in New York for one more night, and like a switch was turned on, I squinted at him playfully and said, "I have an idea."

I went to the freezer and grabbed a pint of Ben & Jerry's.

"Dahlia, it's midnight. I have an early flight tomorrow."

It had long been a silly tradition of ours. Whenever he had a bad loss, we'd do a bath and ice cream. Whenever we had a fight or a debate to be solved—some of our biggest decisions had been reached that way, in our oversized tub with Triple Caramel Chunk and a spoon.

I shrugged. "Okay then. I see how it is."

I went to go put it away, knowing he wouldn't let me, and he came over behind me and closed the freezer door.

Yes. My heart lifted like a yo-yo racing back up its string.

"You run the bath. I'll defrost this and meet you in there?" I moved my eyebrows up and down and made a stupid, sexy pouty face as I held the container.

He cracked a smile and before walking away, he kissed me on the cheek. "I love you. Even when you're being crazy."

It prickled a little, and I resisted the urge to disagree that I had overreacted. Or that it stung when he said she was pretty, even though it was true, and I had said it first.

"I know," I said.

Waiting for the microwave, I resolved to get back to being cool Dahlia. The wife who doesn't get upset by much and lets most things roll off her back. The fun version of me who is the picture of patience and understanding. Did I feel threatened by Regan? Since when was I jealous? I had delighted in my skills at ignoring the women hitting on my husband on social media, or the groupies who waited to see him after games. I had recognized early on in our relationship that if I smiled about it all and told him I trusted him I would make him feel far too guilty to ever make a fool out of me.

And I knew he wanted me to be happy when all I wanted was for him to keep picking me. It was infuriatingly meta and hard to convey.

With the meditative power of a monk, I dismissed my resentments, and for the rest of that night at least, we remembered who we had been.

16

Sabrina

S abrina arrived at the next filming day in a rare and foul mood. Perhaps not rare. Not anymore. She was going to have to apologize to Lexi, but that would be difficult since she meant every word she had screamed at Tom.

She was miserable because Robbie was officially recirculating in the cultural zeitgeist as an attractive bachelor, re-released into the wild, and onto potential future conquests. Sabrina had become adept at avoiding any news about him, but every so often his press found her. The temptation of one breadcrumb, and she was deep down the trail. It seemed the most popular photos of Robbie that had cropped up were of him and Aubrey taking in a West End show. Aubrey looked beautiful, if a bit too thin, and a bit too much like young Sabrina. She stared at the photo for a few full minutes before even considering Robbie. She couldn't believe how long it had been since she'd seen her daughter in person. She couldn't believe Aubrey wanted to stay over there with him.

When she tore herself away from that photo, it seemed that Rob had been spotted out with several women, all of whom were age-appropriate and known for their intelligence. They were not bimbos. Clever. He had no doubt been advised to make very careful selections going forward. Robbie would have to be with women who had good heads on their shoulders, who would never be fool enough to spend time with him if all the issues hadn't been absolute and utter lies.

He was most recently seen with Lorna Thurmont, a once-in-a-generation actress who could travel from comedy to drama and never seem out of place—in fact, seemed to define whatever genre she was in.

Landing a publicity shot with her would go a long, long way for Robbie. People loved her. The British press adored her. As neither had never, ever treasured Sabrina.

When it came time to sit down at Taverna Makrakis in midtown, Sabrina was in no mood.

Upon seeing Sabrina's face, Budgie did a double take. Half an hour later when the scene prep was through and they could talk, she made a beeline for her cousin.

"What happened?" she asked, pulling out a seat for Sabrina.

"Lorna."

"Oh, drat. I heard about that."

"Why didn't you *tell* me then?" Sabrina snapped back.

Budgie gave her a look. "You asked me not to."

"You're right."

"Listen, it's what he does. In fact, we could have guessed this would happen, right? Pattern-wise, it makes sense."

"Tell me, is she a nightmare to work with?"

"Allegedly, she is lovely."

"Damn."

"I don't buy it. Something in her eyes tells me she yanks the legs off of spiders that dare to crawl through her mini-castle."

"Alright ladies," said a clapping Zoe. "We're getting ready to start rolling, please do any last-minute face checks, make sure those phones are silenced."

"She doesn't have a mini-castle, does she?" Sabrina whispered.

"She might have a proper castle."

"Damn."

"It was featured in *The World of Interiors*."

"I hate her."

"At least you know Lorna's new boyfriend is an absolute pig." Budgie looked around. "Hey, aren't we missing someone?"

"Save it for filming, Ms. Budgie!" said Zoe.

Once they began, Mariana piped up, "It's my event and I felt we deserved a night out without all the *drama*, you know what I mean? It's nothing personal against Dahlia, I don't believe she understands what it's like to be one of us. You know? Is she even verified on Instagram?"

The conversation was frenetic and awkward as everyone tried to steal some screen time. Budgie's one-liners were too good to be missed, and they had to back up a few times to catch what she said.

"Dahlia is a gold digger and thirsty," said Nicole, out of seeming nowhere. "There, I said it."

"What makes you say that?" Sabrina asked.

"I see how she treats him. We have a mutual friend in common, and … I don't want to be disrespectful," she folded her napkin over in her lap, "I'm not going to say anything specific, I don't want to break that confidence, but yes, trust me, Dahlia is not what she seems."

"She seems like a bitch. Maybe she is exactly what she seems like," said Mariana.

The whole, long dinner was like that, catty and badmouthing. At one point, when the conversation grew stale, Zoe had them pause and told Sabrina to talk about what had happened at Lexi's apartment the other day.

Although Sabrina looked like she detested the idea, she played along.

"Lexi, I'm sorry about what happened the other day. I should have kept my mouth shut and left if I couldn't. I apologize."

"What happened?" asked Mariana, hungrily.

Everyone waited to see who was going to give the rundown.

"Sabrina and I had a super great time the other day, and then my man came home, and he was in one of his stupid *moods*, he gets like, in this work-mode and he's impossible." Lexi explained, "It's best to meet him on like vacation or something, I see him for who and how he is, but most people never get to because he comes off stiff. He and Sabrina sort of got into it because he was a real douchebag about Sabrina and Robbie. You don't need to apologize, for one thing that was between you two and for another thing you were right."

Lexi tossed Sabrina a genuine smile and then started off talking about the cocktail she had ordered and what spirit she ordered it to be made with, and it became clear she was talking up a brand with which she was involved. Given this permission, soon Mariana was off and running and talking about her sex toy line.

By the time they got everything they needed for the scene, the sun had almost set. The street was dark and shadowed, though Sabrina knew that if she was home right now, she would have been able to bathe in the last bits of sunshine. Not that she would. She would have likely been curled into a ball, watching *Bridesmaids* again.

Budgie asked her if she wanted to get a real drink, and the pair went down the block to a bar off the beaten track enough that it wasn't filled with tourists who thought Times Square was *the city* and not the belly of the beast.

Budgie ordered for them both, getting Sabrina a vodka soda with three limes squeezed, one left in, and getting herself a Willet Old Fashioned with a few extra bitters.

"What's really bothering you about this Robbie bullshit?"

"It's Lorna bullshit, not Robbie bullshit."

"Sure, the Lorna and Robbie bullshit then."

Sabrina winced. "No, don't put them together like that. Oh, that's very good. That's very good, sir, thank you."

"No problem," the bartender said, and then something spread over his face as he seemed to realize she was *somebody* though he couldn't place exactly who, "That one's on me."

"That's not necessary," Sabrina said.

He flushed red and walked off, pulling his phone out of his pocket.

Budgie laughed. "Look at that, you're still star-striking the young folks, that ought to make you feel better."

Sabrina gave her cousin a look.

"It should, honey. You wanted to be a star, right? You might not have become a movie star, but … this is still something, right?"

"No, it's not, that's the point. There's nothing that I'm passionate about anymore. Once upon a time I *thought* I wanted to be an actress once upon a time I wanted to make a living doing something I loved. And I suppose it feels like maybe I could have either gone all the way up or I could have settled all the way down. Now I've done neither, and I can't do either, and I can't for the life of me figure out what the hell I'm supposed to do next."

"Bri—"

"Was I even good, Budgie? I don't even think I was very good. Was I?"

She had never asked this of Budgie. Never asked her to give her professional opinion on something that could be potentially explosive.

Her cousin drew a deep breath. She paused for dramatic effect. "You were great, Sabrina. You were. You gave up. That's the problem, not your talent. Cheers."

"Cheers."

They clanged glasses.

"You're not placating me are you?"

"Saying that you were good? No, I'm not, but it doesn't matter. Because you're still the one who gave up and didn't try anymore. You had a shot there. One bad movie does not end a career. Ask *everyone*."

"Maybe you should have given me this tough love routine back then."

"You weren't clear on what you wanted then. It only seems clear to you now."

"You have always been so sure. So clear. You knew when we were kids that this is what you wanted to be."

"Yes, I knew one thing about my life and I achieved it. The rest has been a fiasco at best and a disaster at worst. I've got a good attitude. That's the only difference between me and a lot of people."

"Yeah, well we also grew up with wealth, didn't we?"

"Oh, *buckets!*" she laughed. "But I could have failed. Hell, I *did* fail. Lots. I got here eventually, and at times my advantages set me back and at times they made it easier. It's the case for most of us. But we're not talking about me. We're talking about you. You who was once full of life and who now thinks her life is over. And it is."

"Leave it to you for a plot twist."

"You gotta be born again, hon, that's it. You don't have much left over from that old life, the resentment, the anger, the bad reputation. You need to stop living in your heyday, if that's what we're calling it."

"Oh, is that all?"

"That's all. You gotta let go of it. When was the last time you did something that was about the *next* part of your life? When was the last time you did something that wasn't a *response*? When was the last time you wanted something in real time and took it and lived it out?"

"I'm doing this show."

"That's not what I mean and you know it. This show is about repairing the past, not about you *wanting* something and going for it."

Sabrina shook her head. "Maybe when I was dating Robbie and he ignored me that one night in Milan and I told him in front of the whole crowd that he could have me or he could lose me. That was right before he proposed."

"Damn, that bastard even has ownership over the last time you did something for yourself? I'd say that doesn't seem possible, but I hate to say that it absolutely does."

"That is terrible. Isn't it? Terrible."

"It is. You must change something about it," Budgie insisted.

"Your phone has rung three times. You can answer it."

"I loathe people who do that."

"I want a moment to think anyway. It's fine."

"It's only Oliver."

"*Oliver* Oliver?"

"*Oliver* Oliver."

Oliver was in advertising. Oliver was a silver fox with the squinting wrinkles of Clint Eastwood. His tailored suits never missed a stitch, and he had a boat, a plane, and seven cars. Before he sounds like a total jerk, he also donates an annual quarter-million to charities and does pro-bono ad work for any business that can't afford him. He's a wonderful man. He was the first man to ever propose to Budgie. They were sixteen. She said yes, but they didn't do it. Not until Budgie's first marriage ended and she was ready for a second one. Then after ten months, they called it quits. Budgie was the breaker; she claimed he loved her too much and that she couldn't stand watching him love his work less from distraction.

Their divorce was a whirlwind.

And now, it seemed, he was back. If he was calling her, he was back.

"Alright, I'll step out, I'll be right back."

Her cousin stepped out front, and Sabrina watched her talking on the phone to him. She got the same dumb lovey look on her face she used to get when they were teenagers together. She was always smitten. Even during their divorce. The night the papers were finalized, the two of them went to a gala together. A *gala*, what could be more sarcastic?

She came back in a few minutes later and had those perky cheeks one can only attain when trying not to smile.

"And what did Oliver want?"

"He's got a table at Balthazar and hoped I could meet him for a late dinner."

"Your ex-husband wants to take you on a very romantic date?"

"Yes, what's wrong with that?"

"I don't know, what's wrong with that, Budgie?"

"Come now. For one thing, I told you the rest of my life is a fiasco. And for another, I'm not going, I'm here with you."

"Budgie."

"Yes?"

"Go."

"Please, you're acting like there's any reason in the world Oliver and I should spend time together."

Sabrina had adored Budgie with Oliver and never understood why they divorced. They had been the kind of couple that people call *you two*. She had always suspected they'd end up together again.

"I swear I cannot think—and I mean this—of anything in the world that would make me happy right now but to know that you and Oliver are out having a date like you did when you were kids."

"Okay, are you—okay. I'll go."

"Go."

Budgie finished the rest of her drink. She handed the bartender a rolled up hundred-dollar bill. "Buy her another round with this or keep it if she doesn't. Alright, Bri, I'll see you soon. Are you sure you're alright?"

"Budgie get the *hell* out of here."

"I love you."

"I love you too. Leave."

"Leaving."

She left, and Sabrina was downing the last sip of her drink when in walked the blonde Aussie himself.

Leo.

He recognized her right away, which shouldn't—perhaps—have surprised or flattered her. But it did. He gave her a big smile and asked if the seat was taken beside her. Sabrina replied, "My cousin just left. What a coincidence running into you here."

"Not really, I was with Lexi before your shoot, and I spent a few hours working down at the coffee shop on the corner." He lifted the strap of his messenger bag off his shoulder and set it on the bar.

"Can I get you a drink?" asked the bartender, this time trying to figure out if this guy was also someone he should know. A Hemsworth, perhaps.

"I was drinking vodka soda. I might switch to wine."

"Red or white?" asked Leo.

"I'm a red drinker, but it's about a hundred degrees out there."

"Sauvignon Blanc?"

"Sure."

"Let's do a bottle of Cloudy Bay, eh?"

"Coming right up."

"A bottle?" Sabrina's surprise was growing by the second.

"Listen, I need to celebrate. I was willing to do it alone, but then I ran into you. No pressure, of course, if you want to have a sip or two and then leave me to my celebration, I under—"

"Sir?" she said, and ad the bartender turned. "Forget the Cloudy Bay. Bring us your finest and coldest champagne."

"Finest? It would be … Krug, we have—"

"That'll be fine."

"It's on me," she said.

"You really don't have to. You don't even know what I'm celebrating. I could be celebrating the dropping of murder charges."

"Any celebration is worthy of champagne."

He laughed. "If you're sure, then I can't say no. But you let me pay next time."

Next time? "Alright."

His gaze lingered on hers as her smile faded, and then, a skip of her heartbeat.

Once the champagne was poured, she asked what they were celebrating.

"Damn, that's good. I've never had good champagne, I don't think. I think I've had Mumm's once in my life." Sabrina feigned surprise. "Struggling entrepreneur raised in the countryside. Not a lot of bubbly. Or celebrating, for that matter."

"I love good champagne. I never tire of it." She looked at the bubbles bouncing in her glass, shrugged, and took a sip.

He smiled at her.

"What?"

"Nothing," he said. "You're sweet."

"That is contrary to the general opinion."

"I'm pretty comfortable on the other side of popularity. And I'm sure they're wrong anyway."

She blushed. "Tell me what you're celebrating."

"What *we* are celebrating is that I finished my book."

"What? That's ... unbelievable, what do you write?"

He went on to describe in detail his passion for travel and wellness that had shaped his life for the past twenty years, and how he had been mentored by a monk in Sri Lanka who changed his life with Ayurvedic medicine. Sabrina listened and found herself focusing on how his lips moved over his perfect teeth more than his explanation of how he had realized he had been gifted with sacred knowledge. He had compiled a series of essays and believed with all his heart that "even if it only improves the life of one person who reads it," awareness was not meant to be hoarded but shared.

He cut himself off. "Sorry, I'm rambling."

"No, no, I love it! Please. I promise I'll still buy the book, but tell me ... I don't know, tell me everything."

When she drank alone at home, she got tired. But here she felt alert and buzzing.

He was interesting. He had had a life. He was not fulfilling anything for anyone else. Even when he talked about his past partners, it was with such quiet respect and appreciation for the time and the impact of her, whoever she was.

He didn't wax rhapsodic. He didn't speak as though he had the whole world figured out. He was another lost soul on a completely different path than she had ever been allowed upon.

Leo was warm and friendly and pleasant to the people who struck up conversations at the bar. He had an inside joke with the bartender by the time Sabrina returned from the restroom. And when they left, they went out onto the hot, muggy streets and were hit with a wave of the city's mineral smell and the rich smell of candied nuts for sale on the corner.

They walked for block after block.

The streets of Manhattan have a strange and beautiful palette. The warm glow from the headlights, the dusty blue as the lights reflected onto the night sky. The striking reds, purples, and every other color in the fluorescent rainbow. There were always puddles; there was always steam and smoke. Something nearby was always moving fast, and somewhere else nearby there was always something still and steady.

It was one of those perfect summer nights that Sabrina had forgotten about so completely that she thought she might be dreaming. Girls had their hair thrown up into ponytails; women had an extra button open. Boys smelled like sweat and soap; men had their sleeves rolled up. The drinks on the patio tables sweated condensation onto table surfaces and were refilled quicker than if it were chillier.

"I love this city," said Sabrina, shutting her eyes briefly as a rare breeze crossed her cheek.

When she opened her eyes, he was staring at her.

She started to ask *what*, again, but before she knew it, he had taken a step toward her, planted his hand around her chin, his fingers in her hair, and his lips on hers. There was an eagerness to his touch, but he was gentle—almost too gentle. She put her arms around his neck and pulled him closer. Her legs felt shaky, and her body was hot and cold at once, and her stomach was filled with pop rocks.

He broke away. "Sabrina, I hope this isn't a kiss goodnight."

She shook her head. "No."

"I know a place, a fun place. I've been looking for a reason to go back. You up for it?"

"Sure, yes."

They hopped in a cab that he whistled for and wrangled quick as a whip. In the backseat, he put his hand on her thigh. High enough that it felt dangerous and against the rules. It was a big, strong, well-worked hand. Not soft as silk like *he who must not be named*. Not now, not when she had Leo here.

She put a hand on his and moved it up a little higher. Beside her, he turned to look at her. Each of their faces was lit by the strobe of passing lights. She felt as though she could not breathe.

She felt nervous and more herself than she could remember being.

Men had always fallen for her. And she had *loved* that feeling. *Loved* knowing that she was in control. That she could do anything, say anything, tease them, make them wait, tell them to hurry, anything, and they would do it. Until her marriage, she had always been fulfilled that way.

Leo squeezed her leg.

How had this happened? Why did he want her?

No, she reprimanded herself, *do not lose confidence*.

They pulled up out front of *Ito's Hideaway*—an underground Tiki Speakeasy.

It was dim inside, all warm dark wood, the tables had small tealights under red lampshades. The vibe was very retro. Up front there was a stage, and there was a show going on, hula dancers with fire and golden spotlights.

"This is *wild*," said Sabrina.

"Isn't it? I came here for a mate's bachelor party. I didn't know him that well and I didn't know any of the others. Bit of a strange place to get to know a bunch of men."

She laughed, and the noise of the place carried away the sound of it.

He reached for a menu and put it on the bar. She leaned on it, reading, and then felt him wrap his arm around her, reading too, but standing close enough to her that no light would be able to get through—if there were much to begin with.

Her heart and her inner thighs ached at this proximity. She pointed to a drink on the menu. "That looks good."

She turned around and looked up at him. His blue eyes looked back at her, and he smiled. "Looks good?"

She nodded.

"Okay," he got the bartender's attention, "two of these Tiki Ritas."

The drinks were sweet and delicious; they smelled like fresh nutmeg and lime. He carried them to a small table in a shadowy corner, where his hand found her leg again, her lips found his.

They stayed for that one round, and then neither of them could stand it anymore.

"I'm going to settle up, okay?" he said, in her ear. "Don't leave without me."

She wouldn't, she never would.

She got out her phone and texted her driver. She had already warned him half an hour ago to be handy—she knew they wouldn't be long and she wanted to be prepared.

He returned promptly, stuffing his copy of the receipt in his front pocket. He grinned at her and then tilted his head toward the door.

She scooted up the steps as he followed right behind her.

"He should be here any minute."

"He?"

"Sorry, my driver."

"Your driver." He shook his head. "I'll never get used to that."

She reached for him and kissed him again. Her arms around his neck, his hands on her waist, their kiss deep. She thought she might get lost in it.

That is until the explosion of flashing camera bulbs bathed them in blue light and cast any private moment into the spotlight.

17
Dahlia

The next few weeks were like a deep dive back into high school and far and away from anything that resembled an adult life with female friendships.

I met Mariana for another apology, this time while shopping at a boutique on Greenwich in Tribeca. She apologized for not inviting me to the dinner everyone else was invited to, and I tried not kick her hard in the neck for being cringey and weird about it.

They filmed Lexi and I out to get our nails done—she got two-inch vividly decorated electric blue tips and I got a gel extension French manicure, which she then said was so 'retro' of me. I didn't understand but couldn't ask without being more embarrassed.

There was another all-cast event wherein I hosted everyone for cocktails during happy hour at an insanely Instagram-friendly bar called While We Were Young. It was tiny, with only us there, which made the experience even more unconvincing.

And I met up with Sabrina and Budgie at a release party for a book about Budgie—none of the other women "made it." It had been arranged that they would not come but we had to act like it was both strange and rude of them.

It was the best filming experience I had participated in. It was at a little bookstore tucked away in the village. They served expensive wine and had the most beautiful meat and cheese spread I have ever seen. Inside was all golden glowing lights and book-smell. It felt Hallmark-worthy. And that night we had actual *fun*. Sabrina's spirits had mysteriously lifted, and Budgie was always entertaining.

It didn't feel awkward. If anything, it felt like I wished this *was* my life, instead of feeling like the show was representing some off-base life I don't have anything close to.

I also did my first interview. I thought it went okay. The guy asking the questions said he felt like he was 'witnessing a new star emerging.' I was happy with my answers. I got to detail my former life as a professional soccer player, albeit for one season but it still counted. I also shared about the Achilles injury that sidelined my rising athletic career before it really started—"The irony is, knowing when it's time to quit and walk away is what separates pros from amateurs." The story of how Mick and I met—"I was at an *NFL Honors* party with some other girls from soccer and I swear I did not know who he was, and once I found out, I didn't care!" My philosophy on marriage—"I love Mick. He's my soul mate. Marriage *shouldn't* mean you give up all your dreams—it's supposed to mean that you'll have someone waiting for you when you get home."

I didn't feel witty. I'd seen other women deliver great puns on these types of reality TV confessional interviews and because I was preoccupied overthinking what I said, I couldn't come up with anything. The interviewer guy helped me out and fed me some lines for me to repeat back, like "They're playing *fantasy* football," "I'd say he throws his balls around pretty well," and "I wasn't interested in *her* vagina monologue." It felt weird because they weren't my own words, but I was assured everyone else was doing the same. He said I did well at adding the right amount of inflex to make them sound like my own. Thank you, to Mr. Bevans and his 9th grade drama class.

And now I was off to my first one-on-one with Nicole.

I was still weirded out by the fact that fifteen years ago I was coming up with moves to dance to Nicole Trace songs and now I was filming with her. It might be easier to wrap my head around it if I was doing anything to be on her level. Like if I had become,

I don't know, a music producer or even a publicist and gotten to know her. But instead, I was supposed to be side by side with her when I had done nothing but play one season of pro soccer and go on to marry an NFL player. I knew it was illogical, but it was sort of fun anyway.

I was trying to remind myself that it was okay. I talked to my best friend, Cassie, back home in Florida, the morning before the Nicole date. We laughed when Cassie reminded me how she'd been right there beside me, synced up in tweenage dance moves. But it was hard to explain the whole *cast* personality situation in a ten-minute rundown. To bring her up to speed without being self-absorbed on the call was frustrating.

Nicole was hard to get a read on. She seemed like she was perhaps a good time? We all knew she had 'partied' pretty hard for a lot of her career, she no doubt liked to 'have fun,' unless that was all a mask. But unlike the brooding photos of Sabrina, the ones of Nicole were all bright pink and excited. Hands in the air. Every picture smelled like strawberry lip gloss and sounded like *whooo!*

And she seemed like she might be fun these days, but she also lacked that down-to-earth thing. She didn't break character to act human. She always seemed like a deer in the headlights, like she didn't want to be *caught*.

Caught doing what is still up for debate.

She didn't talk much to me, but she didn't seem to like me. It was Cassie's advice to recognize that I was most likely all in my head about it. I told her that I *didn't* feel that way about Sabrina and had obsessed over her as much. But the answer there was that they had different personalities and not to worry about it.

I met Nicole at nine pm at one of those sleek Eurotrash bars where the floor seems perma-sticky like the dirty cloth they "clean" your table with. And nothing is made in-house and there may as well not be a food menu. Oh, and the beat of your hangover is guaranteed to match the *whomp whomp whomp* steady bass of the techno crap that plays the whole time you're out.

Not to hate on it too much or anything, but they're usually filled with the worst people, and they always look like spaceships to me.

It made sense of the sequin mini dress Zoe had encouraged me to wear out. It was super short with a high neckline and long flutter sleeves. I never wore it because every time I *actually* went out, my vibe was more jeans and pinot noir and less tight dress and racy cocktails.

Either way, that was where we met. And that's what I was wearing. No one said reality television was real.

They had Nicole already seated at a tiny round low table. She was wearing black shorts and a black tank with high platform sandals. It was early enough that we had the room to ourselves.

After the mandatory *hello, you look great, so do you* she started, "I bought into partial ownership of this place about two years ago as an investment and it's done really well for me."

I was glad I didn't say anything negative, but I had come close.

Zoe cued a waiter to take our order.

"What do you say we do a shot of Jägermeister?" Nicole said.

Let it be known, I would go on to say in my next interview, I hate Jägermeister more than anyone on the planet. Also, I had my answer—she was off the wagon or is it on, I can never get that right.

"No, no I can't do Jägermeister, Nicole."

"Cool. Southern Comfort then?"

I scrunched up my face.

She kept going and from Hypnotiq to Crown Apple, she covered everything I stopped being able to drink in my junior year of college or *never* had.

"I got you ladies. How about some *Jamo* shots?" our server suggested. His delivery was bursting with all the fun energy you could insert into one line.

"Yes. Sounds perfect," I lied.

It didn't matter that I hated *Jameson*, I was aware of how much footage they had of me looking not-fun, saying *no* to everything, looking like I was too good for it.

After two shots of what tasted like graham cracker cigarettes, Nicole wanted to go dance.

No, I didn't want to dance. For one thing—remember those dances I used to come up with? Yeah, those were the extent of my interest in the bodily rhythmic. I can keep a beat, sing on key and everything, but dancing isn't my thing. I boast spaghetti arms, tight hips and mechanical, forced moves.

But I had to say yes, though I considered saying I wanted to *go home*. Which I did. Which I had always wanted to do in bars like these. When I went out to them—always dragged by not-real friends, like Nicole—I could draw on the excuse of some sort of early morning practice or training I had to attend.

This, I could not get out of.

We danced to a club remix of her last big hit, Nicole Trace and I … alone. Those shots proved themselves necessary because the whole scene was awkward, and I could never have done that sober.

They looped the song and took us in at every angle. We danced until I was sweating in my sequins and until my face was flushed. Nicole looked rocker chic cool and composed. She ordered us each two more shots of a Buttery Nipple, which I vaguely remembered as having Irish Cream and butterscotch schnapps and tasting like a Werther's candy but might as well be served with Excedrin as a chaser.

And then we took a break and went onto the roof. Nicole explained the area was set up for the show. They'd done a good job to make the space look like a real rooftop bar using rented hedges and the same kind of tiny white lights from Budgie's party.

She lit a cigarette and offered me one, which I said no to—another no, on camera—and we talked.

Nicole went on about her ex-boyfriend and I tried not to identify him by the story, but it was too easy. All her ex-boyfriends were famous, and I knew who all of them were. It was impossible not to. Everyone did. But here she was, giving me the weepy ins-and-outs.

Speaking of ins-and-outs, I was dizzy. I hadn't had drinks with sugar in them like that in ages. Nicole seemed bright and buttoned up, perfectly together, but I noticed I was starting to get drunk. I was a little friendlier, I was making more faces, I was less conscious of the camera, and I wanted to go home more than ever.

"But then again, your relationship is perfect, isn't it?" she was saying, when I realized I was supposed to be answering.

I don't want to make it sound like I was wasted. I wasn't. But sugar-drunk is a different drunk. It brings on anxiety for me. The sugar races through my metabolism and warns my brain to *panic* because a debilitating headache is on the way. It's distracting. It makes me sleepy. It makes me hungry. It doesn't make me want to have my first heart to heart with any stranger, much less one who had been smiling from a poster in my bedroom a decade and a half prior.

"My relationship? No. We got into a disagreement the other night. I mean it was perfect. But then we moved. To somewhere I hated. No offense to that city, but I hated it, and it wasn't right for me."

She prodded me for more. I revisited my soccer career, its end, and thoughts of my potential foray into personal training and nutrition. Then, as is the thing that happens every time me and DeKuyper meet up...

I blacked out. Can't remember a thing.

18

Zoe

What bothered Zoe the most about Nicole was the fact that she had the distinct attitude of someone who had been handed *everything*. Not that most of these bitches on the show hadn't been handed *everything*, and still managed to fuck it up, but Nicole really *acted* like it. And not in that cartoonish, somewhat fun, Lady Gaga–type way. She was legit aloof to her bones. She got famous young, and her parents let the nation sexualize her.

She was one of those superstars who, Zoe believed, would still be performing in shopping malls if not for a hands-on team of agents and managers propelling her through her landscape. When Nicole's publicist, a colleague of Regan's, let Zoe know Ms. Trace was signing the participant agreement, Zoe was certain Nicole would deliver the most outrageous content. It only took filming one interview with her to reveal she had the personality of a moist towelette. It wasn't like the Sabrina confessional, in which she didn't want to reveal much about herself; Nicole wasn't that interesting. She talked about her role models for the most part. Zero TVQ. God they were going to have to script her throughout the filming, if she was going to come off as anything.

Outside those Q&As, all they had to this point was what looked like a lame extended Rocky training montage of her trying to get her life back on track. It was awful. They had footage of her spending a thousand dollars in a vitamin shop and of her singing while running on the treadmill. They had her practicing mediation.

Fiona suggested they play up her woo-woo stuff and make her look like a whackadoo. She had a crystal orb she charged herself with a spell *"Clear and strong, full of light, may this crystal increase my might,"* a deck of Angel Cards she consulted for every decision, including what to eat, and she purified her shoes with sage before wearing them. They could work with that.

They had filmed her going to a psychic and crying because she told her she was still going to get married one day and have a child. That made Zoe and Milo both cringe since she didn't look like the sort of person who had an inhabitable womb. But then again, meth heads have kids all the time.

Not that Nicole is a meth head. But maybe they could allude.

Ugh, not even worth it. Nicole was coming off as a big bust. All she could be now was a Pathetic Mess character.

The problem was Zoe knew Nicole *had* more in her.

But all the drama from the night at the club? Oh, it was solid. And Nicole came to *Zoe* with the idea. Mostly, she said *let's get Dahlia white girl wasted and talk shit about her relationship.*

And what do you know?

Get a little too much sugary booze in Dahlia's system and cut all of Nicole's shots with water. (She had rejected the idea of staying completely sober. Respect.)

All it took was a few shots of high-proof, high-sugar crap booze. Zoe wondered if Dahlia remembered telling Dr. Steiner about how she tended to black out whenever she had any drinks college kids can afford. And okay, whatever, was it only the booze? No, Zoe might have slipped her a little something extra.

Don't judge me, Zoe said to the audience in her head. Everyone has to get their job done; in fact, she was *doing* Dahlia's *for her.*

She was welcome.

Dahlia spilled her own tea, all over herself. She talked about how things had been much better before they moved and how much she hated it there in *that* place, how they've got separate lives now, and—when prompted—she confessed she *didn't* trust him as much as she wanted to. She was terrified he was cheating on her, even though she had no reason not to trust him. Even though *she* was the one who was lying to him.

Lying how?

It turns out Little Miss Gold Digger is also Little Miss Secret Birth Control. He thinks they're trying to have a baby—or at least not trying *not* to—but Dahlia was taking birth control pills every day. Her tearful monologue, albeit slurred and would require the use of subtitles post-production, included a long-winded confession that, unlike all the other players wives, and maybe it was because her sports background had rendered her somewhat less feminine, she remained unable to find that internal desire for motherhood, while Mick was out there oozing potential *big dad energy*.

Zoe barely stifled her laugh when Dahlia mentioned Regan.

Ah, now *that* was rich.

19
Sabrina

"How did you get in here?"

Budgie had woken Sabrina up by tearing open the curtains and allowing in an absolute tidal wave of sunshine. She flung open the French doors that led to the balcony.

"This place is as stuffy as a mousehole. You need fresh air."

"I'll be fine. I'm fine." Sabrina said.

"You're sleeping late. You didn't happen to—" she squinted at her cousin. "Makeup still on. Hair was curled last night. Shoes right by the bed. What did you do last night, dear Bri?"

"Nothing, I met up with an old co-star downtown and then… you know, came home."

"I don't buy it."

"It's true."

"Something has been off about you lately." She looked at the other side of Sabrina's king-sized bed. "You sleep like Julie Andrews, sitting straight up in bed, not ever making a fuss or a muss. And now your whole bed is a mess."

"Am I not entitled to that?"

"Of course you are! But something is off, you're lying to me."

"Certainly not. And it's far too early in the day to be accused of such a thing."

"I've had twenty-year-olds lying to me for as long as I can remember. *It must be a bug*, they say, when I can smell the whiskey from last night. You are lying to me, and I can't imagine why."

"I am not lying."

"Then someone must have broken in. Maybe it was that anonymous Adonis you were caught creeping around with the other night? We never did dissect that."

"I already told you that was nothing more than a drink with a new friend."

The two of them stared at each other.

"Fine then. Suit yourself. But it's time to get ready."

Sabrina yawned and pushed off the Coeurs Pink D. Porthault sheets she'd bought the second she didn't have to worry about her husband and his taste.

"Ooh, lovely tan," said Budgie.

"Thank you, I bought it yesterday."

"The crew will be here within the hour, your hair and makeup are waiting in the foyer. Better start getting ready, you don't want them seeing the *actual* whole process, do you?"

Budgie herself was in a pale violet blouse with a high collar, a low chignon bun, sparkling lilac earrings, and a pair of purple, high-waisted pants. Her shoes were the same lilac as the earrings. She looked as though she had rested for forty-eight full hours.

Not like Sabrina, who had spent the last few days in a romantic whirlwind with a man she never would have thought she'd like.

Within an hour, Sabrina was ready, which Budgie commented on with admiration as usual. People always told Sabrina she was naturally pretty, but whether that was true or not, what she did specialize in was looking drastically different with or without makeup—not worse and then better, but different. She got a lot of press for being a chameleon when she was young. One second, she was Heroin Chic, the next she looked worthy of Grecian royalty, the next she was straight out of old Hollywood.

That was the choice for today.

Her hair was curled in what she always thought of as the Grace Kelly look. Her makeup was subtle.

The Grace Kelly look was not quite right.

At her request they adjusted things for a few minutes; she asked for a few extra curls here and there, and ended up with something closer to Veronica Lake.

The crew arrived and set up, and Zoe was absent, having been replaced for this shoot by Fiona. Sabrina was not a fan. Between the deliberate insertion of British expressions into the conversation and the encyclopedic knowledge of the minutia of Sabrina's life, she reminded her of those pandering journalists Sabrina endured when she was first married.

After a monologue with content of zero interest to Sabrina, including a reference to how *knackered* she was feeling today, how that's the price for producing *factual programs*, and how she was missing her lover back home, whom she hadn't seen *in a donkey's years*, she took Budgie and Sabrina through the breakdown of the scene.

They were to talk about the other ladies, specifically Mariana and Dahlia.

"What are we supposed to say?" asked Sabrina.

"The two of them sort of get into it, don't they? Dahlia said Mariana looked like she'd gotten a whole rack of plastic surgery done? And Mariana *hasn't*," she put the last word in sarcastic air quotes. "There was that. Oh, also feel free to talk about Lexi's thing with her man, that whole … arrangement. Also, how was it spending time with Dahlia at the book party?"

"Is there an arrangement?" Budgie asked, looking delighted.

"On camera please."

Sabrina and Budgie got into position on the settee on the balcony. The wind was blowing a little, and the sun was at its most golden.

When they got the go-ahead, Budgie began. "I have always loved it up here. You ever think about the fact that you've got a monopoly on sunshine, while half that city is in the dark?"

"I do, actually," she said, scrambling to think of something to say that wouldn't come off as elitist. "I don't think I'd have the strength to live in this city if I couldn't have a little nature like this."

"You couldn't live in the city if you weren't rich as sin?"

She wanted to bite back *you are too, Budgie dear,* but instead she gave a polite laugh. "I guess not."

"And that's coming from someone who was born here. What are all these transplants doing living in broom closets if even you can't stand the idea?"

"Trying to make their dreams come true, I suppose," said Sabrina, tone sharpened. "For a lot of them, it's up to you if they do, isn't it?"

"Sad, but true," Budgie acknowledged. "The worst outcome is when all those fresh-faced kids off the bus from Minnesota start getting themselves all faked up in an effort to keep up. The only thing that ever makes a star is if they stand out. All these kids start blending in with all the others. It's not as big in theatre, but it's still a problem."

Sabrina nodded, understanding it was her cue. "You say that, but wasn't it you who had a plastic party?"

"Don't get me wrong, I don't think there's anything wrong at all with getting yourself *done*. But it should be about yourself, not about trying to *succeed* or fit into some mold that'll change in two hours."

They both took a sip of rosé at the same time, and as the pink liquid caught the rays of the sun, they exchanged an undocumented look that meant they had both done about a hundred things in their past to keep up with the Joneses, including Sabrina's nose job at fifteen. She would *never* let Aubrey do that. How had her mother?

It made her cringe.

That the camera probably caught.

"What do you think, is Mariana full of it?" asked Budgie.

"I think she's a bitch."

Budgie almost spat out her wine, and Sabrina's gut plummeted. It had come out of her like water from a geyser. It was the wine on an empty stomach, it was the cloud-high head she still had from last night, it was the way she felt compelled to defend Dahlia.

"Ha! Well tell me how you really feel, kiddo."

"I'm sorry, I shouldn't have said that. She…"

"Is?"

"Is."

Budgie laughed. "Ah man, remember when you were younger, you never used to hold back."

"Got into a lot of trouble for that."

"You sure did. Such a sweet kid, and then puberty hit and you had a tongue like a razor blade."

"Would that were true, I would be less worried about Robbie being out there in the world right now. If you catch my drift."

Budgie's eyebrows looked like they might disappear into her hairline. "Ha!"

"Great, great, that's great stuff," said Fiona halting everything that had, for a moment, flowed naturally. "If you could talk a little bit about Lexi and Tom's weird relationship, we'll have everything we need."

Sabrina and Budgie paused before trying to get the rhythm back.

"You went to Lexi's? What was that about?"

"I did." Sabrina said. "It wasn't what I expected. It's her partner's home, not hers."

"Did you meet him?" Sabrina nodded and took a sip of wine. "And?"

"He is a terrible, despicable man. I can't say much more than that, because he is not worth the breath. Quite truly."

"Considering how many words you had for Rob, I'm surprised."

"They are cut from the same cloth, I promise you. And that girl deserves better."

"I didn't get the feeling you were all that fond of Lexi."

"I'm not *not* fond of her. I see myself in her. An absolute reflection of modern times, like I was, except perhaps I dislike where modern times have taken us. Or perhaps I'm angry with myself, and that's all it is. Or none of that."

Sabrina paused after that, wishing perhaps she had kept it lighter, and Budgie took the opportunity to try for her.

"We all feel that way, sugar, but I guess when you're the icon of a generation it's easier to feel more than the rest of us. Lexi's the kind of kid I want to kick in the rear and make her start thinking for herself."

"Especially not to be a sugar baby to a chauvinist asshole."

"Sugar baby? I thought her boyfriend was some blonde guy with a bun and the abs."

Sabrina's lungs felt like they collapsed, her stomach turned. "No, that's her yoga teacher, or spiritual coach. Her boyfriend is an older man."

"Spiritual coach?" Budgie teased. "She has a private yoga teacher?"

Sabrina shook her head yes. "He's a good-looking guy. His name is Leo."

"Leo."

"Leo."

"Did you … meet Leo too?"

Sabrina tossed her a glance that told more than she meant to. "I did."

"And how was he?"

Sabrina fought the girlish smile that was threatening. "He wa—he seemed very nice. It was brief."

"Aw, too bad."

"I only met him for a moment. That day. I mean, that day, I met him briefly." Sabrina explained.

"Mm."

The conversation went dead. Sabrina knew Budgie had figured out Leo was the blurry face from the *Post*. She avoided eye contact with her cousin. She'd always been a terrible liar. It was something she had wanted to scream at the press when they accused her of dishonesty. All she wanted was to tell them that she could not lie to save her life.

After what seemed like five minutes, but was closer to fifteen seconds of dead air, Fiona broke the silence, "Okay, we have everything we need here. Let's head to the party. And Sabrina, before you go, might I grab a word with you?"

When Sabrina agreed, Fiona asked the crew to pack up.

Once alone on the balcony, Fiona leaned against the banister. "Listen, can I be honest with you?" She didn't stop to give Sabrina time to answer. "You have to let your hair down. Be yourself, even if it isn't yourself, find a self to be. Remember the *it girl* you always were? We need you to be *that* Sabrina Verroye. This girl here, who called Mariana a bitch? We need more of *that*."

"That's because you want someone to throw a drink in my face."

"No, it isn't! If you do *that*, that's *you*, that's what Aleksandr wants. The truth, *not* all the posturing. Find the old Sabrina that Budgie was talking about. Let loose."

"If you want her, I hope you have about a pound of cocaine and a time machine."

"I can't get my hands on the time machine, but—"

"God, I'm kidding. A hundred percent kidding. I hear you."

"But more than that, we need you to do something."

"What do you need me to do?"

"We need you to be the confidante. Get the others to tell you their secrets. We know they've got them, but we can't do anything with it unless they tell someone."

Sabrina waited for the ethical pull downward of her gut, but nothing came. Perhaps she could no longer feel very much.

"Why would I do that?"

"Because we want to make you look good. If we want to do that, we need other people to look like they've lost the plot. That's how this works. Reveal or be revealed."

"That doesn't sound like you're working hard on anyone's side."

"Oh, I am. You have no idea. You're the star here, and they can make you go one way or the other, and I feel very strong about everything you stood up against."

Sabrina scanned Fiona's face for deceit but found nothing but her blank stare, a tinge of hope.

"You're going to look trustworthy, like a good friend. Any prodding you do to get them to tell you, of course we can edit that out. We get—Aleksandr gets—what you're going for. You want redemption, and you will be redeemed. Trust me. I wouldn't lie to you."

"Why wouldn't you lie to me?"

Fiona shrugged and smiled. "You were one of my idols growing up over there. I loved you. I hated the way the press made you out. Trust me. I'm going to see if my mom has any pictures of my room to send me, I made this whole wall collage of Sabrina's Style. It's embarrassing."

It always made her feel strange when people said that sort of thing to her. It always gave her a shade of discomfort and violation, but a much bigger part of her…

"That's still not quite…"

"Look, Sabrina," Fiona was very serious now. "The truth is *they* decide how you look. *They* do. If you want to look like anything other than a malicious wanker, you'll help them get what they need. Otherwise, you," she leaned in close enough that Sabrina could smell her coffee-breath, "you don't always come off that great. You need to either play along or stand by your principles and look like the bitch everyone already hopes you are."

The blood drained from Sabrina's face.

"It'll be far easier to be against you, Sabrina. And eventually, you aren't even love *to hate*. That's when you're done … finished."

Sabrina had gone stiff and numb.

It was too hard to even think, to admit to herself.

She had loved it. She wanted it back. She needed it. And it made her sick to imagine those days were gone forever.

20
Zoe

Fiona texted Zoe and told her Sabrina was down to extract as much information as she could from the other women. No reply, but then Zoe sent the group chat a text sharing *her* good news—they had all the women's phone passwords. It took some trickery. It was a group effort. Milo filmed Lexi using a "literally amazing" face mask and hand treatment, a promo for one of her brand partners, then waited a few seconds for her to need her phone, which she could not use facial recognition or touch ID to open. Boom. Budgie simply gave it to Zoe when she had to borrow her phone. Mariana did too, when her nails were drying, and Zoe asked if she had any photos of her dog. Nicole couldn't get her touch ID to work half the time and had an old phone; eventually, one of the crew members saw the code. Sabrina had been the hardest since she rarely touched her phone. But when they filmed a phone call with Mariana, she put it in, and Fiona had seen it.

Zoe also let Aleksandr know and texted him: *Taking the ladies' phones away later, got all the passcodes. We're in.*

Aleksandr sent back a double thumbs-up. That was all. No text, no affirmations.

It disappointed Zoe and wasn't enough. She needed more. He was such a withholding douchebag. She couldn't believe she had to clamber for his approval.

21
Dahlia

When I arrived at Mariana's party stone-cold-sober, I intended to stay that way. I was pretty sure I had never quite shaken the hangover from the outing with Nicole. Zoe comforted me by saying I didn't say or do anything embarrassing that night, but frig—I hadn't had such a horrible experience since college. What was it about drinking on *this* particular job that made it that much worse?

Maybe I had rounded some age curve and my body was unwilling to take it anymore. Or perhaps it was because this whole process was sketchy.

Mariana had a penthouse in the top of one of those old apartment buildings that looked like it would be at home in one of those sappy seventies tragedy romances that still had enough old-school glamour but was starting to pick up the tasteless details of coming decades.

The crew with me had to take the elevator before and after I did, since it was the size of a coffin. Zoe rode up with me, doing something that felt a lot like coaching. She was telling me that the party was going to have a surprise twist and that Mariana was surely going to be a bigger bitch than usual, but not to let her get away with it.

Things were still rocky with Mick at home, but I wished he was with me. Instead, he was having another meeting with Regan. Regan, the cool girl who was undoubtedly ripping the meat from a chicken wing with her perfect veneers and ordering another pitcher of cheap beer.

I am, "I can't drink cheap beer."

She is, "let's fucking *go*."

I used to be the "let's fucking *go*" girl. What happened?

The elevator opened once we arrived at the PH, and I swear that apartment looked familiar. Like it had been in a thousand movies. It had a long hallway as a foyer with a mirror and decorative table that had a picture of Mariana and others who I supposed was her husband and child. I hadn't considered that she had either of those things.

The crew was filming my entrance.

"Welcome," said a girl in a stiff white button down, a little black bowtie, unflattering black pants, and shiny black shoes that looked like they came from Mickey Mouse's closet.

"Champagne?"

"Sure."

Dammit. Okay, I'll have to be careful.

"The hostess requests all shoes be left by the closet there. New carpets."

I looked at the girl. "Did you ever see that episode of *Sex and the City*?"

The girl smiled, then hid it like she wasn't supposed to, but nodded. I smiled back, hoping I came off human, instead of elitist and trying in some misguided way to *connect with the people*.

The apartment looked decorated by a previous generation, stately, untouchable, as if Mariana and her family had merely moved in when it was vacated by some rich old grandmother. A grandmother with taste, but the sort of taste that involved a zillion crystal candy dishes and ornate gold framed mirrors, uncomfortable looking furniture that was Lilliputian-sized.

It didn't have a touch of the modern aesthetic whatsoever. If I had ventured a guess at what Mariana's place might have looked like, I would have pictured bright colors and abstract art (possibly of herself partially clothed or naked altogether).

Maybe some animal print pillows or crystal chandeliers. But instead, there were no shoes allowed inside and I was sure that was a Fabergé egg on the mantle.

The others were already there, along with a few people I didn't know; rookies who were sitting uncomfortably and trying not to look at the camera. That had been me only a small time ago, now I felt a bit like the pro.

In other words, I was being smug. I guess that meant I was in a good mood. You can't be smug in a bad mood.

Sabrina and Budgie were looking über-Verroye with their timeless style. Lexi was in a cropped top and a matching skirt with a high slit and had a sky-high bubble ponytail. Mariana seemed to be channeling Sharon Tate in a kaftan and a half-up half-down, teased hair. She even had on the black liner and pale lipstick.

Nicole wasn't there yet.

"Ah, there's Dahlia, come on in, love," said Mariana, sweeping over to me, her flowing dress out like wings.

"Hi, this place is so nice!" I said, through double cheek kisses.

"Oh, thank you! Yes, okay, now come, come—oh, there's Nicole!"

Nicole got the instruction on the shoe rule, looked confused and irritated with the poor catering girl, snatched a glass of champagne from her tray, and came in smiling.

"Okay, now that we're all here," announced Mariana, "I have a little surprise for everyone, if you could all follow me into the *parlor*, we can start!"

Start?

It took half an hour of stuttered film setup for us to actually follow her, and I regret to admit I had made it onto a second glass of champagne.

I couldn't help myself. I would never get used to having all this good champagne on tap. My family used to get a nice bottle every big holiday, and we would savor it like it would light on fire if we drank too fast.

Once in the "parlor," we were faced with a big table covered
in.... Perhaps someone else might have guessed what was coming,
but I did not.

"Sex Toy party!" screamed Mariana.

Please. People still do these? I knew it was her business, but
I didn't think ... we would be faced with it.

There was a gasp of prudish shock from some of the other ladies
that I didn't know. Lexi squealed, "*oh my god no way!*"

Budgie laughed and picked up a bright red, translucent double-
ended dildo that reminded me of sickly-sweet hospital Jell-O.

Nicole looked downright offended. Sabrina looked blank,
which I guessed was her only alternative to pleasant. Well-trained
in diplomacy and tact.

Behind the table, there were two girls in matching pink T-shirts
with a heart logo. Employees of Mariana I gathered, from how the
three interacted and huddled off camera. When one of them turned
to close up a cardboard box, I saw that it was the business name and
logo: *Come Get Some.*

The two girls got our attention by clapping—yes, clapping—and
then the taller, thinner, uglier of the two said, "Hey ladies! Thank
you all for showing up today, this is amazing to see everyone! Okay,
first thing's first, let's all make a vow right here and now to be
totally open! This is a judgment-free zone!"

She spoke in constant exclamation points, even without
shouting.

"Right!" Agreed the other girl. "We're all women trying to feel
good, you know what I'm saying?"

She seemed too young to call herself a woman, and too immature
to even notice that she was not sexually fulfilled without a little
something extra. When I was twenty-one, which I assumed was
around her age, I was still imitating porn and pretending everything
felt shudderingly good. It wasn't until Mick that I even had an
orgasm. And even then, it took as much commitment, work, and as
many learning curves as mastering trigonometry.

With a lurch, I had a vague memory of sharing that with Nicole at that awful bar.

Dammit.

If I said that, no doubt I said worse.

"But first let's all start with a round of…"

The two of them turned to the server from the front hall, who had made her way in with a silver tray of glow-in-the dark pink shots.

"Wet Pussy shots!" the two of them exclaimed together. Mariana whooped with her arms in the air.

We all took one, and then the two girls—who were starting to remind me of the twins from *The Shining*—said, "to our pussies!"

When no one repeated it, they paused filming and told us we had to, for the toast.

"To our pussies!" we all said, but I made a sarcastic face when I said it, before miming a gag and then taking the shot.

Zoe paused filming for a second and approached Nicole. She showed her something on her phone and Nicole nodded. Once Zoe was out of the shot, we resumed. Nicole said, "You know Dahlia, you need to get more at peace with your body. After everything you told me the other night, it seems to me this party is perfect for you."

She did not, it is important to note, whisper this.

"I—did I say something that makes you to think I'm not?"

"Wait, you didn't black out did you?" Mariana piped up. "How collegiate-chic."

"No, okay, I didn't—I—why are you saying that?" I looked at Zoe who refused to make eye contact.

"If you want me to repeat it, it's downright sad that you can't get yourself to orgasm without a toy. A woman ought to know herself better than that, don't you think?"

My whole body flushed a deep scarlet. Why did I tell her that?

It's a job, she's not your real friend, come up with something…

"Oh, maybe I could, but I can't be bothered. Why reinvent the wheel? They made those things for a reason."

I said it with a gesture at the front table.

It made everyone laugh, and Nicole gave a squint and a smile.

For the next three hours—*three hours*—we had to react as the girls demonstrated and talked about all manner of different ointments, creams, gels, and instruments of every shape, color, and kind.

The worst part was that most of the vibrators were called The Mariana followed by a roman numeral.

The last thing I wanted to think about when, well, you get the picture.

"This chocolate body paint is *vegan* for any vegans out there—or if you have a vegan partner!"

"This one has fifteen settings—*whoa*!"

"This one we love because it's one hundred percent discreet. It looks like mascara, but—surprise! It's a vibrator!"

"This one is called *O, Baby*! And it's a tightener that I *swear* it'll get your lady pocket tighter than it ever started out!"

A) Lady pocket was about the grossest thing I'd ever heard.

B) "Than it ever started out," called to mind another inappropriate implication.

"This warming liquid is am*azing* on winter nights!"

"This cooling liquid is perfect for hot summer days and nights like this!"

Temperature didn't feel like a real relevant problem to me.

"This one tickles!"

"These whips are also vegan leather…"

"These handcuffs are *beyond* and we have them in pink, black, and cheetah."

It was endless, and we all had to laugh and squeal and rub things into our palms and wrists and feel things as they buzzed. Torture.

The big surprise for me was how much Sabrina played along. She wasn't acting all aloof and disgusted but kind of curious. Budgie's zingers were endless.

At the end the girls handed out forms we were supposed to fill out. It was a risk to put your name down on an order Mariana would certainly see. Nothing was so innocent that it wouldn't be possible—and likely—for her to judge. She could say all she wanted that she was the most open-minded, she started this business because every woman *blah blah blah*, but there was no way.

I put down an order for an aphrodisiac pheromone perfume (that I had private hopes might work) and a pocket vibrator that seemed innocent enough but wouldn't make me a puritan.

I was going down the list looking for anything else I could want, thinking how bizarre it was to throw a party where all your guests had to come buy something from you, when a man entered the room.

He was in a paisley button down and white, slim-cut pants. My immediate assumption was that he was gay.

"Girls, hello!"

What fresh hell…

"Sorry to crash ladies' night, but I simply *had* to. Isn't all this a *hoot*?" he said, feeling too familiar. "I hope my beautiful wife has shown you all a great time tonight, don't forget to pick something out for your hubbies and boy toys!"

"What the…" I said out loud by accident. Only Sabrina heard me, and I could see from her tight cheekbones that she was resisting a smile. Budgie beside her had a look on her face that seemed, somehow to say, *ah, another gay husband*.

Afterward, we were all to mingle. While some of the women went up to the Shining Twins and asked them for details on products, I flew to the side of The Gay Husband, desperate to understand more about him.

Who was he, why was he her husband, did he think we didn't know? Did he not know? Was I a bitch for naming him gay without knowing him?

Maybe.

He introduced himself to me by saying, "Hey, hi, hello! I'm George, look at you, what a *great* figure!"

Straight men don't call it a *figure*.

"Thank you," I said, taking another glass of champagne, and smiling at the girl serving it. "Your house is lovely."

"Ugh, I know, mother decorated it. It's such a *perfect* place for us, it makes me think of Paris in the twenties. I want to recline on a couch nude and have Picasso make a mess of me. You know what I mean?"

Wow, what *even* was this man?

"I say do it!" I said, leaning forward and then laughing. He cracked up.

"You're a trip!" he said. "I like you! We could cause some mischief together," and he gave me a wink and a side hug.

"How did you and Mariana meet?" I asked.

"I used to be in a band, and she used to come to our shows. That was about twenty years ago now."

"A band? What kind of band?"

I thought of my own short-lived high school groupie days. Boys in skinny jeans with mediocre voices, when I earned street cred saying the lead singer was my boyfriend (and would be for a total of two weeks max).

"A cabaret band at this little jazz place down in the village. What a fun year that was."

"A cabaret band, seriously? How cool," I said, wanting someone else to be hearing the conversation.

"Yes, I'm having a bit of a fan moment with Budgie Verroye here, if I'm honest. It was my *dream* to work in theatre. Now I'm stuck in publishing, running one of the top fashion books in the world, but who *cares* when it's not your dream?" He cracked up, and his voice reached pitches higher than mine could. "Got close though, working at that drag bar off 6th was *heaven*."

Okay, I quit.

22
Zoe

Scheduling the group trip was a nightmare. Usually, the trip would be to a far-away lavish destination, but Nicole's schedule didn't line up with Budgie's, and Mariana had a morning-show spot to film that further conflicted. Aleksandr needed to be close to the city for post-production he was doing on another project, so it was decided that since the Verroyes had a home in Nantucket and Nicole had committed to a luxe summer rental there, that would suffice. Close enough to buzz back to New York, but still a short plane trip away enough to allow for someone to get into trouble.

The first several hours of filming were spent on the walkthroughs of the compounds. The content felt like filming for HGTV, which was the last thing in the *world* she would ever, ever want to do. The best she could do was to force Budgie and Sabrina to point out different luxuries, but the most interesting edit she would get from that was to make them seem braggy and boastful of their wealth. Dull. People wanted to see the glam for sure, but it wasn't the kind of barefaced manipulation she preferred. It was like playing checkers instead of chess.

And it had nothing to do with the fact that these women seemed *over* their beautiful digs, while the staff was relegated to the cheapest motels—literally *Barnacle Bill's Bed & Breakfast*, which included no breakfast and barely a bed. More like a canvas bag of metal springs.

Mariana did a good job as usual. She made all sorts of faces behind their backs and tried to exchange a few words with everyone about Dahlia, who wasn't being the bitch they'd hoped. Mariana had stepped into that role for sure. Dahlia was going to need to be something else. Zoe was thinking martyr, victim.

Oh, and maybe alcoholic. Former athlete—it would be perfect except for some reason she had the tolerance of a bootlegger unless they gave her a little something extra, like they had at Nicole's bar.

Sabrina was also quite the lush, but it was far more depressing on her.

Nicole had rallied. She was, after all, how they got some of their biggest drama for the season. Not that they could use that until the end … they had to wait to use *that*.

Lexi was there as a trope and a joke. She was plugging her shit all day long. Paid sponsorship Lexi. Eye *roll*. She was in an athleisure phase, but give her time, soon she'll have a sprinter van she got for free and be all hippied out in Joshua Tree.

The explosion with Sabrina and Lexi's old Sugar Daddy had been solid too. It was good enough that Lexi's "boyfriend" was a fat, ugly, rich, monster, but to find out he was a misogynist as well? It had been clutch to get him on board for the beach weekend. Didn't think they were going to nab him.

Budgie was still comic relief. Her scenes at the theaters were good. They'd get that old, bored, *Glee* audience to watch for those. And all the desperate Broadway wannabes could hope for a clue as to what it was that the Great Budgie Verroye looked for. The audition scene they filmed with her had been great. She had been snarky and cruel, but in that likeable way that Budgie had. Which was perfect.

And Mick. Oh, Mick. He had unwittingly done his job beautifully. Dahlia hadn't even begun to notice.

Aleksandr had finally texted *one* comment that indicated a modicum of approval.

Wow.

That was it. And Zoe knew she was on the right track.

23
Dahlia

The crew filmed me getting ready for Nicole's dock party. Since Mariana had taken up residence in the guest house, I was in a room upstairs in the main building of Sabrina and Budgie's *incredibly* bougie beach house. Their compound had better visuals than the hotel suite Mick and I were staying in. Budgie had described the property as a cottage, but … yeah, no. We had a beach house when I was a kid that served the opposite purpose. You had no choice but to call it a beach house, but anyone who visited would find that it was on a crappy beach and smelled like mildew and had bunkbeds for maximum sleeping capacity.

Mick and I had flown up and together listened to a funny podcast in the car to JFK; we were laughing, but we didn't talk. That sort of summed up our *lately*.

Tonight, I poured everything in to trying to be beautiful.

We were told to dress beachy cocktail chic. I had bought a midi dress in a pale moss green color they called *Delirium Green*. It was feminine and sexy without showing off all the goods. The cut-out details flaunted my abs which looked phenomenal thanks to all those planks and star planks. I paired it with neutral heeled sandals and twist gold tone leather hoop earrings.

Sabrina shared her glam team with me and we went for simple and clean. My hair was styled long and loose and they used a technique I'd seen on Instagram to play up my lips. It worked—they appeared even pillowier than usual.

The whole look was working.

Perhaps I'd get a compliment on the internet for once.

As soon as I married Mick Irvine, the internet took to disassembling me into insult-able chunks.

She's sooo not hot enough for him!
OMG he can do way way better than her.
She looks like a bitch.
She was clearly a gold digger … talk about jackpot. Classless.
Dahlia Irvine is a GOLD_DIGGING SKANK she ain't even cute.
She's had tons of work done.
She has money, why doesn't she get some work done?

It was endless and all I had to do was exist. Well, exist and get the guy. They were shielded by the internet and its façade of anonymity. It's not anonymous at all, in fact, given the right amount of time, wine and wrath, I could get to know them very well.

For example, Little Miss *She was clearly a gold digger.* Her name is Sara, and she is a single, living in Atlantic City, working as a server. In her Insta profile she describes herself as a dancer and a foodie (interesting combo). But that's not all—she also notes that kindness is Key! With little emojis to match. Smile=Key emoji. When not posting photos of her thonged ass covered in sand in Cancun, she posts gym selfies with sideboob and thirst-trap captions. And it's her fault I went through her Insta with a critical eye. She's the asshole. Not me.

Mick matched my wardrobe mood. He was in a tan suit, white shirt with a Mandarin collar. He was wearing the sleek, shining chestnut loafers I bought him for his birthday.

He looked good. And all I wanted was to hug him, kiss him, and have him love me back. He still didn't feel like the Mick I knew. He was distant, even when he laughed and joked with me.

You'd think I had cheated on him and he was trying to forgive me but couldn't.

He kept telling me things were okay. He kept telling me I was worrying for nothing. Worse than that, I did not *dare* tell him I was

worried about all the time he was spending with Regan. A lot of
work stuff *was* changing with him, which would make sense for
why they were together as much as they were. But still, something
didn't sit right. I was trying to say to myself that the discomfort
came from the suspicion—and the suspicion could be wrong. But
it didn't matter, my instincts seemed to be kicking in.

And what do you do when you believe *your man* might be trying
to leave you? Well, as easygoing and feminist as I'd like to be, as
much as I'd like to say you don't *need* to play games once you have
committed your life to someone, I'm sorry I cannot say that. The
truth is, you don't act like a bitch, you don't nag, you don't call
him out and scream at him until he admits it. You try to remind
him why he loves you. You hope that you are still that amazing,
transfixing, super fun girl he fell in love with, and he comes back
to you, horrified and admits it because he can't bare to know he's
hurting his sweet, sweet girl. And the best-case scenario is that you
were wrong, and you needed to put a little pep back in your step.

Or? You nag him until he says, "Yes, okay, you figured it out."

Neither gets you the guy. Not really. The only other option is
that you be your awesome self, and he gets back to normal. Then of
course, you never know for sure if he was cheating or not.

Ain't love grand?

Moving on.

I had spent a whole lot of time smiling and being *chill* Dahlia
with Mick right now. It was making me resent him for a whole
rack of new reasons.

Once we were ready, we met Mariana, Sabrina, Budgie, and her
friend Sam down on the dock. We would be taking the Duffy to
Nicole's rental property. I had never even heard of a Duffy but
was curious.

It was an electric boat with a striped, fabric top, and a luxurious
interior. The name on the rear read *Watts of Fun*. We all had to
remove our shoes before boarding to protect the gleaming wood
from scratches. Plastic flaps kept out the wind. It was outfitted with

butter-soft leather (could it be real leather on a boat with open sides? It sure felt like it) and plush pillows. One out of place toss cushion read "*What Happens on the Duffy Stays on the Duffy.*" I didn't suspect a lot happened on the Duffy, the cushion must have been a hostess gift.

There was a small bar, I was told, behind my left elbow, at the back of the boat. I pressed a button and found a cavity filled with expensive bottles of liquor.

It was different from the super-fast gas guzzlers we'd buzz Star Island on, when in Miami, or the noisy pontoons we used to float around on with the other footballers and their wives in Texas. I was expecting this to be painful in an outdated sad way. Production's nod to the *past her best-before date* idea of Sabrina and her roots. But the Duffy ride was incredible fun. Sabrina was laughing and smiling lots. Budgie leaned over and acknowledged this, by saying she'd always been happier at the shore.

It was nice. Sam was catty, playing a character, but pleasant and at least *seemed* to like me.

He reminded me of Mariana's husband.

Speaking of Mariana, even she seemed to take a break from being horrible. Mind you when the camera was on her she ignored the rest of us and stood up making her way to the front of the boat to do her best *Titanic* "King of the World" pose, aiming her boobs heavenward. I think she thought she looked like a Bond girl, but it was closer to an outdated bronze figurehead. When she was done, she returned to join us at the back.

We had a bottle of Dom Perignon on the way, and Zoe sat down with us and shared that she had gotten news that the edits of the show to date were *perfect* and the higher-ups at the network *loved* it. She went on to say that the four of us were playing especially well, but not to tell anyone else.

***

When we arrived at Nicole's, we had to wait for them to find her because they needed to film her greeting us. She did, along with a girl who looked Eastern European in a uniform that would have looked at home on a yacht, except that it looked like it may have come from Party City. I didn't want to be judgmental, but it was too easy around these people.

The girl held a platter of pretty drinks she said were margaritas with some Blue Curacao for color, and we each took one. The house was massive and ultra-modern.

It would have been more at home on the moon.

I leaned over and said this to Mick, who gave me a polite laugh. Gave *me* a polite laugh. I'm his *wife*. I need this brand new, weird awkwardness to stop.

"Are these all of your closest, most personal friends then?" Mick asked Nicole.

Nicole laughed, forced and loud and patted him on the chest, "Oh my god, you are *too* funny! I knew you were hot, but not this *funny.*"

Oh! She's flirting. Okay.

Whatever.

I wasn't worried about it.

He didn't give back the old "let's not touch, though," smile that he usually does. He sort of cocked his head and smiled. Flirting back?

No. *Stop.*

Sort of regretted the fact that Cassie and I had split headphones in the back of class listening to the Nicole Trace album fifteen years ago, since one day she was going to hit on my husband. But whatever.

I wasn't worried about it at all.

She wasn't the Nicole Trace she once was.

Dammit, I was growing mean again. Critical Dahlia.

You know, when I was in college and early in my soccer days, I had a teammate, and together we were mean, judgmental, and standoffish to other girls. We would text each other in the locker room about other girls *in* the locker room. We laughed a lot, which is nice, I guess. But one day, we talked about it and decided we were disgusted with ourselves for how rude and nasty we'd been. We decided then and there to cut it out. Quit cold turkey.

And ever since then, I'd done a pretty good job of sticking to it.

Sure, I could watch some embarrassing crap TV or have an unpleasant exchange with someone at Target and make a snide comment or two, but I was nice. Even in the privacy of my own brain.

This was making me hateful and cynical, and it was all coming back to me. Even if I couldn't stop the thoughts, I knew I must resist letting them slip.

"If everyone can stop by the phone check right up there, that would be cool," said Nicole. She seemed far more alert than usual. When I noticed a rabbit-like twitch of the nose, I wondered if I knew why.

"Phone check?" asked Sam.

"Yes, it's like a coat check, but for your phone," she said it with a mute *whoever you are.*

"Really?" asked Budgie. "We do that sometimes at shows since people can't seem to *resist* taking pictures and videos and throwing off the actors. But for a party?"

"I value my privacy," said Nicole, with a sickly-sweet voice I remembered from the days of her youth, but which hadn't appeared in real life yet. "Thank you for understanding."

Weird as it was, we accepted her conditions, and walked up to the phone check, where we each received a ticket in exchange for our phones, which went into Ziploc bags. They looked like evidence.

"Plenty of hosts do this, I think it's *so* civilized," said Mariana, taking her ticket. "It's wonderful to not have everyone on their phones. Living in the moment, you know?"

"God, Lexi's head might explode," I said.

Only after I said it, did I realize *that* might sound mean.

Everyone at the party seemed young. Early twenties max. They almost looked like—and might have been—hired models, but not the quiet brooding ones. These were the kind with big boobs and orange fake tans, and the guys had great bodies and average faces. Did she hire people to fill it out? Otherwise, who would these people be?

Within an hour, I had a theory. The 'kids' as I could only think of them, made the party *wild*, *crazy*, *loud*, and perhaps *epic*! They danced, they squealed, they did shots, they fell in the pool. I supposed in that case, I understood.

Maybe part of this was the contrast—a good way to make Nicole look a little more put together than usual.

I know that's not the nicest thing to say, but she flirted with my husband and didn't say a word to me.

Not only that, but the pretty drinks were *strong*. I didn't notice until I realized I was getting *loose*. I was up in front of all the women, telling some story about the high-end hookers in Geneva who used to come into the hotel bar where I stayed.

"… and I swear she saw Obama come out of one of the ballrooms from a speech, and after that, he's in the lobby and she tried to pull the *same* move on him!"

Everyone laughed because my delivery was Full Personality. I wasn't wasted, but I was bursting with False Charisma.

I might have started to wonder if I should be embarrassed, but thankfully, Nicole took the cake.

Shortly after sundown, the live band stopped—as it did periodically to accommodate filming—and someone climbed up on stage to say that there was a big surprise for us.

"Oh no," I muttered, grabbing Lexi's shoulder beside me, bracing for what I hoped was about to happen.

An unidentified voice boomed, "Everyone, put your hands together for Nicole Trace!"

There was a teenage me inside somewhere who was excited to see Nicole Trace *live*. And there was another side of me that feared/hoped it would be the disaster I could only imagine it would be.

Nicole took the stage in a *tight* bodysuit studded with rhinestones and diamonds. Her hair was in slicked back high pigtails, and she wore coordinated boots. To her credit, she did still have a great body, and there was something about seeing her on stage that made it seem like whatever *it* was, she'd never quite lost it.

She took to the mic and thanked everybody.

"This is so weird," I said.

"It's *so* weird," agreed Lexi. "I mean she used to do this like *all* the time, right? She used to sell out Madison Square Garden, like … what?"

I shook my head, a frozen smile stunned onto my face as I watched her with wide eyes.

"*Ooh,*" she began.

I looked around for Mick.

He was nowhere to be found.

Dammit. I hoped he was at least seeing this…

"*Baby, oh baby, I saw you at the club and knew you were the one, oh baby…*"

I was trying not to be a jerk. Don't laugh, Dahlia, don't laugh… take another sip of your drink.

Sabrina appeared at my side. "Is she using a backtrack?"

"Oh my god wait," I said, "if you listen, you can hear her actual voice on top of it."

By the time it got to the chorus though, the backtrack had been turned down, which she looked surprised by. She kept singing, but it sounded … a lot different.

I was *not* laughing at her. But what was I supposed to do? If I saw that on TV I would have died.

She was dancing too, with backup dancers. They were all younger by many years, and far more flexible. They shifted and popped from position to position with fierce energy, and she couldn't quite get there.

I had a hand over my mouth and didn't even notice.

When it ended, I looked to Budgie, who looked placid.

She felt my gaze, smiled, and said, "Honey, when you been in the singing and dancing industry as long as I have, you get used to keeping a straight face."

And that said it all.

We all laughed like witches, and I knew I would feel guilty the next day. But for now, it was hilarious.

Mick reappeared, and I was trying not to laugh, but it was harder because everyone else was also trying not to laugh.

"Oh my god, honey did you—did you catch Nicole's performance?"

"I did."

"She was using a backing track for like half but then it shut off, and I mean…."

"Are you *making fun* of her?"

This sobered everyone.

"What? No, I—"

"She got up in front of people she thought were her friends, and now you're standing here laughing at her?"

What I couldn't say was that it was for sure all intended to be great footage, and what I also couldn't say was that Mick always cringed with me. He was my partner in cringe.

'*Thought were her friends?*' Did any of us think that?

"You have to admit, it was sort of surprising."

He stared at me, not a glimmer of humor on his face. "I don't even recognize you, Dahlia."

He walked straight over to the phone check, handed in his ticket, tossed one more glance at me, then went inside.

Everyone was looking at me.

"I wasn't laughing at her," I said. "Not really."

Everyone looked embarrassed. Embarrassed *for* me, which was the worst feeling.

"It was crazy to…"

There was no defending it.

Mariana sucked on her straw until it made dry, bubbling sounds.

Seeing as the party itself had no music, there wasn't even anything to hide the silence. It was quiet. And awful.

Mick was out front waiting for a car. The camera crew followed me, which I thought would piss him off, but it didn't.

"Mick, I'm sorry, I wasn't being catty, or I didn't mean to be. Please stay and take the boat back with me. It's—"

It's *TV*, I wanted to say.

"I'm not going to stand around and watch you act like this."

I barely knew her. But I couldn't say that either. The car pulled up.

"Look, let's go home and talk. I'll go with you."

"No, I don't want to talk. You can stay here." Mick slammed the door shut on the car and it pulled away.

I never thought I'd feel this way again. This is what it feels like right before you break up. When you can tell that your boyfriend has lost interest or that you have pushed him too far and that you're about to be thrown back into the sea without a life vest.

That can't be what's happening. It only feels like it. It's not real.

24
Zoe

Zoe, Milo, and Fiona crouched in a dimly lit guest bedroom on Nicole's property with a pile of phones and an iPad each.

"Anyone getting anything?" asked Zoe.

"I found a text from Duane Reade about an anti-depressant."

"Who?"

"Lexi."

"Lexi! Okay screenshot, send, delete, delete from recently deleted. And make a note to add a scene with Nicole talking anti-depressant addiction to her. Hurry, we got to find good stuff. Check their DMs, their texts, their photos. If it's something we can't use without it being obvious, we're going to have Lexi or Mariana 'find it.' Make a note if you find a good nude or something."

Milo was staring at Zoe. As was the GoPro on his chest, meant to capture party b-roll. Zoe was used to the gaze of the camera catching behind the scenes stuff. But still…

"What?" she asked.

"This is a little messed up."

This wasn't necessarily kosher. She wasn't sure if it was the kind of thing that Aleksandr would flow with or not.

It must be. No, for sure it was.

"Yeah? It's the job. Do you want to start over, Milo, do you want to quit or get fired from a project with Aleksandr, or do you want to shut up and find some gold in these bitches' phones?"

He shook his head. "You got it."

They found a lot. A receipt for a stole that was *real* fur on Budgie's phone. A *fake* Birkin purchased for Mariana. Nicole's Arizona concert getting canceled for low ticket sales. Lexi's dog was not a rescue but a fancy purebred flown in from Virginia.

Hours of conversation on text between Dahlia and some Cassie, about her distrust in Mick, her impending fears, her insecurities over Regan. Good, that was great.

Sabrina's communication with Leo. Loads of blue text bubbles to Aubrey, all unanswered, "I miss you." "Heading to the summer house in Nantucket next week. Wish we could be there together again." Zoe was hoping to find some scoop on the whole Robbie thing, but Sabrina had learned to protect herself a bit more. She had been in the game longer.

But they had enough.

25

Dahlia

Holy mother of pearl.

I didn't know hangovers could be this bad.

My head was splitting, I was nauseous which I *never* was, and I was dead tired.

Zoe had scheduled all of us for MorningAfteRX, a company that sponsored Lexi. It was one of those mobile services that brought IV drips to the house and tried to bring you back up to normal. The name was dumb and called to mind Plan B contraception before hangover cures, but whatever. They would show up on the breezy back deck of Budgie and Sabrina's place. Hopefully between the fresh salty air, a couple Excedrin, and that I would be back to normal.

The only agreement I had to make was that I would do it on camera.

I would have agreed to anything. I could not feel like this and go in to work. There is no calling in sick when you signed up for your life to be filmed. Even if it's not your real life.

The show must go on.

I was determined to be *up* for the filming, and to do that, I spent as long as I could in bed. I didn't remember much from the night before—again, strange for me—but I knew I'd been an ass. I usually took such pride in being the one riding a happy buzz, watching the fools make themselves. But this time, I was the embarrassing one.

It had to happen every once in a while, right?

The only thing I was nervous about was Mick. He had been out for a run.

When he came back in, I sat up in bed and looked at him with puppy-dog-eyes, hoping he wouldn't give me a tight-lipped nod before silently going off to the shower.

He didn't.

He shut the door behind him, came over to the bed, and took my hand. He then lowered his forehead to my fingertips the way he sometimes did when he needed us to be okay and we weren't.

Relief surged deep in my nervous system, and I swear half the hangover was cured.

I ran my other hand through his damp, hot hair, and bent to kiss it. I sat back up and so did he.

"I'm sorry, Dahl."

"I'm much sorrier."

He cracked a small smile. "You look pretty sorry."

"I'm a mess."

He squeezed my hand and then stood and walked to the balcony to open the door, letting in the salty breeze. The day seemed cool and bright now.

"I'm sorry about last night. You were right, I was wrong, I was being catty. I should have known better. Been better."

"I know that's not you. I don't know what I-I don't know what's going on with me. I think I've—"

He looked at me like he might ... what? Confess something? Something was there, resting on his tongue, unwilling to come out.

I wanted to pry. Instead, I shook my head and tried to look forgivable.

"I don't know what's going on with me either. The show might be bringing out the worst side of me."

He sat down next to me again. "It's okay. You don't owe me the apology. I shouldn't have left. Especially on camera. That's not us."

"It's not." I shook my head. "We haven't been us lately, and that makes me act and feel crazy." Tears filled my eyes.

Hangovers gave me the blues, and they made me loving and emotional. So did making up.

"I know."

"It's not an excuse, I'm not saying that. And how drunk I was last night wasn't either—you know I never get like that. Something about this show, I feel like I'm always wasted."

He nodded and bit his lip. "I was wondering if they pulled the Everclear trick on you. Didn't you say you saw Zoe doing that before?"

"Do you think? But I didn't taste anything. I mean, *you know* I never get like that. Maybe a headache in the morning or the occasional silly drunk, but never *messed* like that."

He nodded again. "How are you feeling now?"

"Awful. But Zoe and Lexi got one of those IV doctor people to come. Lexi is in partnership with the company. She's their Brand Ambassador."

He laughed. "Haven't we made fun of that?"

"Yes, and I love that she's sponsored by booze companies *and* hangover cures."

Mick stood up, still holding my hand. "I don't want to hurt your feelings, but you need a shower."

"Do I?"

"You've got hair like a banshee and you smell like booze."

"Ew, I hate that smell. Booze through pores. Do I really?"

"Kinda. But I want you to come take a shower with me." He winked.

My heart surged. I swear, Mick is the only man in the world who can still give me those *beginning butterflies* that usually die out or mature over time.

I threw off the white cloud of a comforter and followed him into the shower.

It steamed up, and he stripped me down before stripping down himself. He looked *good*.

A little advice: marry an athlete. As long as you can trust him, marry an athlete.

I hopped into the big, beautiful shower—Mick smacked me on the ass and said, "damn you're hot."

I laughed, flattered as always, but knowing how impossible that was right now given the state of me.

And then we had some of the best sex I could remember.

A bit of it was the delirium, a bit of it was some of the unresolved anger at each other, and I like to think the rest was *us*.

When we finished—and he made sure we both did—we laughed with cringing faces, feeling certain we had been overheard.

Then we spent the next half hour luxuriating in the steam, cracking up as we experimented with all the dials and levers and nozzles. When we got out, I felt good again, even happy. I still had a crushing headache. Mick went out to get me coconut water and digestive cookies, and I hoped that I was being paranoid when he returned from the errand and shade passed across his face again.

Please stay, Mick. Please stay right here, with me, in this, together.

★★★

The IV scene we shot was fun. Lexi came over to Sabrina and Budgie's, and we all sat on the back porch. I had thrown on some makeup, but Zoe asked me to tone it down a little, saying I looked too glam. That was *not* true, I knew I looked sunken and not anything close to normal. But I guess she wanted that.

It took ages, we had to film our sleepy, hungover entrances a few times each, my entrance including walking in with a giant Evian—which forced me to have almost *too* much water and meant that the final cut included me stopping for a moment, for fear I would projectile all the liquid.

They even filmed the needles going into us more than once. That part was a little excruciating.

I had to repeat my joke "can't we please pour a few Bloody Marys and call it a day?" five times. They had me say it in a few different tones. It lost all sense of humor by the end.

But whenever things got annoying, Lexi managed to lift us back up. She may be a vapid, young thing, but she had a way of making people feel at ease. Maybe it was how disinterested she seemed in the unpleasant or deep, but on days like this, that worked for me.

After we were hydrated, we were shuttled in a Sprinter Van to the yoga studio in the solarium at Nicole's place. We all had on our yoga pants, and we looked like a parody of rich bitches. It was all still new enough for me to find it funny and cute.

Lexi went missing, and when she showed up again, she was with someone I assumed was the teacher. He was fit as hell and had a tan that would have looked more at home on the west coast. He was defined and muscular, but not in a hulky way. Sabrina caught my attention, when she choked on her water at his arrival.

I tapped Budgie. "Does she know him?"

And with a big stage wink she answered, "I think they've met. At Lexi's sugar daddy's house."

"She went to his house?" I had forgotten that all the while I was drownproofing in Dahlia's world of crazy, everyone else had been filming their own stuff.

"Yes, it seems Miss Lexi lives in an industrial three bedroom in the Financial District with a nasty mother fucker."

I cracked up and then was told to quiet down, as it was Lexi's turn to speak. With a weak apology I switched to stretching my left leg.

"Ladies, this is Leo," Lexi introduced. "He's going to be our teacher for today. He's going to lead us through some poses before we have our light lunch on the veranda. Let's give him a round of applause, shall we?"

We all clapped along, not quite sure why.

He looked bashful, as he took to the front of the room.

"Hello, girls, how are you all doing this fine morning?"

"Oh my god, he's *Australian*. Ladies, hold me back, hold me back!" Mariana reached for Nicole.

I hoped the camera didn't catch my eye roll. The thirsty old cougar act was tired.

"Alright, so who here has done yoga before?"

Everyone but Budgie raised a hand.

"Perfect, I'm going to do some relatively basic stuff, but if you need an adjustment get my attention and I can give you either a more advanced position or one that better suits your level of experience."

Budgie laughed. "I'll need you to come by and help me back into a seated position."

"I'm sure you're capable of more than you think you are, Ms. Verroye." He smiled and then went to his own mat at the head of the class. "Let's start in a seated position. There are blocks beside each of your mats, if you need to, feel free to prop with those and ask how, if you're unsure."

I still wasn't at the top of my game and when I said that to Budgie—who looked very out of her element in the athleisure wear—she said, from a clumsy downward dog, "don't worry honey, I'm popping some lunch champagne after this. We'll have earned it."

I laughed, got shushed.

"Oh Leo," said Mariana, "Is it true Lexi isn't your *only* friend here?"

"Ooh!" said Nicole.

Leo blushed. "Now bring your right foot forward..."

"I heard you and Sabrina went *down under*."

What a tired Australia-plus-sex joke. But wait, really?

"Is that true?" asked Nicole. "Oh my god, Sabrina, I had no idea...!"

From Nicole's unconvincing delivery of feigned surprise, I knew two things: (1) Nicole was fed this line by production and (2) Nicole didn't have an acting career in her future.

Sabrina didn't lift her head. "I don't know what you're talking about."

"Now bring that foot back, let it float, reach back toward the doors, keeping your hips parallel with the floor."

"Sounds like you kept your hips parallel with Sabrina's!" said Mariana, who then let out a *whoops!* before falling to the ground.

"Did she?" I asked Budgie, who was in child's pose.

She looked up at me. "I think she might have."

"Now bring that foot down to the earth, not forgetting to keep your weight evenly distributed."

"Easy for you to say, you don't have Triple D boobs," said Mariana.

"No one told me today was The Mariana Show," I said. "But keep it up, you're a wealth of giggles."

"I'm full of 'em, Dahlia."

"Deep inhale…"

"I'm jealous, Sabrina," said Mariana, sounding not-jealous at all. "I'm having trouble getting a handle on your type though. First a proper Brit, now a hot Aussie. What's next?"

"And now walk or jump to the front of the mat, rising slowly, one vertebrate at a time."

"I'm guessing an old rich American, because you've gone broke, right?"

"Stretch your arms out to your sides…"

"But that's sort of Lexi's bag, isn't it?" Mariana said, laughing at her own joke.

Lexi, bless her, laughed and said, "my man is taken!"

Budgie and I exchanged a look. Sabrina looked the way she often had in the press. Stoic, statuesque, and impermeable.

★★★

Before we wrapped, Sabrina invited everyone to her place for the evening event. We already knew that was on the books, but every invitation had to be on camera or it "didn't happen," Zoe had reminded us. The plan was a small outdoor dinner party.

There would be a few other people coming, though I didn't know who that would be.

When the cameras stopped rolling and the mics collected, Budgie pulled me aside and narrowed her eyes gesturing at Zoe.

"I don't like how happy that one looks."

"What do you mean?" I asked.

She shook her head. "She's got the same look in her eye I see in the vicious understudies at the playhouse. Waiting for their opportunity to break a lead's leg to get in the spotlight."

Zoe's cheeks were tight with a resisted grin, and she wasn't making eye contact with anyone or anything but her phone. Budgie was right.

The girl who controlled us all looked a little too happy.

26

Sabrina

Sabrina had always had hosting anxiety. She was good at it, and that was due in part to the very fact that she was always anxious about it. It was her mother's voice she heard when she tried to get things in order. The cameras circling her all felt like her mother's permeating gaze, watching, watching, waiting to catch a mistake.

Her mother had been famous for her hosting. She even put out a book once, *Host Like a Verroye*. It had massive sales, the advance and royalties falling in heaps into their black hole of endless wealth. Now that she was gone, the royalty checks still showed up, but they arrived addressed to Sabrina.

Her mother, Victoria Verroye (ViVi), had been a socialite when that mattered. It wasn't the same world anymore. But when she was a young mother and wife, she had thrown some of the most lavish parties the magazines had ever seen. There were always squads of cameras crouching and taking close-ups of her perfect, fresh-flower centerpieces, her impeccable tablescapes, and every other detail of her ever-gorgeous presentation. She always had immaculately groomed servers passing silver and crystal platters of tiny, beautiful, expensive food. Before influencers, there were women like Victoria Verroye. As happens with the exquisitely wealthy, they seldom pay for the tins of caviar or the same-day fresh lobster or baked-this-morning pastries that show up. All anyone wanted was to get mentioned in the corner caption of one of her photos. It could make a small business into an iconic stop in the city. Florists, small vineyards, bakeries—countless companies had made their big breakthrough by getting a nod from ViVi.

To this day, Sabrina got handwritten letters from aging owners of now-quintessential shops, restaurants, and companies that credited all of their success to the "generosity of the Verroye family."

It had been a long time since Sabrina had hosted anything at all, and this was the first time since losing the title and the marriage. It had to be perfect.

Sabrina was running around checking completed things and panicking about the things that were not yet done.

It wasn't even a big party—dinner and cocktails on the lawn.

But, as ViVi would say, *there is no small party; only elegant gatherings, and they begin when one is joined by another.*

If she couldn't pull it off with perfection, then she wasn't ViVi's little Sabrina.

Budgie was helping some—always the fun, smiling one who could balance out Sabrina's contagious high tension. While Sabrina was likely to look at a slow-moving delivery man and ask him what *had happened to him* that made him move like the air was molasses, Budgie could get away with saying, "look, Ryan, is it? I'm going to be straight with you, hon. You're movin' in micromotion, and we need you to step it up. Sound good?" At least, she'd toss him a wink and, at most, a crisp hundred-dollar bill, and the job was done.

Sabrina couldn't pull off copying her style. It didn't work coming from a woman like her. She was the skinny, irritable schoolmarm whose *joking* was often considered rudeness. Budgie was the beloved who had all the success and none of the wrinkles.

She was always telling Sabrina to breathe and let it be, it would happen, it was a party, but it didn't relax her. It never did. Even if she could take a moment and breathe deeply while Budgie walked her through a breathing exercise, fifteen minutes later, Sabrina would be screaming internally again.

Budgie even managed to keep the staff laughing while they all signed NDAs, ensuring that they wouldn't post unauthorized pictures. One of the PAs passed them out, and Budgie made it fun. Sabrina could never have.

The setup for the party was finally coming together around four. They were on schedule.

The table on the deck was exceptional—everything white and pale pink. The food was coming along, even though the chef had—in some quite certain terms—indicated he would rather deal with Budgie for the rest of the evening.

Sabrina hadn't shouted at him or anything, it was simply the magical power her pluming stress had on people working against a clock.

It drove her nuts that she couldn't have music. Music always set the tone of the party. Her mother had always said that—it had its own chapter, but it was explained there were licensing and sound issues.

The wine was chilled. The glasses were too. Everything was nearly there. The food wasn't ready, and half the serving team was flirting with each other, shirts untucked and bowties loose around their neck. One girl in particular had her white shirt unbuttoned very low, and Sabrina could see the brand of her bra between the cups.

At five o'clock, two hours before dinner, Sabrina went to her room for glam. When she held a hairpin for the stylist, she noticed her hands were shaking. She was uncertain why.

At 6:30 p.m. they were done, gone, and she was dressed.

There was a knock on her door.

It was Lexi.

"Come in," she said, opening the door all the way.

Lexi did, hands behind her back. "Oh my gosh, you look amazing."

"Thank you, so do you."

There was a small hesitation before Lexi said, "I have something for us. Please don't get mad at me."

Lexi brought her hands to the front, exposing a miniature zip baggie decorated with a few smiley face stickers and filled with white powder.

"Oh, lord, Lexi—"

"Before you say no, can I pitch my case?"

Sabrina laughed. "Okay, good luck."

Lexi sat down on the edge of Sabrina's bed with a galumphing bounce.

"You seem a little stressed out. I feel like everyone else is having fun around you, and I know part of why you're doing," she lowered her voice to a whisper, "*the show* is to get back to being the old Sabrina Verroye that absolutely *defined* a decade."

"Did I say that?"

Lexi rolled her eyes. "Look, I have a doctorate in celebrity. Of course that's what you want. You're in bad—well, sort of awful—straits right now with the press. You need to *wake up*. You need to get *driven*. You need to be on *point*. And this is some good stuff, I promise. It's clean, it won't do anything but what you remember. I know you used to do coke. Weren't you sort of famous for it?"

"No—well … not intentionally. Intentionally known for it, I mean."

"Why did you do it then?"

Sabrina should have thrown her out. Told her she was an adult, not the stick figure nineteen-year-old she used to be who felt immortal and would try anything once, twice, ten times to be sure.

But somehow, she couldn't. Perhaps it was the little, small, tiny addiction that she had fed like a feral cat for years.

"I did it then because I never wanted to sleep, I wanted to be alive all the time. Ironically. And because I believed it made me … well I felt *on*. Back then. When I did it. But it was stupid."

Lexi shrugged. "Come on. You only live once, and I'll do it with you. I do it all the time. It's the only way I'm getting anything done."

Sabrina resisted asking what an Instagram "celebrity" had to get done.

"This is ridiculous. I can't. I'm—"

"Don't you dare mention your age. Remember when we talked? I said you were aging yourself like *bad* and you really are. You have to remember you still got your life to live."

It struck a nerve in Sabrina, who had lived in desperate fear of getting old, unimportant, and ugly for most of her life. An unfortunate but likely outcome when a girl is told she is young, beautiful, and full of promise for the foundational years of her life.

All day she had asked *what would ViVi do*? Was there anything wrong with asking *what would young, vibrant Sabrina do*?

Maybe she missed that wild mess.

"This is crazy. Alright, yes. But only a little."

Lexi squealed. "You're going to feel much better. By the way, everything is done downstairs, I knew you were stressed so I asked, to make sure, before coming up. It's done and it's effing beautiful, obviously, and they're taking pictures and filming it right now. Zoe called in photographers to pitch some spread in *Town & Country*."

Sabrina's heart lurched. *Town & Country*. Just as though ViVi was watching.

Hopefully not *right* now.

Lexi was a professional. She took a mirrored jewelry tray from the vanity, removed the Van Cleef bracelet, saying, "ooh, fab!" and then dumped out a small pile of the powder.

"Okay wait," she said, and for a moment Sabrina thought she might be thinking better of it, and she couldn't tell if she was relieved or disappointed. "What's your favorite song?"

"My favorite song?"

"Wait, hold on two secs."

She clicked and scrolled through her phone until an Ed Sheeran song started playing through the Sonos system.

"Music sets the tone, isn't that in your mom's book?"

"Did you *read* that?"

"Are you kidding? I'm a gold digger trying to land a rich man, of course, it was my textbook. You should see my dinner parties."

It was hard to imagine her playing housewife. But if she read ViVi's guide, she must have picked up a thing or two.

She used a black card she had conjured from nowhere to efficiently cut up the powder and then shifted the pile into two thin lines. "It always tastes better cut with a black Amex and a hundred-dollar bill!" she said to herself. Then she magicked a bill and rolled it into a makeshift straw and offered it to Sabrina. "You go first." Lexi instructed.

"You're going to be fine, don't stress," she said. "Tonight is going to be fun. I'm excited to see the real you."

Sabrina took a deep breath, feeling equal parts excited and young and stupid and old.

Apparently, the art of doing coke never leaves you, as Sabrina swept up her line neatly, handing the money tube and tray back to Lexi.

Sabrina gasped and felt her body electrify in a strange and familiar way. She wanted to cry and laugh. She felt young and stupid again.

Lexi cleaned up her line as well, with an "ooh!" before she scrunched her nose up and rubbed it.

"Alright," she said," ready to go have a great night?"

A smile had crept onto Sabrina's face. It was like time travel. "Yes, I am."

She started laughing, thinking how ridiculous she was in her somewhat-conservative dress doing cocaine in the beach house. Last time she'd done any drugs *at all* had been here, when she was in the early days with Robbie.

"You know what?" said Sabrina, feeling energized and suddenly sexy, as it had always made her feel back then. "This dress is too stuffy."

"Yass girl!" said Lexi. "Makeover montage."

The two of them went to Sabrina's closet, where they found a short red dress Sabrina hadn't worn in years. It was sleeveless and gathered up top, Grecian style, with a deep V. The sides were laddered, revealing a tasteful amount of skin. It made her look like she had curves while showcasing her small waist.

Or at least it had.

"Oh, I don't even know if this still fits."

Lexi rolled her eyes. "It totally does. You're being dumb, put it on."

She reminded Sabrina of her daughter in that moment, and she felt a wave of affection wash over her, followed by a quick spasm of guilt.

She ignored the guilt—it was of no use to her. Lexi was right. She needed to get happy.

The dress, as ever, fit like a glove.

"Holy *moly* girlfriend," said Lexi, from the edge of Sabrina's bed when she emerged from the dressing room.

"You think?"

"Um, yeah, I think."

"Once upon a time this was my Jaw Drop dress," Sabrina found herself admitting. "It was made for me by Azzedine Alaïa a few years after I was married. The style was called The Goddess, but he dubbed it my revenge dress."

"Literally, Sabrina, this is your night. I swear. That man-child ex is going to see this, and he's going to cry and jerk off and resist texting you, that's what's going to happen. Let's hope he doesn't follow through and actually make the call, right?"

Sabrina laughed.

There was a knock on the door, and then Budgie let herself in.

"Whoo, mama! The revenge dress?"

Lexi and Sabrina exchanged a look and burst into laughter like schoolgirls.

"I love this," said Budgie. "Where has this Sabrina been hiding? I swear it's been all modest Dior and Chanel, nothing feisty. I love it!"

"Isn't that asshole going to *die* when he sees this?" asked Lexi.

"Hasn't that been the goal along?" said Budgie with a smile.

"Maybe it has," said Sabrina.

"Wait," said Lexi. "You need a choker. I have the perfect thing downstairs, it's Bulgari, it didn't work with my outfit. Do you wear gold?"

"She does tonight," said Budgie.

"It'll be so good, because Robbie will see it and be like, *I didn't give her that, does she have a new man?*" Lexi squealed, "Oh my god this is *so fun.*" And ran off to get her necklace.

27
Dahlia

I almost did a spit take with my cocktail when Sabrina walked outside.

She was *stunning*.

Made even more stunning by the fact that she was smiling and looked happy.

We were positioned beside the pool for a round of drinks, where a gorgeous male bartender was working a shaker with rolled up sleeves and a charming smile for each of us.

The first scene we shot was Budgie, Sabrina, Lexi, and me. We got to film *simply* having fun, no prompts to trash-talk or fight with each other. I would have been relieved if I didn't always feel the presence of a giant blinking *yet* following that relief.

Nicole arrived, wearing a soft blue latex dress, and she did that little, double-handed castanet wave at everyone. She looked confident, like she thought she'd earned everyone's respect after the night before.

Be nice, I told myself.

Mariana arrived last, looking far overdressed. I wondered if the reason for her absence was that her "glamsquad" had been working on her for extra-long. She seemed to have undergone a facial treatment that resulted in a fresh glow, and her hair was runway-sleek and straight.

Everyone had stepped it up tonight. And there I was, fighting against the hangover undercurrent to look my normal.

Even though the sky was a pretty, drenching gold, they had hot, blinding lights on that made everyone look washed out. Hopefully in a good way, like a soft Instagram filter.

That's what I hoped every time they turned them on.

"How were things with Mick this morning, Dahlia?" asked Nicole, in a commiserative friend-tone but with a distinct frenemy grimace.

"Actually great," I said, defensively. "We had great sex and I'm pretty sure he's not going to divorce me."

There was a stunned silence, then laughter that started with Budgie and Lexi.

"Is that how you keep him, then? The sex?" she said with a laugh, looking around at the others.

Everyone else was in a good mood, and they laughed too. I had no choice but to choose not to take every word she said as poison. I shrugged, "use what you got, right?"

"I suppose you have to *stay* the best then, yes? Do you take classes?"

"I could teach them," I said, before a big sip of my cocktail. I hated that the hair of the dog *worked*.

Budgie guffawed. "Cheers to that!"

"I would take your classes, I swear, a man like that?" Lexi said.

Overall, the night was off to a pretty good start. Even being the butt of the joke wasn't as bad as it could be. I had kept it light and recovered the moment.

After that initial scene, around eight o'clock, the guys and the rest of the guests were to join. This included Budgie's friend Sam, Mick, and a man I didn't know.

It became clear that this bigger, grey-haired man with a red face was the person Lexi was dating. She gave him a throaty kiss, and he looked annoyed with her.

Sam had observed the whole thing from Budgie's side, sipping a drink through a paper straw and loving every minute of the drama.

Mick gave me a cursory kiss on the top of the head, and when I smiled at him, he gave me the tight lips I had feared earlier.

Seriously, what was going on?

The red-faced man looked like he would give anything not to be there, but clearly not, since he had no obligation to be.

Lexi held his cheeks and told him not to be such a stuck-up prick. She followed it up with another big kiss, and he pursed his lips but let her appease him.

I wanted to give Mick's thigh a squeeze—the one that usually meant *oh we'll talk about this later.* But now I was afraid it would make me seem bitchy all over again.

Wasn't a little bit of teasing okay? Especially when it was at the expense of an old man willing to date a young girl like Lexi, and vice versa.

It was hard to tell right now. The only thing I knew for sure was that I was not able to be myself.

But I was going to try like hell to have fun anyway.

★★★

Dinner was picture-perfect. Sabrina had arranged a tapas-style menu but with delicious Italian cuisine. We had caprese salad with burrata and the freshest tomatoes and basil I'd ever tasted (the cheese was flown in from Puglia I heard her say), prawns with a balsamic reduction, a lemon sorbet to cleanse our palates, then bucatini with Bolognese. Not only that, but each portion had been paired with region-specific wines. The wine was flowing.

The sommelier who poured for us explained that when you have a true Italian meal, you should be able to taste the region's soil, climate, as well as anything else that can differentiate one piece of land from another. The olives should grow on trees near the bulbs of garlic, the tomato and basil should have been raised together, and the wine should be from so nearby that the roots might "hold hands" with those of the olive trees. The chef had nodded along, piping up in Italian every once in a while, with something he wanted to add.

The meal was impeccably paced, not dragging on too long. I would have enjoyed everything much more if Mariana hadn't continually leaned over to me and often across me so that Mick could also hear her say that she wanted to go skinny-dipping. She said it over and over, and always like it was a new idea.

You know the annoying drunk guy hitting on you at the bar who won't stop, won't drop it, until you get firm and tell him to stop? That was Mariana. Except I didn't want to go full-bitch on her and tell her to stop. I needed to save a little face.

After the main course, we were presented with the chef's family recipe lemon cake and shots of limoncello.

It was one of the best meals I had ever had. Not only that, but it was gorgeous. Eating out on the deck and looking at the Atlantic wasn't quite the blue and white Tyrrhenian Sea, but it was good in a pinch.

At one point I had leaned over to Mick and said, "Do you think we can plan that trip to the Amalfi coast now?"

He squeezed me on the thigh, and said, "sure."

As dinner was being cleaned up, filming paused for a reset back to the pool area. Zoe approached me and asked to speak with me privately.

She then said, "Before we go back down to the pool, we need you to apologize to Nicole."

"Apologize?"

"Yes, it seems someone told her what you were saying at the party last night."

I looked back to the rest of the women. Who would have said something?

"Dammit, really? I don't even remember exactly what I said."

"You'll be fine." Zoe smiled, "She's being sensitive."

I didn't completely agree with that, even though she was trying to be on my side.

"Okay, I'll talk to her."

When the group began to move downstairs, I grabbed Nicole and cringed as I said the words, "Hey, could I steal you for a sec?"

"Sure."

We went to the sunroom, where a ceiling fan spun and the night breeze swept through the screens. Under different circumstances,

I might be happy vacationing in this place. As enjoyable as the meal was, and as alright as today had been, it was all good with a neon asterisk.

We sat down, cameras crowded us, and a boom lurked overhead. "Look, I heard that someone told you I had said some things during your performance yesterday. Honestly, I could never do what you do. I could never get on stage in an outfit like that and sing. Ever. Anything I said was because I would be so scared, I couldn't do it. If it was me, I would be terrified I would mess up. I guess I was braced for you in the same way. And that wasn't fair. You're a professional, I mean, I listened to your music all the time, I loved you when I was a kid. Why do you look like you don't know what I'm talking about?"

"I didn't know you were making fun of me."

Dammit, Zoe.

"No—no, I wasn't making fun of you. I was blown away that it was happening and was overwhelmed by all the nervousness I have whenever *anyone* gets up to perform. I'm zero fun at karaoke."

"I'm glad you thought it was such a mess. You know, I've been wondering why Mick is with you. And now I really don't know. But this does explain what Mick said to me last night."

My gut twisted. "W-what do you mean, what did Mick say?"

"He said things weren't going great between you guys. And he said he thought I did amazing on stage."

I took a beat. "You were amazing. I wish I had guts like that. Sincerely."

"I'll tell you something." She leaned forward. "You never will. Because let me guess. You made fun of me last night, like it was *totally* embarrassing, but that's because you're fucking jealous. Aren't you?"

"I—"

"No, really," she held up a finger, "because as *humiliated* for me as you were, you're not *great* at anything anymore are you? Sort of funny, kind of smart, relatively independent, and confident, but that's it, isn't it? When you cook, you follow a recipe, when you sing it's only good in the car. You never found your niche after soccer ended for you. I bet your parents were unimpressed with your second act. Maybe you even have a sibling who they try not to compare with you." She laughed.

I stared at her, dumbstruck. No one in real life would ever gut another person like this.

"Yeah," she went on. "And then you married a hunk, and now he's starting to see you didn't have anything else left in your arsenal. He's starting to see you for how unoriginal you are and I bet he's looking at you like, *what* am I going to talk to *her* about for the rest of my life?"

"Okay, that's enough, Nicole. How dare you. You should be ashamed to talk to me like that."

"Should I? Why? You're *nothing*. You're a has been that never was. You're *incredibly* average. And you're awful to that wonderful, wonderful man. We've talked a lot lately you know, before last night. I met him a couple months ago." She stood up. "I might know far more about you than you think. I might even know the color of the sheets in your bedroom."

I let out a spike of terrified, defensive laughter. "Please, stop."

She was about to leave the room. "They're vanilla with hotel stripes. And the duvet is that soft grey. I should get something like that for myself." She looked as though she was thinking. "I'm going to join the others. I wonder if Mick needs a drink. His favorite is a virgin mojito when he's training, right?"

My jaw felt like it might start to crack from tension and my heart was pounding. My blood was hot as magma, and I was at such a loss for words that I felt like I might explode into a dry, gasping pile of dust. I downed the rest of my wine and prepared to pretend none of that had affected me one bit.

But she was right about some of it. For one thing, I had been that girl in high school who had never quite made it to popularity but knew everyone in school. Never excelled at music or drama and played sports because I was told to.

I was going to have to act my face off tonight. I was going to have to pretend there wasn't a thing in the world Nicole could say to hurt me.

Why did she hate me?

I wanted to go through my phone, see if Mick or I had ever posted anything from our bedroom, where the sheets could be seen. Even thinking like that started making me feel like *I* was the crazy one.

It was my worst quality. I had an inability to ever believe the worst of people, even when I saw it in real time. I am far more likely to believe I had imagined the whole thing, misunderstood the tone, or asked for it in some way.

Even now, when Nicole had been an undeniable cunt.

And I didn't ever use that word.

But, sorry, "bitch" wasn't strong enough.

I wasn't sure if Nicole's rant was bad timing with Mick and me being on such weird terms or … was there something going on that I had missed?

How and *when* had they seen each other that I didn't *know* about? Why hadn't he said anything to me?

My fury was beginning to bloom in earnest.

Zoe came over to the couch, taking her headphones off.

"Are you okay?"

I shook my head. "What the *hell* was that? And why didn't she know what I was talking about? I thought you said she'd heard what I said last night."

"Honestly, I thought she had, but I must have misunderstood. Looking at all that, she must have been talking smack for some other reason. It's *her* issue."

I resisted asking if Zoe thought it was true, any of it.

Instead, I tried to rally—now *that* I had always been ace at.

"I'm sorry, but we have to get you downstairs. Can I get you another drink?"

"No. Maybe water. Thank you."

I went downstairs, where Zoe followed. I asked the bartender if he minded if I got my own water. He scooted aside with a "be my guest" gesture. The cameras found me, of course, and filmed it all.

"Why are you behind the bar, Dahlia?" prodded Zoe.

I thought of how to phrase it. I couldn't say I didn't trust production not to roofie my water. "I need to be sure of what I'm drinking." Dammit. I looked back at the bartender while I removed the metal cap from my bottle and poured it. "No offense."

I sat down with everyone else, and for the next hour and a half, I tried to look and act normal. I did not want to explode.

I would not explode.

I could not explode.

In other news, Sabrina was on fire tonight. She had comebacks, she was witty, she was positively lit up.

She did, however, seem a little frenzied. Like someone told her she had to step it up and be fun *or else*.

Sabrina tended to drink every time we filmed, but this was the first time she seemed tipsy and not like she was, I don't know, self-medicating.

Our small party was in full swing when Mick tapped me on the leg and pointed. "That the guy?"

Leo was emerging from the house, carrying a tray.

Lexi saw him next and screamed, "Leo's *heeeere!*"

"Evening, ladies."

"Ooh, what did you bring us?" asked Mariana, leaning over and taking on a new *sexy* look.

"I brought some wellness shots. They're kombucha, cayenne, fresh lemon, apple cider vinegar, and of course," he said, setting the tray down and handing one to Sabrina with a wink, "a little bit of Mezcal, distilled with damiana. I consider that to be full wellness."

All the girls laughed, and he lifted his glass.

"Cheers," said Sabrina. "To feeling good."

Leo cocked an intrigued eyebrow. "Indeed."

28
Zoe

The greatest gifts God ever gave the minions of reality television? Drugs and alcohol.

Zoe hadn't thought the Lexi/coke plan was going to work out. But evidently Sabrina still had enough desperation to reclaim her youth.

Meanwhile, Leo was perfect casting. It was too easy to convince Lexi the addition of a love interest would make Sabrina more relatable. He needed no arm-twisting. Worked for Zoe. Now she needed this party to escalate.

But she worried Dahlia might be onto the old *add a little something* trick. Dammit.

The good news, the others weren't. Fiona and Milo had to walk Nicole down the steps to the pool area. She wasn't *totally* messed up yet, but in those heels and with those steep wooden steps, she was unsteady. Of course, they had it on film. She had taken the shot Milo handed to her after the attack on Dahlia, and it seemed it hit her fast.

As for Mariana, the production had started serving her cocktails during the 'getting ready' scenes that had begun hours before dinner. The PAs told her it was her big chance to talk up her business, and they filmed and filmed. It was more about getting enough footage of her wine getting refilled again and again at different stages of her hyper-vanity.

It was fucking great. She paid however much and spent all the time to look perfect, and all the viewers would see was this slurring, over-injected, mess leaving lipstick on all her glassware.

The whole gang was hitting the mark tonight. A dinner preceded with cocktails, served with multiple wine pairings, then followed by shots and cocktails—who could have guessed it would be a recipe for disaster?

You would have thought a bunch of adult women would.

But no, because deep down they all knew they were boring unless they had something in the mix to keep it interesting. If anything, all these women owed Zoe a big fat thank you at the end of all this.

Zoe gave Leo a signal, and he asked Sabrina if he could talk to her alone.

She blushed—like, actually blushed. Of course she did. She also said yes, because of course she did.

They went to a small part of the courtyard, surrounded by hedges with a settee and a team of three there ready to film.

They sat together and then the crew placed them closer than they naturally wanted to be.

Fifteen minutes of lighting and arranging later, they were set.

Once they got the go-ahead, Leo started.

"I have to say, it's nice to see you."

"You too."

"It was nice seeing you in the city, but I didn't expect to see you again."

"We need him to talk about what they did," Zoe said to Milo. He ran over and whispered in Leo's ear.

"Keep going," said Zoe out loud.

"I have to say," Leo began again, "it's nice to see you again." Only this time he delivered the line he looked her up and down with a devilish look in his eyes.

"Perfect," Zoe said to herself.

"Er—you too. It's nice to see you again." Sabrina laughed.

"That last time, things were a little wild."

Sabrina couldn't help but smile.

Gag.

"The class was nice."

"You know I've done a lot of one on ones in a lot of nice places, but never in a penthouse like yours. That was the fanciest one I've ever seen."

Yes, perfect, play up the *poor little hippie* angle.

"Oh, thank you. It's big. Too big for just me."

Recut as innuendo, and they've got something there.

"You and your husband used to live there, then?"

"We never *lived* there, no, but we used to stay there with our daughter whenever we stayed in the city."

"I'm guessing you designed the whole place. It felt like you. Fragile, and beautiful," he swept a hair off of her face, "but a little cool."

"I–I don't mean to be cold."

"You're not. I can tell." he pointed at her heart.

This is unbearable, thought Zoe.

"I didn't used to be cold."

Yes, more about your golden days, more about the past you miss so much.

"You know, I don't think I told you this, but I saw *Lily of the Alley* about five times. Some of the scenes," he made a face like it was too hot to mention, "I grew up to them. If you know what I mean."

"Leo!"

"That might be a little too weird. I'm sorry."

"Cut," said an exasperated Zoe. She went in herself and crouched whispering in Leo's ear, "You're going to have to make it a little more obvious here. How about, *ah, don't be shy, you know you're sexy* or something like that?"

And by *how about* she meant *do that.*

"I don't know, I wouldn't say that. It was enough already saying the *Lily of the Alley* thing."

"That wasn't true?" said Sabrina, smiling.

"It was, but I wouldn't have said it."

They both shared another look.

"Leo, can you please … we're on a schedule here, let's go."

They both looked a little surprised, and then Leo turned to her and asked if she would feel comfortable with him saying that.

She said yes, thank fucking god, and they started the scene.

"Don't be bashful. You know you're sexy."

"Leo…"

"Especially tonight. That night, at your place, when I—"

"Hang on. Cut. Sabrina, don't look at the camera, please."

"I-it's, are we really going here?"

"We don't have to," said Leo quickly. "I won't say a word if you don't want."

Who even was this guy? It wasn't a difficult task. Deliver your lines, bone the movie star, cash your check, and move on. *This* was exactly why Zoe knew she was stronger and more rational than most people. Emotions make you weak and get in the way of everything.

"I don't … I don't know why we…"

Zoe went over to Sabrina. "Listen, this is all part of it. Trust me. Okay?"

Sabrina couldn't hide her excitement at the attention from Leo. "Okay…"

"Take it again. Leo, go."

"Especially tonight. That night, at your place, when I stayed over. That was … *whoo*. Unbelievable. I had no idea you could let loose like that."

She was beyond blushing now, and Zoe couldn't help but laugh inside that Sabrina was turning red all the way to her clavicle.

"You were a maniac," he said.

"I may have had too much to drink." She seemed frenzied. She was both aware and not of what was going on.

Leo leaned in. "You know it wasn't that. It's us. Our chemistry. It's undeniable, don't you think?"

Sabrina was reaching swooning. She was transfixed by his perfect bone structure, piercing eyes leaning in toward her.

There was no way Leo was into her, right?

No. There were plenty of girls Leo's age. He could hook up with any young thing.

Zoe, for example, actually *did* yoga. She had, of course, stalked his Instagram before she approached him for the job—which wasn't a wealth of anything, since he used it only for his business. Lots of shirtless fitness videos with disgusting comments from desperate women like Sabrina.

You know, Zoe and he had far more in common than he would ever notice.

Zoe was a maniac in the bedroom too, for fuck's sake. And gorgeous men like him would never even know because they never took a chance on a girl like her.

Sabrina had years on him—a couple, anyway—and yet *that* was what he went for?

She was too thin. And Zoe didn't believe she was *wild* in the sheets. She was too frail-looking. Too martyr-ish. She'd make a guy feel like a rapist for spanking her.

That's probably what happened with Robbie.

And yet men like them still looked for women like her.

Fucking men.

And this, as Zoe thought nightly, was why she would die alone. Because there was no one on the planet good enough, and they never saw her, regardless.

Leo put a thumb on Sabrina's chin. "Can I kiss you again?"

Sabrina's eyelashes fluttered and Zoe's eyes rolled.

"Yes," she said with a small nod.

He kissed her. Deep, and like he meant it.

Yuck. Perfect for the footage, but *ew.*

He put a hand on her ribcage, and she ran her brand-new manicure through his hair.

Zoe hoped he was a clout chaser. He was too hot for her.

"Yeah, okay, enough, we can cut there." When they didn't break away, "um, hello?"

Sabrina pulled back first, clearing her throat, and touching her lips. Oh, now she's shy.

"Alright, back to the others."

★★★

It was nearly ten-thirty when Zoe's earpiece crackled and she got the word.

"They're here," she said to Aleksandr, feeling very official.

He gave a curt nod, not taking his eyes off the monitors, pressing the headphones into his right ear.

Zoe pressed the button on her radio. "Tell Mariana it's her cue. Wait, is Sabrina in position? Yes, okay, go ahead."

Leo was sitting on a chaise, and Sabrina was between his legs like the quarterback and the cheerleader. They had fully forgotten they were on camera. But again, that made it even better.

"Got it," said Milo.

In the yard, he gave Mariana a nod.

She didn't notice, prompting him to duck under the camera and go to her. He squatted at her side, waited for Mariana's acknowledgment, then ran back out of scene.

"I'm going in!" she screamed.

Next thing you knew, she was shimmying her underwear off from beneath her dress and jumping in the pool. Once in, she peeled off the rest of her clothes and sank beneath the steaming water.

Lexi squealed, took off her top and unzipped her pants. They landed in a pink lamé heap on the ground, and she jumped in beside Mariana.

Lexi yelled for Budgie's friend Sam to jump in too, and he did, laughing and saying Lexi was *so bad! So bad!*

Nicole asked Mick if he would get her zipper.

Dahlia stood up and pushed Nicole into the water.

Mick gaped at Dahlia. "What the hell are you *doing*?"

"Shit, that's gold, they had to do that now?" said Zoe. She turned on her radio. "Hey—tell them to wait. Hold. Hold."

Dahlia shook her head in absolute impatience and took a sip of her water.

"Dahlia, what is going on with you?"

"I'm messing around! It's *fun*, right, Nicole? I'm *pretty funny*, right? Mick she tore a strip off me inside, she was horrible, I'm sorry, she's got this whack idea that she's ... that she's like, I don't even know going to take you from me. Says you guys have been hanging out."

"You're doing this here?"

Dahlia looked surprised. "Are you saying there's a *this* to do?"

Sabrina and Budgie stared on in utter disbelief. Budgie looked composed and had on that *mad teacher* face, but she could never shake the ghost of a smile.

Sabrina looked like she'd seen a ghost.

She hadn't. But she was about to.

Nicole floundered around in the pool, her latex dress trapping her legs together.

She called for help.

"You've got to be kidding me," said Dahlia.

Lexi and Mariana laughed, doing that *oh, no! but it's funny!* Sort of laugh.

"For fuck's sake," said Mick, kicking off his shoes and leaning over the edge of the water. Nicole reached for his extended arm and he pulled her up and lifted her out of the pool.

"Oh my god," she said, shaking, looking at him with *my hero*-eyes.

"You're fine, you're fine, here you go." He set her down on one of the cushioned chaise lounges.

"Mick?" asked Dahlia. She was tipsy—better yet, she seemed angry-drunk. *Hell yeah.*

"What?" he said, tone raised.

"Have you and Nicole been *hanging out*?" she had a look on like it was all unlikely.

Mick looked at Nicole.

"Don't look at *her*, look at me, Mick, what is she talking about?"

"I've seen Nicole a few times, yes."

"H-how? Why?"

"We met because she did some promotion stuff for the team, and … that's all. It's like me seeing Regan. It's nothing. But then you're pushing her in the pool and everything you said about her the other night, I mean, what is your problem?"

"Mick, what—" she shook her head. "Mick, please." She gave him an imploring look.

Zoe made a note on her iPad: *Mick and Dahlia poolside. Fantasy football interview line.*

"I don't know what happened to the girl I knew. You're not the same."

Dahlia looked like he had slapped her.

Too bad he didn't.

29
Sabrina

Mick left the scene, going back into the house. Nicole loafed after him a conspicuous moment or two later, saying she had to dry off. Dahlia watched in awe, heart pounding so hard that it showed.

She went to the bar and took a shot.

Fiona approached Sabrina.

"Okay we need you to get her alone now. We still have the hedge set up from you and Leo. You can go do it over there."

She talked into her two-way radio, giving instructions to the cameras to be prepped for the scene.

Sabrina did not want to. But when she hesitated, Fiona added, "Listen, be the chum she needs right now. It's a win-win for you both. You're compassionate and she has a chance to tell her side of this."

Sabrina bit her tongue—which hardly had any feeling left from this repetitive action.

"Dahlia," said Sabrina, gently. "Let's go over there. Yeah?"

Dahlia followed, and Sabrina felt like she was leading her to slaughter.

Once settled, they took only two minutes resetting the scene before telling them to speak.

"Is everything alright between you and Mick? It seems a little tense."

"Don't worry about it. We're fine."

Dahlia kicked her shoes a few feet away. The grass was growing dewy. Sabrina knelt to pick them up. The cameras made themselves scarce but remained present.

Being filmed seemed to be the last thing on Dahlia's mind.

Dahlia started to cry. "I'm sorry, you don't need to talk to me, it's okay, I'll be fine."

"It seems like this might be a bit more than an argument. Is something going on?"

"I don't know. I don't know! For one thing, I'm drunk, and I've never been drunk like this until … lately. I don't get like this and I hate it. I'm dizzy and feel awful and I would never have—it feels like Mick is acting like he doesn't even know me anymore. Maybe he doesn't. I don't know. I'm on eggshells all the time."

She rested her head in folded arms.

"Things do seem a little tense between you." Sabrina stopped herself from saying that she remembered the point in her marriage where pins, needles, and eggshells seemed to constitute the floor wherever they walked. It indicated that she was hitting milestones along a path that would lead to one and only one possible destination.

"We've been bickering which we never, ever do! I don't understand. It's like we're totally different people And I've been impatient. It's not all him. I don't know what all that stuff with Nicole is about, I can't even … I can't even. And I'm insanely moody lately, borderline manic, because of these hormones."

"Hormones…?"

Dahlia kept her face covered by an arm but then leaned back in the chair. "No, it's birth control and I can't tell him because we're supposed to be *trying* to have a baby. Half the time I'm all whacked out from the pill and the pill makes me *crazy*. But it's him too, he's different—"

With a start, she seemed to remember the cameras were there. Worse than that, Milo had retrieved Mick who was now standing on the sidelines.

If only Sabrina had any clue what was about to be said, she would have stopped her. Sabrina should have known.

Dahlia saw Mick. Mick looked shocked.

Dahlia's face cleared to blank, and she shot up. She looked to Sabrina, then to Mick, then to the cameras. "Shit," she whispered.

Mick's face had fallen. He looked like he might break someone in half. The two of them looked at each other, and it was like watching the earth crack open between them, an irreparable chasm forming in front of them.

Zoe looked like a cork ready to burst out of one of Sabrina's champagne bottles.

30

Zoe

Yes. This was *too good*.

Mick stormed inside.

"Mick!" yelled Dahlia, starting to follow him.

"Dahlia, we need you to stay out here."

"What? No! I have to—"

"What you have to do is go back over to the pool. You're working, don't make me remind you, you're *under contract,* right now. We are on the clock and we need to finish here. K?"

Dahlia looked stunned.

Zoe motioned toward the pool, and like a zombie, Dahlia went.

"You too please," said Zoe to Sabrina.

Sabrina looked as though her skeleton might burst from rage. Zoe wanted to laugh.

Once Sabrina had gone to the pool, and was seated again with Leo and out of earshot, she lifted her transceiver.

"Okay, go for Aubrey."

God she was like a damn maestro.

You could hear a record screech to a halt when Sabrina's gaze landed on the figures of two girls, who had appeared, silhouetted on the lawn by the indoor light.

"Who is that?" asked Lexi, squinting.

Sabrina turned transparent. "Aubrey?"

The trek from silhouette to the bright lights felt long, even to Zoe.

"Hey, mum."

"This is fucking amazing," said Zoe.

"Shh," snapped Aleksandr.

Zoe's blood boiled. She hated being reprimanded.

Sabrina rose slowly, and everyone else watched in uncertainty as she went to her daughter.

She was silenced.

"Oh wow Mum, what's *this* get-up?"

Sabrina stifled her attempted hug and instead smoothed down her dress. "Aubrey, what are you doing here?" she looked to her friend. "And, I'm sorry, I don't think we've met."

Her friend said, in a British accented *hot girl* voice, "Bailey."

"Bailey, hello. Ah ... welcome." Sabrina shook her head at Aubrey. "What are you doing here, honey?"

Aubrey bristled at the affection. She shrugged. "I haven't seen you in a while. Heard you were having a party."

"Oh, not really, a little thing."

"Didn't Gran say there's no such thing?"

"It's wonderful to see you."

Sabrina hugged her daughter and glanced at the cameras over Aubrey's shoulder. Aubrey stood stick still, not returning the embrace.

"Don't look at the cameras, you cow, how many times... ?" said Zoe under her breath.

Aleksandr looked at her witheringly.

Zoe stepped back and consulted her iPad, only to mask the embarrassment.

One of the servers came over with a tray of champagne and offered it to the girls.

"No. We're fine." said Aubrey. "We had a few cocktails in the back of the car on our way here."

Bailey snort-laughed. The server gave a small nod then started to go back inside.

"I'll take one!" screamed Lexi.

The champagne was delivered to the pool and Sabrina looked like she'd rather be dead than here.

"Gee, I have to ask, what is even going on here?" said Aubrey. "Getting a real weird vibe."

"I don't know what to say. I wish I had known you were coming."

"Is this what you've been doing since you and dad broke up? Getting messed up and trying to reclaim your youth or something?" she laughed, as did her friend. "Like who is that boho wannabe, and why are you getting all gross with him? I saw you from inside, all cuddled up. Like what even?"

"Aubrey, that is *enough*."

"Oh, don't try to pull that on me. You don't *get* to tell me what's enough." Aubrey swayed in a small circle and steadied herself on the back of a lounge chair.

Sabrina looked betrayed and livid.

"No one here is doing anything wrong, you do not get to walk in and be disrespectful. That is not who I raised."

"Raised? That's rich. But oh yes, what a classy group of chums you have here. I should be more respectful, you're right."

Budgie, for once, looked uncertain of herself. She pushed past Dahlia and got to her cousin's side.

"Hey, honey, what brings you to the cottage?" she tried for a smile, but the glare of the angry eighteen-year-old diminished it.

"I thought there might be some space to reconnect with my mom in person here, seeing as this is the one place on the planet she ever said was *holy* to her. I thought, if I were to catch up with mom at the cottage, there was no way she could disappoint me. Again."

Mariana let out a would-be girlish *whoo* and started jumping up and down in the pool, her fake, medicine ball breasts splashed again and again on the surface of the water. *Yuck*, thought Zoe, only barely not saying it out loud. "Join the party, hon!"

"This is so typical of you," said Aubrey. "Do you seriously wonder why you disgust me? Because you've always been American trash. I can't believe I got out as intact as I did."

"Aubrey, stop it, right now."

Huh. Sabrina had a scary-mom voice.

"No, I will not stop, I am thrilled to see such undeniable proof of who you are. It's what dad always said. He said he scooped you out of a gutter, coke-crazed and half drunk. You know, I went to your room before I came down here."

She pulled out the rolled bill-tube placed with the drug evidence Zoe had made sure to set before sending Aubrey through the unoccupied house for some "soulful childhood memories" footage.

"Are you still doing drugs? I don't know if you're trying to reclaim your garbage youth or if this is simply who you are. I mean, were you on drugs when I was a kid? When you were *pregnant with me*?"

Ugh, that was perfect.

Zoe could edit that with a lingering silence and really spin it. She could see the headlines now. Could see the articles with the rumor surgeons vivisecting the hesitation and reexamining Sabrina's entire life and Aubrey's subsequent upbringing. They would find tons of circumstantial evidence.

The show would be blasted all over the internet for months. Maybe longer.

It could only mean good things for Zoe following Aleksandr to his next project.

Aleksandr even had the crew filming themselves and each other. They had so much behind the scenes footage it was an airtight case—she had all the evidence to prove that *she* had been the one to do it all. She had been the one to make the show happen.

Now they had two fights ready to explode. This was good shit brought to you by Zoe "The Life Ender."

Sabrina, Budgie, Aubrey, and Bailey stayed outside as instructed. Sabrina was shaking. She looked like she'd give anything to be off camera, but fortunately, Aubrey wouldn't talk to her anywhere but.

Zoe had learned a lot about Aubrey from Fiona's thorough intel. From what Fiona found, Aubrey loved being a rich bitch and had no intention of leaving her titled life behind.

At eighteen when she could now choose, she chose glamour over her mother.

Zoe could understand that. There was a part—albeit microscopic—of Zoe that could see feeling sorry for Sabrina. She lost her kid when she tried to do the right thing.

Someone should have told Sabrina long ago that being a good person got you fucking nowhere.

31
Dahlia

I was shaking.

My ears rang as the crew now ushered us inside, leaving Sabrina, Budgie, Aubrey, and her friend outside. Once we were in, they tried to start setting us up for another scene.

"No, no, I need to talk to my husband," I said.

"No, you need to keep doing what you're contractually obligated to do, here, Dahlia, please, you're the only one I have this kind of trouble with," said Zoe.

I was stunned and clearly in some sort of bizarro-world.

"Mick?" I said, when he came into the room. He wouldn't look at me. "Mick!" I went to him, grabbed his arm and he wrenched it away. It broke my fingernail—my fake nail and my real nail, right down the middle.

"Dahlia, Jesus, let go."

Mariana gasped, and Nicole looked sympathetically at Mick.

"Did you hit him?" Mariana asked, scandalized.

"Did I—no, Mick, can we please talk?"

The cameras weren't quite set, but they were filming alright.

Mick, a stranger to me now, looked at the floor, his hands on his hips. "Dahlia, you need to calm down."

"I cannot calm down, I don't know what the hell is happening, are you like—what is going on with you and Nicole?"

He looked to Nicole, who gave him some sort of commiserative look I didn't understand. Her makeup was not running, and someone had given her and Mariana robes. Her fake blonde hair looked orange when wet.

"No, you don't look at my husband, look at me."

"I'm sorry, don't *look* at your husband?" she looked at him again, like they'd talked about all of my *antics* before.

"I feel like I'm being gaslit. I didn't know you two were friends much less whatever this is. Mick, why are you being like this?"

Tears welled in my eyes. Mick, once again, looked to Nicole.

"Nothing happened, Dahlia."

"What ... does that mean, *nothing happened*?"

"It's not like that. Things have been off lately between us. So messed up. You know that."

No. No.

"Mick, things are a little weird, but you haven't been home—"

Oh my god. I was hearing it. He was never home anymore. Was this why? Was I the blind wife who had missed all the signs?

"You cannot be—" the tears spilled and I wiped them away. My finger was bleeding and I squeezed it. "Are you saying ... what are you saying?"

"Nicole's been there for me, Dahlia. As a friend. That's it. We've gotten close. Nothing more. Nothing physical."

"That makes it sound like—"

I could not find the words. I would never use words like *emotional cheating*, but what was I finding out right now?

I looked to our hungry audience. Zoe looked like it was her birthday. Mariana looked like she was watching a movie, only missing the popcorn. Lexi looked like she wanted to help but had no idea what to say. Leo looked awkward, like he was cropped into a scene he wasn't supposed to be part of.

I was sure all this read like drama to him and his free-spirited ideals. But this wasn't drama, this was my life and it felt like it was ending.

In front of cameras. In front of all these people.

"Dahlia, this isn't how I wanted to have this conversation."

"Have *what* conversation?"

He looked at me like I already knew.

This was a blindside. A complete and utter blindside.

"Mick, we need to talk in private—" I forced a laugh.

That, at least, he could not say no to. If he didn't say no to that, I could deal with whatever else was happening right now. I started to lead the way but he didn't move.

"Dahlia."

I felt fully removed from my body, and like I might throw up.

"I think I should go," he stood up.

"You thi—I'm sorry, *what*?"

His last glance before leaving the room did not go to me.

It went to Nicole.

32

Sabrina

It had been almost a year since Sabrina had laid eyes on her daughter. Their last in-person encounter was one of the standard visits Sabrina was granted in London. Aubrey looked older. Thinner too. Sabrina called her all the time. Texted her daily. She had even called Robbie a few times, hoping to talk to her. Everything went unanswered. She had gone through many different iterations of *trying*.

She had tried being the angry mother, demanding contact.

She had been the cool mom, who understood how her daughter wanted space.

She had been the miserable parent left behind, who begged and pleaded.

Sabrina had no idea which demanded the most humiliation. All of them. All of them and yet, what was a mother supposed to do? She had tried to explain why their lives would change and had to.

Aubrey, in one of the very few conversations they ever had about the divorce, had responded like Robbie. She had been horrified, disappointed in Sabrina that she would publicly declare a division. To side with the press, as they had both phrased it.

Ironic that as soon as Sabrina tried to do the right thing, the press turned against her. Sabrina knew that was no coincidence. The conspiracy theorists are right that money rules the world.

"Aubrey, honey, why wouldn't you tell me you were coming?"

"You somewhat invited me in one of your 'miss you so much' texts. And then Dad seemed to think it was a good idea to come find you and try to spend time with you here. But I didn't think you'd be having a rave when I showed up. You know, my friends' mothers are like, actual adults. Bailey here? Her mother works for charities and cooks dinner every night she can. She gardens, she reads, and she didn't, oh I don't know, detonate her entire family and her daughter's future because she's decided to hate her father."

"I did not detonate anything. Your father did."

"Right. Right, because my father is a *predator*. Right."

It was such a fine line to walk. Sabrina had known plenty of women who got divorced, and they always talked about how hard it was to stay neutral. She didn't get to walk away gracefully, quietly, and tell her daughter—grown or not—that it hadn't been right. That they were better apart. The decision to leave Robbie was based on more than Sabrina's emotions. She was disgusted by him, she was horrified by his actions, and it had certainly contributed to her own personal inability to look at him and see anything but a monster.

"Aubrey, I had a responsibility. I could never have stayed with your father after learning what I learned."

"Because you're such a role model? The spoiled Upper East Sider who took her clothes off in a smut film before she turned eighteen, and got impregnated to score a title?"

"Aubrey, stop this now," said Budgie, in her best, booming stage voice. "You're crossing a line."

"I am not crossing a line. My mother did, *Aunt* Budgie. She could have left him if she wanted, but she didn't need to completely soil his name for the rest of time. And by the way, my name. You know *I'm* related to him, right?"

"Your father did that to himself!" Budgie held her hands up helplessly.

"Lucky you, Aubrey, because he didn't come out looking that bad, did he? No one believes the women, no one believes me, your father is the only sane one in a world full of crazy women."

A million memories raced through Sabrina's mind. All the times Aubrey had been a normal, growing girl, and he had called her despicable names. He called her conniving when she was six years old. He always had a criticism for Aubrey. What she said. Did. Wanted. He was fixated on her *appeal*. He feared, as though it were a girl's only currency, that Aubrey would never be pretty enough for all the inevitable press they would get.

Aubrey was beautiful, but she didn't look like every other girl in the world.

How many ways did Sabrina have left to say, *your father is a bad man, and I left him because the women he abused needed an advocate, and after what I learned, I could not spend one more day by his side or appearing to be beside him?*

"Dad has been picking up all the slack. Making sure I still have a nice life. He acts like every day is my birthday. All I get from you is a bunch of tragic texts begging me to forgive you for ruining his life and trying to ruin mine."

Sabrina could not begin to defend herself. Treating her like it was her birthday every day?

One day, Aubrey would see it for what it was. Sucking up. Cheap affection, bribes. And the problem was that when Aubrey did realize it all, she would feel abandoned by him in a whole new way. Realizing one parent was wrong did not make a child understand the other parent who left. It made her feel more alone. Things were not that black and white. Sabrina and Robbie would never swap places as the golden parent, and even if they did, it would not last, because that sort of grief was inherently muddy for any child.

"Aubrey, I don't know what to say."

"Perhaps because you're too messed up."

"Aubrey. I'm sorry that you feel left by me, I'm sorry you think I did this. I'm sorry it's all so public. I'm sorry your own life was splattered all over the news like blood on concrete. Honey, I am."

Sabrina's daughter sucked in her cheeks, and she knew from Aubrey's childhood this was what she did when she didn't want to cry. She would bite the inside with her molars until the tears stopped threatening.

Aubrey cleared her throat and looked up to the sky before saying, "You dragged him through the mud because you became high on your social justice warrior drivel. Everything to you is some big *point*. You aren't happy without pointing out all the great big world injustices. All the *wrong*. And the second someone pointed a finger at dad, you were more than willing to jump on board. I don't even know if you were waiting for something to hate him for or if you had to make sure no one dragged *you* through that mud. Pretending you didn't sully your own name long, long ago."

"Maybe I did, but that's not why I said what I did. That's not why I left, and that's not why I made sure it was public. It's because—" she hesitated, and Aubrey waited for the next toe to be stepped on, "because your father did it. Those women are not lying."

"And you're little miss perfect over here, drinking, doing drugs, and groping some younger guy. Sure, you look like the absolute picture of the perfect mother."

"I never said I was."

"No? But you're saying my father is a criminal. So, what, I hail from two disasters?"

"Maybe, Aubrey." Sabrina's blood pressure was rising. Not at Aubrey. At Robbie. Always at Robbie.

"Listen, kid, your mother might have a lot of causes, but I've known her a hell of a lot longer than you have, and I can tell you for certain that she would never do anything to hurt you. If you're hurt from what happened, you should trust her that it was the lesser of evils."

Aubrey scoffed. "Aunt Budgie. You've been married three times to men who gave you the life you have now, forgive me if I don't value your opinion much."

Budgie laughed. "Honey, I'm a Verroye, I was born gagging on a silver spoon, I make no bones about that. We can talk some other time about the failures of my romantic life, but in the meantime, you need to reconsider all this anger you have at your mother. And you know, you can talk to your mom like an adult, and maybe see if you can understand her a little bit."

Aubrey looked at Bailey. "Can we go?"

"Sure."

"We are going to leave now. Great to see you and catch up. Have a super rest of the night mother."

The two of them left, and one of the cameramen hopped to action to follow them. Sabrina felt like she took a breath for the first time since seeing her daughter.

"Oh, honey, I'm sorry," said Budgie. "She's a kid. She'll figure it out."

"Budgie, you don't have a daughter, you don't understand, don't try to," she said it as sharply as a knife and regretted it immediately, but could find no more words for an apology.

Sabrina shook her head and looked to Zoe. "I'm done. No more. Get everyone out of here."

"We have one more—"

"I don't care, I'm going to bed. Get the cameras out of here."

"Sabrina, go inside, I'll deal with this," said Budgie.

Sabrina walked away. She took the outside steps all the way to her room and hid there in the dark, smoking from a hidden pack of cigarettes until the property went quiet.

33
Zoe

Once packed up for the night, the crew decided they had earned a drink. Zoe was positively elated. Some of the others seemed to think things hadn't gone *entirely perfect*. Or at least, Zoe guessed that was the problem judging by the fact that they weren't jumping up and down.

Fiona turned out to be a real powder puff. She fled the location after the whole Mick–Dahlia showdown, before the Aubrey scene, saying she had a sour stomach. Zoe could tell it was guilt over the set-up. Loser. She had a lot of toughening up to do if she ever wanted to make it in *this* business.

Even Aleksandr had stopped furrowing his brow for the moment and had cracked a smile. She put on a little makeup on her way to the bar.

Maybe tonight was the night she could try flirting with him a little.

Awkward to plan out flirtation like that, but at this point Zoe was used to doing things in a prescribed, planned, and manipulated way.

Living the life Zoe had, things rarely happened that surprised her. Think about it. The good surprises are things like:

- finding out the guy you like likes you back, or better yet, a secret admirer
- a marriage proposal
- desired pregnancy
- financial windfall
- unexpected job success

Well, she seldom had a crush anymore. She gave that up a long time ago. As for the financial windfall, she didn't play the lottery. The job stuff was pretty much her only focus and goal, and it would not be a surprise when it happened.

Bad surprises:

- getting dumped
- undesired pregnancy
- financial loss
- unexpected job failure
- illness

Due to the same reasons, she was unlikely to have romantic or family-life surprises, so she didn't have to worry about those. Financial loss—she bought almost nothing and had no real earthly possessions. Illness could strike her; that was true. But since she always assumed the worst, she could pretty much count on being emotionally prepared (read: dead inside) to handle whatever.

When she found out she got the job on Aleksandr's project, that was a good, unexpected twist. And tonight went better than she could have ever predicted.

She would get his attention, try to stand out. Make sure he knew she was the reason for his success. Like, what was he even doing? He was editing, which was way beneath him. Zoe was sure he was a magician though, and she was eager to see what he had put together. The crew hadn't seen any of the footage; they only made notes on the scenes they wanted to manipulate.

The bar was a total dive—the ironic destination for the tipsy rich and the "right at home" place for the vacationers who were packing twenty people into an off-shore house.

Aleksandr ordered a round of shots, and they raised them high and said, at Zoe's suggestion, *to the ladies who will make us richer than them!*

It was a lofty and unlikely goal for the others, but Zoe thought it quite likely this was her *real* ticket to the big time.

"That wasn't Everclear, was it?" Zoe asked Aleksandr playfully. "If it was, I'd think you were trying to get me to spill all my secrets or take off all my clothes."

Aleksandr shook his head, then looked at her for a moment before calling, "Jason, get your camera, I want to do some more behind the scenes stuff. Everyone mic up."

Jason grinned, gobsmacked—but didn't move.

"Jason, what's the problem?" Aleksandr asked.

"No, yeah, I'll go get my gear."

Milo followed, "I'll get the mics."

Within fifteen minutes they were all wearing one—they were pros after all—and Jason was behind the lens.

"Carry on as normal," said Aleksandr, with an easy, breezy air. "This is mostly for us at the end, and I'd like to show—show how human we are."

He winked at Zoe.

She didn't know what the wink meant, but she smiled at him before ordering a Long Island Iced Tea and drinking a quarter of it quickly to cool her nerves.

It was after midnight when she was finally alone with Aleksandr.

They sat out by the fire pit in the sand. She was on her third Long Island, and he was on his third gin and tonic. At least that's what it looked like; she knew he often drank them, and he was drinking something clear and bubbly with a lime.

His hair was a little mussed. He wasn't much different tipsy or being social, but he did seem to be in a good mood.

"What did you think of filming tonight?" she asked, tossing her hair and leaning toward him from her chair.

"We got a lot of good footage didn't we?"

"Yeah I'd say so," she enthused.

"That was all you, wasn't it?"

If she were the type of girl who blushed, like Sabrina, she would now. But she wasn't.

"I can't take *all* the credit. But I can take most of it." She laughed.

"Let me ask you something," he said, leaning closer.

Zoe leaned in. "Yeah, what's up?"

"Do you ever feel bad about it?"

"Bad about what?"

"The manipulation. These are real people, real lives. Real marriages, mother-daughter relationships. That doesn't bother you?"

Zoe screwed up her face and shook her head. "Let me tell you something, these people are stupid enough to fall for it. And they willingly signed up, they knew what they were getting into. Okay maybe not this bad, but we have to keep elevating things, that's why we picked such—"

"Such what?"

She took a sip, "Not to be an asshole, but that's why we picked people the world already doesn't like. People love to watch an antagonist get what they deserve."

"And you think these people deserve this?"

He was testing her, seeing if she had the guts to back up her actions. And she did. It wasn't her first time being questioned. "Look, if they wanted it easy, they could stay private. But they chose not to. They should know by now a little arguing isn't going to capture the attention of a viewer. We want to see things collapse."

"You think that's sort of human nature, is that what you're saying?"

"Absolutely. Look at *gladiators*, now we have running water and electricity, but that didn't change our truest nature. People love watching other people suffer. Reality TV hasn't made it decades by showing a bunch of *best* friends *getting along*. Nope. We can't send them out to the dust of a colosseum and let them kill each other anymore, but we *can* watch them break, cry, insult, throw drinks at each other. Think of them as our gladiators of emotional warfare." She let out a sigh. "If you let it be human, let them destroy each other and themselves, it's more fun."

He nodded. "Got it. So no regrets."

"No regrets." She held her cup up to him. "Cheers!"

He clicked his plastic with hers, and took a sip, never taking his eyes off her.

"I wonder about the privacy you're taking away from them. By getting them to tell their secrets for the world to hear, or broadcasting an affair—"

"At this point it's an 'emotional affair,'" she said with sarcastic air quotes. "And that was the start of half of this. Mick Irvine needs new press. Mick Irvine needs to be with a celebrity, not some small-town ex-soccer player. My friend is his publicist, you know that right? I wrote it all up in the emails."

"I don't think I do."

Zoe was getting too buzzed to realize how unlikely it was that he didn't know.

"My friend Regan, his publicist—she's had a thing for Mick forever—and she doesn't want him with Dahlia. Even in sports, you need press, you need a story, you need celebrity. Tom Brady married a model because he could and because it kept him relevant. All the religious and political stuff, that's a way for these players to get people to pay attention. Anyway, Mick needs a reinvention. This guy is a white wall; you can paint him any color you want. Regan met him, before Dahlia was ever on the scene, and he was all in. But then I guess Dahlia broke him down and broke him down."

"You look like you admire your friend's method."

"I do! She told me that a few years ago she asked him what is the most important thing to you, and he said *football.*" She splayed her fingers. "Football. That's his—that's what he said. Not love, family, friends. Which I also admire because really it's honest. So yeah, he said that and when he got traded, things weren't the same between Dahlia and Mick, and Regan *got in there.* She was doing her job. She introduced him to Nicole. Told her to act this way, act that way, and she came off like the perfect girl for him. And now here we are, he's going to leave his real-life-wife. She can go back to nowheresville and he can get on the map as part of cultural history instead of ending up some football player no one ever remembers."

"What about Dahlia?"

She scoffed. "Oh please. She's got a bunch of girlfriends, I'm sure, and they'll all build her up and tell her how *crazy* he was and how *right* she is, and then she'll marry some normal guy that she'll appreciate. Look, if she knew half of this, she'd *want* to leave him. He's not even a real person, he's whatever people tell him he is. That's what you get when you're raised to be, *groomed* from a very young age, to be a star athlete."

"I had no idea how valuable you would be, Zoe," said Aleksandr.

She *beamed*. "Thank you. I try. It's an art. To get her to be the crazy bitch, have him come out on top even though he's going to leave her to be with another girl? We're doing them all big favors. And I'll tell you something better."

"What's that?"

"That's not even the biggest twist for the end of the season."

"It's not, then what is?"

"I can't tell you that. I may not even be able to tell you how I do it, either. It's like a magic trick. I'm something of a magician, you see, Aleksandr." She crossed her eyes and pursed her lips at him.

He smiled. "I'm going to need you to tell me how you do it."

"Maybe if…"

"If what?"

"If Jason isn't crouching behind me while I'm mic'd up."

Aleksandr laughed and the two of them turned to see Jason and his camera filming.

"He is good though, you are good Jason, I only noticed you a minute ago. That's why they pay you the big bucks, right?"

Jason, who was not paid big bucks shook his head. "You're something else, Zoe."

She shrugged. "You'll thank me when we make history."

34

Dahlia

Mick was not there when I got back to the suite at the hotel. His things were gone, and it occurred to me that he must have packed up before he met me for filming. I'd shared enough hotel rooms with him to know how long he took to collect his belongings and still leave behind one rogue T-shirt. That meant he knew he was going to leave.

My head spun in practical, logistical questions, where did he go, how did he get home. It was easier to be irritated because it was too unsafe to access my utter, absolute grief. No, not even grief, *fear* of grief—putting me further from resolution. I didn't even know for sure yet what was happening.

So often in our marriage I had been marooned, during training camp or certain team-only events, but this instance of separation seemed radically different. There was a finality that left me feeling paralyzed.

How did this man who I had spent years with … how did he change so immediately?

This is what the internet will say about me and Mick. She managed to hold onto him for six years and then one day … he was gone. Not even a note.

Or was it more brutal than that? Would my marriage end—the gravity of which was still well out of reach of my mind's grasp—and then the few friends I had left and my family would sort of do that cringing, "yeah, I was afraid of that…" or "I can't say I'm surprised…".

The only closure for me being that I had tried my best.

I couldn't tell what was worse: the shock of him being gone or the revelation that there had been clues along the way that I likely missed.

All of it was worse. All of it was worse than when, a few months ago, I would have confidently thrown my relationship to the wolves, knowing it would come back in one piece.

That's what I'd done by going on this show. And here my broken relationship was, returning limping, bleeding, torn apart, and hobbling right past me.

Despite the dizzying reality of the exchange with Mick, I kept feeling like I was being dramatic. Irrational, over-reading into things to imagine there was any way a *marriage* was ending without me seeing it. Relationships, like *cheap* relationships, young ones, those end in a second. But how can you have a life together and then one day find out you can't have it anymore. We were *married*. Everything else felt unimportant, like what it might mean for Sabrina that her daughter showed up; and stopping to remember any of the night made me sick to my stomach.

Each time I tried to call him or text him, I reminded myself that I was his wife and had every right in the world to try to reach my husband. My attempts went straight to voicemail, his location tracker disabled.

Cool Mick, I remember high school.

What kind of man—what kind of man did any of this? But what kind of man walked away, really *left* after dropping a vague bomb like that?

He never answered. My options here were limited. Leave and go back to the city. Stay, make the ones in charge of my edit happy and film day after tomorrow—the last day before a break.

Dig a hole, climb in, wait to die?

That sounded best, but wouldn't work. My anger would unbury me too fast.

This show might be the worst decision I'd ever made. Whatever future scenario played out in my mind, it circled back to the show. The show. The worst mistake I ever made. Looping thought.

After a silent hour of sitting motionless on the sofa, staring at my phone waiting for the call or text that never came, I decided to change and get into bed. I washed my face, used all my products, and brushed and flossed my teeth. Routine always centered and calmed me. In my soccer career, a strict timetable of workouts in the morning, scheduled meals and practices in the afternoon gave me a sense of control in an otherwise unpredictable situation. Train your body what to expect and what it should be doing, sports psychology 101, you'll perform best when the game is on the line.

I got into my side of the bed and made a wall of pillows around me. Ridiculous as it was, I needed a physical way to feel less exposed and vulnerable.

Early the next morning, sleepless and hazy, I devised a plan: pack up my stuff, and Uber to Sabrina's. Returning to the scene of last night's events might help me find a piece of evidence, a conversation, anything that would assure me it wasn't as bad as I remembered.

The property was dead quiet, when I got there, like a sleepy town seconds after a tornado has ripped through and destroyed lives; those moments before everyone emerges to take stock, and the EMS vehicles arrive on site.

Inside the house was dim and so different without the frenetic crew around every turn. The stillness of *real life* was now unfamiliar to me.

I found a vanilla cupcake in the kitchen, bit into it like an apple, and walked out onto the deck. The temperature had dropped, and the sky was leaden. Sabrina's housekeeper and another man were tying down the umbrellas in the pool area and collecting the outdoor cushions. When you prepare for inclement weather, nothing gets damaged.

The smell of cigarette smoke lured me toward the cluster of Adirondack chairs positioned to look out over the water. A stone pathway through the short grass guided me to them.

Clearing my throat so as not to startle whoever it was, and hoping it was anyone but Mariana, relief washed over me as Sabrina turned in the chair. She beckoned me with a lazy hand, patting the arm of the one beside her.

"Take a seat, Miss Lonelyhearts."

Sabrina was barefoot, still in her pajamas and wrapped in an oversized blanket that looked like rabbit fur. Even vulnerable, she was an icon. She swigged from a bottle and then offered it to me. Dom Perignon was the last thing I wanted but I took a sip, because whether you want to keep drinking or not, you take a bottle of champagne from Sabrina Verroye when it's offered.

Having a drink off-camera felt completely different.

"This is all I have to offer you," I said, holding up my cupcake.

She looked at it for a moment, then had a bite, and handed it back. She wiped some icing from the corner of her mouth and let out a heavy sigh.

Her eyes remained fixed on the water. "I need to apologize for my part in last night," she said. "I can't blame Fiona for my own stupidity, but can I suggest I'm acutely accustomed to taking direction? It was never my intention to have everything blow up on you. I believed, maybe *led* to believe, I was giving you a place to share your side of the story. I feel awful for what I did, Dahlia, and I want to fix this for you somehow."

"Please," I countered. "You didn't *do* anything to me. You sped up the big reveal." She made eye contact. Neither of us laughed.

We sat together in silence for a few seconds, watching as the waves slammed the shore with increasing energy. The breeze lifted sand off the surface of the beach down below us, and I tightened my sweater around me, the big chunky sweater wrap I had bought for the weekend, envisioning sleepy mornings with Mick and a cup of coffee by the water.

"I thought I could use this show to change my trajectory," said Sabrina.

The beach was deserted except for a man running in our direction near the surf, and for a millisecond I thought it was Mick.

"When I left Robbie, I never would have imagined that the world would hate me for it. I didn't think I would be left without my daughter. What scares me for Aubrey is that once the press tires of supporting him...," she waved her hand above her head, "and they will. I'll still be the evil fame whore. But they'll come around to hating him, and they'll hate her too."

Saying this she shook her head, winced in predicted pain for her daughter and then lit another cigarette.

"I never understood why you were the scapegoat," I said, feeling small and repetitious. "Four separate women, then you left him and you're the asshole. I'm sure I'm picking all the wrong words, but you were the good guy there. You should have gone down in feminist history."

"Instead, I lost everything, including my daughter."

Squinting at the sunless, lumpy sky I shied away from the clichés that came to mind. This was not the time to fill dead air with say-nothing-things. Silence seemed better. But I was never skilled at that. "Do you think she's angry because she doesn't believe it?"

"I think she can't believe it. And I think the reason she can't," she took a drag, "oh I'm sorry, did you want one?"

No.

"Sure, please."

I hadn't had a cigarette since high school. Athletes don't smoke. Like any girl who had tried out a few different personalities, though, I knew how to light it without looking like a dork, even as the wind picked up and pushed my hair forward into my face.

"The reason she can't believe it is because she has no idea what life might look like if she isn't part of that particular society." She added, "I wanted nothing more than to get out of it when I was her age."

"You did?"

She took a deep drag, held it and closed her eyes as she exhaled.

"More than anything. I was sick of the rules, the perfect place settings. It seemed tedious and dull. My mother made a life of curating perfect moments. The reading nook with the window that looked out over the most beautiful parts of the city." Sabrina flicked her ashes in the heavy green glass ashtray before handing it to me. "She had shelves built into it with a collection of first edition books that cost more than the combined salaries of the entire staff."

"Sounds like a nice nook at least," I took a puff .

"She never sat there once. I don't think she read any of those books. Not in her whole lifetime. Everything she did was like that. The whole place, every corner was *done*. All so that other people envied it. All so some young girl could look through a magazine and dream of a life like ViVi Verroye's. Which ViVi herself never lived."

I did not want to admit I was the girl. "Do you still have that home?"

"We do. The monument to good taste sits there now, maintained, and cleaned twice a week, and I could never stand to move back in. Making me pitiful, since I don't get to complain about not living in a big, gorgeous townhome in Manhattan that I despise largely for its perfection."

"But that's not why, it's because the life wasn't real. Right?"

Sabrina inhaled again from her cigarette, reminding me to.

"That's true, nothing was real. And, somehow, I created an existence that was even more counterfeit than the one I wanted to leave." The flag flapped vigorously against the pole near us, and seemed to applaud her words, as if the wind and the universe were hinting that we were onto something.

"Why did you marry Robbie?"

I had a pang about Mick. When we were engaged, I was unsure if I could commit to what becoming Mick Irvine's wife meant. My head had been filled with stories of affairs and infidelities among the players. Could I survive a day-to-day existence entirely out of my own control? But my heart convinced me that joining my life to his was the right thing to do and that if I loved him enough, we could get through any challenge.

"We were young and," she laughed, "famous, and free to do whatever we wanted. He was handsome, he was fun, and I didn't think far enough into the future."

We had that in common. You can have all the skill, talent, and ability but the unexpected onside kick can be a game changer.

She rubbed one of her temples. "Now all I have is a lifetime of privilege to look back on and hate. There must not be anything worse than an aging brat."

"That's not—I wouldn't describe you that way. You wanted something real, and you don't feel like you ever had a chance to experience that." I shrank down in my seat, crushing the rest of the cigarette into the ashtray.

"And what about you?"

"Ha! Me? I'm a nobody, married to a somebody, and I never minded that, but I thought I could have some small identity of my own. That's why I did *this*."

"I didn't want to ask."

"I have no idea what's going on with Mick. And I keep beating myself up because what if it's all my fault? That I ruined us because I haven't been myself lately."

"You can't ruin a good marriage in a few weeks."

"I don't know, maybe when I think of *lately*, it's longer than I have realized. I don't know."

My phone buzzed in the pocket of my sweater. There it was, the text from Mick I'd been waiting for. But when I looked at the screen, I saw it was only the weather app warning me rain was starting in my area within minutes.

After a moment, the cold bottle of champagne knocked me in the shoulder. I met Sabrina's eyes as I took it from her. This time when she looked at me, it was like looking straight into the light of a star. Her expression made me feel comforted, seen, and understood.

"Dahlia. It's a little bit terrifying," she laughed, "a *lot* terrifying to believe that you can feel as though you know someone, and then find out how wrong you've been, and ever believe you can trust someone else again. You're never going to be sensible when it comes to love anyway. You'll either be right or not."

"That makes it sound like I am getting a divorce." No tears accompanied this thought. Instead I felt empty.

"I don't know what you'll do. I left my husband for much worse. Did you feel like something was wrong? Before last night I mean?"

I started to say *no*, because technically, everything had been okay. But that was not true. The air was suddenly still. It smelled like stone and earth. I felt a single drop hit my arm.

"Yes. And I couldn't put my finger on what it was."

"Ah." She took the bottle back and stood up. No longer shrouded she held the blanket in her free hand. Sabrina wasn't in a hurry to escape and hide from the imminent storm. Instead she took a deep swig. "There you have it. It's no joke what they say about a woman's intuition."

"Maybe not." I said looking up at her.

"You never did like Nicole." She still wasn't moving. Neither of us were. *After all we've weathered, what's a little rain?*

"How did you know that?" The arm of my chair was getting wet. Those juicy fat droplets that seem cartoonish and hit with a splat were coming down all around us. As I got to my feet, one hit me right on the cheek and trickled down my face like a well choreographed tear.

"Intuition, Dahlia. Same as you."

35
Dahlia

Later that afternoon, I fell asleep upstairs at Sabrina's. The downpour and half a Xanax knocked me out, and I slept right through dinner. I was going to leave for the city and skip the last day of the filming, but Sabrina and Budgie convinced me to stay. Our call time for the next day was 9:30 a.m., and thanks to a career involving pre-dawn workouts, I had always been a morning person. When I married Mick, I had learned to stay up late. A social life as a player's wife meant being *up* and *on* for dinner at 10 p.m. You adapt.

When I opened my eyes, it took me a moment to remember why I was alone and where I was. The memory of how screwed up things were with Mick came out of nowhere and hit me like a sucker punch. Maybe a Bloody Mary would help?

God, I was sick of drinking. Every left and right they handed us something. At first it seemed tasteful, then it became like empathy. *Here you go, bucko, I know today's going to be tough, have a drink.* But now the novelty of endless refills of expensive champagne had worn off, and the need for a fun personality was outweighed by the need to feel normal again.

The sun had returned, and I noticed its warmth radiate through the windows of my room. I usually loved the way things felt after a big rain, clean and quenched; it always filled me with a sense of hopeful expectation. Today was different.

Surely my phone would provide relief with a flurry of texts. But tapping his name revealed that his last message was from two days prior. There was nothing recent. Not one. How *nothing*?

This was ridiculous. Breathing through the throbbing heartbeats, I tapped his name and called him. He still wasn't picking up.

I almost laughed.

A text from Fiona arrived, reminding everyone to dress appropriately as the day would be *watersports*, which sounded like a gross exaggeration of what we'd do.

Some tinted sunscreen, a little waterproof mascara, and lip gloss made me look low-key compared to the full face of makeup I had been in for the last few weeks.

No doubt the other ladies would appear in flowing kaftans and big earrings, unprepared for anything but wine and a light breeze. Not me. I was ready to be splashed, dunked, and, worst of all, grilled about Mick. Maybe that wasn't the worst. Worst of all was that I felt prepared to take Nicole out if she pushed the wrong button. Mentally, I was like one of those inflatable balloon men you see flailing outside of a car dealership. But physically I was there. I landed on a fabulous one piece with a low V in front, a pair of sunglasses I was sure I'd lose, cut-offs, and a pair of black flip-flops.

One last look in the mirror told me the sunglasses were going to have to work overtime to hide the pain in my face. The heartbreak in my chest, bones and blood was so soaked through that I looked like I'd been ill for a while, like I shouldn't have been able to get out of bed. Even a courageous smile looked wrong.

Sabrina was already waiting down at the dock with Budgie when I arrived. Fiona attempted to feign enthusiasm and greeted me trying her best to make small talk about the weather and Nantucket while we waited for the others. Eventually she fell silent and stopped. There was too much that went unsaid. *Thanks for the setup Fiona. Wasn't that a huge surprise with your daughter, Sabrina? Sorry your marriage is pretty much over, Dahlia.*

Budgie had the air of a nurse, aware that her charge might collapse at any moment. Sabrina looked mean, but it was her version of strength.

"Hello," I said upon seeing them.

Then, like comrades in arms, they both said a stoic hello back.

Mariana traipsed down from the guest house after not too long, her hair in a kerchief, sunglasses covering most of her face, and the predicted kaftan blowing in the breeze.

Lexi arrived soon with Nicole.

She stopped by me, squeezed me on the arm and whispered, "I'm sorry, I'm only with her because I'm staying there."

Nicole said nothing but was smiling like a teen who found out her crush liked her back. Maybe he did.

The idea that this was the group meant to represent some semblance of friendship seemed bizarre. No one was looking at each other. But yeah, let's all go have fun with watersports!

We were outfitted with lifejackets, piled onto a boat, and told we were going to a different dock where we would be set up with waterproof mics and given the rundown on the event.

After an emotionally freezing boat ride, we arrived. Zoe and the rest of the crew were waiting along with a couple of jubilant teenagers who welcomed us, excited for their time on film, and began giving us our instructions.

Lexi put on her best *Lexi* personality, Nicole was in high spirits, and Mariana was struggling through what looked like a rocking hangover. Budgie was herself, as usual. Only Sabrina and I hid behind icy fronts.

Every time Mick or my anger at Nicole came to mind, I dismissed it, focusing my energy on something else.

"Wait a moment, wait," said Sabrina. "Are we expected to get on *that*?"

Sabrina pointed at a bright yellow banana-shaped inflatable.

"Sink into it, girls, can it get any worse?" Budgie directed.

Sabrina stiffened and I let out an exasperated sigh.

Zoe was standing by the yellow monstrosity, talking to the boy-man who would captain the boat that would pull us.

She was explaining something to him and I didn't like the look of it.

***

They had us climb onto the banana, stacking me—of course—right behind Nicole. Budgie was behind me, then Lexi and Sabrina at the end. Mariana, after letting loose with a not-funny riff about riding water weenies and having things between her legs, had requested the front; she was probably thinking it was a smoother ride. I wished I'd placed bets on whether she'd find a way to bring up her sex toy business, but then no one would have taken the bet against me.

At first the boat pulled us calmly, and only fast enough to get a breeze in the hair. There was a camera on the boat towing us and one on the chase boat following beside us.

I held on extra tight to Nicole's waist, my bad feeling not subsiding a bit. Sure enough, the speed picked up once we hit the real open water. The boat that pulled us was zigging and zagging, whereas the crew's boat was driving in one straight line.

The direction changed frequently, there were other boats nearby, and the *having fun* sounds quieted, even from the women who hadn't arrived at set angry and resentful.

It happened in an instant. I don't remember everything because it was a rapid series of events. Mariana later said it started when we hit a rogue wave or maybe it was cross chop, from a passing boat. The front of the inflatable dipped into the water, and as I let go of Nicole's waist, I felt myself slide off. Ditto for Nicole, who landed on top of me. At that moment, the back of the banana cartwheeled forward-launching Sabrina about twelve feet into the air. Budgie, Mariana, and Lexi had all jumped off already.

Breathless, disoriented, and caught underwater with no sense of where *up* was, I didn't know it was Nicole whose body kept colliding with mine as we both struggled to reach the surface.

It came to me that my life vest had moved up my body and arms, trapping my head within itself. When I righted it enough I was able to get my head above water where I gasped for air. The salt water was stinging my eyes, and blinking and rubbing wasn't enough to clear the blur.

We were all bobbing in the choppy, freezing water, trying to take inventory of what happened. Budgie was giving us words of reassurance, and I was coughing because I had swallowed a lot of water. It was then that I noticed I didn't see Sabrina.

The next while felt how I imagine a spacewalk must feel—slow and out of my complete control, punctuated with sounds of my own thoughts and breath but not much more. The cold water and the frenzy of many people, like what seemed to be twenty or more, moving in many directions, was too much for my nervous system to process, causing it to freeze like a laptop with too many tabs opened.

I was in the water; I was in a boat wrapped with a towel. It was unclear to me whose boat it was, but it was somebody else's boat, not our tow. Nicole, Lexi, and Mariana were with me. Then we were on the dock, and someone was talking to us.

"Everyone okay?" asked the someone, an older guy.

An inch or so of Sabrina's wet red hair peeked out from behind a man's kneeling body, who was assessing her on the dock. She was not moving.

Budgie crouched at her side.

It was a horrible, confusing ten minutes. Half an hour?

Sabrina was lifted expertly onto a gurney and slid into an ambulance like a body in a drawer at a morgue. They drove Sabrina away; Budgie went with her.

The crew never stopped filming.

36

Sabrina

Sabrina closed her eyes for an instant and opened them to the sound of panicked screams from her fellow riders. Of all things, the voice of Zoe rang through her head.

"Remember, the microphones are super expensive and barely water resistant. They are done if they are submerged for more than two or three minutes. If you fall in, you need to get back out as quickly as you can!"

Sabrina's rule-following was ingrained within her. She grasped the black plastic handle in front of her with both hands and tried to stay atop the yellow cylinder best she could, as she saw everyone else fall away into the water.

She felt light and weightless, she was flying and then nothing. It was quiet and dark.

She wondered where Rob was. Then, he appeared in his Vilebrequin swim shorts, the bright blue ones with the orange starfish, and lay down on the chaise beside her. This holiday alone was the first they'd taken in years. The weather in Monte Carlo was ideal. The sea air fought off the humidity and left its salty residue everywhere. She tasted it on her own lips.

"No one will ever love you like I do," he said as he stretched his arms over his head.

The pretty, uniformed steward emerged from the interior and asked if she could bring them anything. Rob sat bolt upright and lowered his sunglasses to engage with the girl.

"My gorgeous wife, do you wish for anything," Sabrina was flipping pages of a French fashion magazine.

True to form, the compliments and love bombs from Rob were reserved for the company of others.

"May I have a glass of that Languedoc rosé from yesterday?" she said.

"Of course and for monsieur?" the girl asked.

Sabrina glanced sideways at Rob from behind her own sunglasses.

"I'd like something young and French. Sweet but still adventurous."

Elodie, as her nametag indicated, smiled, and tucked some hair behind her ear. She was maybe in her twenties, probably from a nearby town like Villefranche, working as a steward to make summer money. Sabrina imagined a girl as attractive as Elodie would be accustomed to the flirtations of the yacht owners, only not like this, in front of the wife.

Sabrina closed her magazine and stood up, tying her pareo around her waist.

"Where are you off to? What about your rosé?"

"I'll take it with me to the room. I'm going to call home and check on Aubrey. Maybe take the car into town to shop. I've had enough for today." Did he even care?

"Excellent idea," he enthused. "You don't want to get too much sun. It's not your friend."

Below in her suite, Sabrina avoided her reflection in the mirror. She had no desire to stare into the dark blankness of her eyes or to notice the lines around every feature that had started to creep in. She'd always had a small frame, but she looked sickly thin, and the effect on her face was what could only be called gaunt.

Everything she did felt like killing time. And the sickest, saddest part was that she had no one left in the world to do anything with, except for Aubrey and Rob. After their marriage Rob had methodically isolated Sabrina from all her friends. It was something of a subtle purge, but he was adept enough to have her believe the severed ties were her own idea, questioning why she had ever been friends with some of them in the first place.

She crawled onto the bed and lay there on her back, arms stretched out and her eyes closed. The gentle sound of water lapping against the dock lulling her to sleep.

A gripping pain under her left arm woke Sabrina up. Her nose burned from all the salt water she had inhaled and she couldn't make out who, but someone was covering her with a towel. Budgie's voice sounded echoey and distant, still recognizable, without its normal gusto "You're okay, sweetie. You're going to be okay."

37
Dahlia

Within days of my return from Nantucket, the separation agreement was filed and papers were in my hands. I was staring at them now, at the sunny table in the kitchen of the New York apartment, where Mick and I used to scroll through social media together and make vacation plans. Where I would set up dinner while I waited for him to arrive in a car from La Guardia. Where I now sat alone, pen in hand, and tears absent.

Ever since the conversation with Sabrina, I wondered how wrong I had been about Mick and me.

Most people see a divorce coming long before it does. They report feeling the break down like an illness. I guess, like anything, it could come on like a debilitating disease, or it can come on as a car crash. Like this.

Now, upon microscopic dissection, it was evident to me how things had begun to disintegrate. Like the arrow in the Fedex logo between the "e" and the "x," the trouble between us was right there all along; the reality was what I couldn't see.

We had begun to communicate like strangers, and the misunderstandings had become infection. We hadn't fought like people who don't like each other. Worse, we had fought like we were people who liked each other but had stopped speaking the same language.

It was *it isn't working*, and no one was exactly wrong. There was no blow up. There was no singular trigger incident. Our relationship had been breaking down, and then he noticed and I didn't. I could not point a finger at him. This really was *no fault*.

The sex had been surprising and unusual, instead of happily routine. The good times had been ones I clung to, with this sense of relief—*oh good, things are back to normal, everything is great, it was all in my head.* The bad times were ones that sent me to the deepest pits of frustration. Days Since Incident wiped away and back to zero, striving for a baseline we could reach that would mean we were happy and could stay that way.

Of course, we couldn't, and somewhere inside, I had known that.

This did not mean that every fifteen seconds it didn't hit me like a bowling ball to the skull and send me spinning.

That's an exaggeration; it wasn't fifteen seconds anymore. Somehow, already, the impact had gotten less regular. Now it was maybe once an hour that I got clobbered by the realization that our marriage was over.

Knowing that I was able to heal sort of made me even sadder. It's odd how when we start to get better we also often get sad—because we start to realize how much we've missed out on, how immensely certain people have failed us. Healing involves grieving. No way around it.

I worried for myself that less than a week ago I had thought I was going to spend my life in a marriage and now I would not, and I also knew that as gutted as I felt now, I would be okay.

Doing what? Taking fewer private jet rides, that was for sure. Our pre-nup was generous. I'd be well taken care of, but I'd be alone.

Budgie called me a few times. She'd report on Sabrina: improving, resting lots, not taking any calls. She'd broken two ribs, green stick fractures, and suffered a nasty concussion, but she was okay. I wasn't as sure about me. I acted like things were *fine, oh, really I'm fine,* and then Budgie would go into distraction mode, talking about some diva in one of her shows. When I had been honest with her, on a weaker day, I had told her I was afraid of what life would be like now. I was going to have to become independent again.

But she had said, "don't beat yourself up for not coming out of this as autonomous as you were before. You joined your life with someone, this is what it looks like when you do that. It's the same for everyone. You'll figure something out, you're a bright young girl. What did you want to be before all this?"

I'd had to think. Then I confessed that I had wanted to be a writer. "Which is such a silly thing these days isn't it? Who even reads anymore?"

"Do you read?"

"Yes."

"Then other people do too."

It gave me a small surge of hope, but I had also become deflated. "But that's such a gamble. If I assume that won't work out, what, I have years of soccer, a *lifetime* of sports behind me? I'm not twenty anymore, I gave all that up."

"You're going to be fine. Worst case scenario, Lexi can teach you how to become an Instagram model. A TikTok influencer. Whatever they call it."

I laughed, and then she went on.

"As for the gamble thing? I work in the industry of high hopes. Think about what you want. You didn't want to move to a fly-over state, but you did. No one can make you do that anymore, right? It's going to take time. But let this be a moment in your life when you realize that *this* is what made you."

Talking to Budgie made me both hopeful and sense the crushing pressure of a world-sized oyster. But between the two, I felt better. Better than I had in quite a while. The stress of thinking I had everything to lose and that I might lose it—that was worse than having nothing to lose.

I signed the papers as the last of my ice melted into my bubbly water and jumped when the phone rang.

Mick was here.

The bizarreness of him calling up washed over me as did the loss. I told them to let him up. He was coming to retrieve some more belongings. We were trying to be *grown-ups* about the whole thing and not passive-aggressively do the pickup when I wasn't home. I had thought we'd agreed on the next day.

We both knew that this visit was going to be one of the last times we saw each other one on one, unless we had bad luck.

The elevator heralded his arrival, and seconds later he walked in. I met him in the front hallway and the scent of my Mick wafted in with him, sending a surge of misery through me.

"Good timing," I said, "I signed the papers."

He nodded. "Yeah," and added "You look good."

"You really shouldn't say that."

However, he was right. I had just returned home after shooting stills and intros for the show and was still in my glam. We had been on a weeklong break from filming anything together until the finale.

After what happened with Sabrina, we had all settled on a compromise of finishing strong. Regardless of Sabrina's injuries, they had made it very clear that if we made the finale a worthless shoot or refused to participate in filming pickups—which must have sprung to mind for everyone as the most desirable choice—then it would be costly for *us*. They needed worthy material, or there would be consequences. Reshoots that, according to our participant agreements, we would be responsible for financing should production deem the material worthless. That contract had become their sword and their shield, and they were very adept at the lunge and the counterattack.

"You do though. You're right. I'm sorry."

"Go ahead and grab whatever you need," I said, pointing toward the bedroom.

For a moment, I thought he might lead the way, but then remembered he was the guest.

I walked over to the hallway that led to our bedroom and paused, "Do you want something ... I don't know this is so weird..."

"I fucked up, Dahl."

I kept my face blank.

"I don't know what … I don't know what I've done."

"Well, we're getting divorced. There's that."

He shook his head and sat down in his usual chair in our living room. "Why are you dressed up?"

"You don't get to ask me things like that anymore."

The streak of rage that pulsed through me like a new jugular throbbed hot and quick before settling again.

"I want to ask you everything. *I* fucked up."

"Okay, what is that supposed to mean, you keep repeating *you* fucked up?"

"I listened to Regan. She's never given me bad advice, and I listened to her, she's been saying it for the last year."

"Wait. Wait, *what* are you talking about?"

"This, all of this is my fault. She got in my head." He put his forehead to his palm and rubbed.

"PR is important, you know? I need the big deals and to stay relevant. I made the mistake of confiding in Regan whenever we had issues, whenever anything was wrong or going on, I vented to her. I told her about everything, and when I told her about how unhappy you were with the move, she said that in her experience, that kind of thing was too big. She predicted we'd have problems, and then we did. We weren't the same, and then once I knew that we weren't the same, I started causing it and seeing it more and," he took in a deep breath and ran his hand through his hair, "I didn't think there was anything wrong with being honest with her about that. She got this idea in her head that if we got a divorce, I would never recover from that, PR-wise, that I would look like an asshole."

Yeah. For sure, he would.

It made me sick to imagine that divorce had occurred to him before recently, and it made me murderous to imagine Regan—Cool-Ass Regan—eating chips and guac with him, cringing about everything I ever said or did, and then building a case against me.

Sabrina had said, *we always know.*

I had always known Regan was shady. But the evidence was never there, only the feeling. And if you don't have evidence, a feeling is either premonition or paranoia, and you don't know which it is until it is too late.

"She said I should get ahead of it."

The look in his eyes told me that everything that had happened to me ran much deeper than I could have dreamed.

"She framed the show like I was giving you something of your own. Like you said that night we argued. I went along with it thinking either way, you would have it. She said you'd show your true self once you were being filmed. She pushed that you were with me for the money. She talked about how we spent the money, the multiple homes, the parties, the over-the-top trips, the cars, all the shopping. She always said that, and I started seeing it that way."

"Wow. Okay."

"Dahlia, I don't know what happened. Everything went exactly like she said it would. It's not because I thought you were—anything, because I never believed you had an agenda. You have always loved me more than I could deserve. You always look at me the way you do, and treat me the way you do, and before you I never experienced any of that. But then she got in my head and it triggered everything."

His breathing was labored through emotion I could hear trapped in his throat.

The part of me that loved him wanted to cry, wanted to touch him. And every other part of me wanted him to feel even worse.

"What exactly caused this revelation, Mick?"

His gaze dropped to the floor.

"Let me guess," I said, a nasty smile turning up the tone of my voice, "Did Regan by any chance try something with you the second you told her we were through?"

His finger tapped on the arm of the chair, and the sound meant he was still wearing his ring. He always did this when he was at a loss for words or felt anxious.

My rings were in my drawer, in their original Tiffany box, which I had always saved, never envisioning that my reason for safekeeping was that one day they would return to the velvet of the interior like they had been rented. Like the whole life they symbolized had been rented.

"Let me guess again, you and Regan got together to drown your sorrows in a limitless night of shots and beer—I bet I can even guess the bar." I shut my eyes, thinking, "Crabby Dick's?"

His tongue traced over his molars.

"That place smells like pee and it's the stupidest name. Whoever opened that thought he was being so clever."

My smile faded as my imagination wandered again and returned to Regan trying something in the darkness of that miserable place. I could see her shaking her head at me and my trespasses, comforting him with a thousand passionately spoken words. All of that cheerleading that people do for each other when they need to perk up someone who has no business feeling better. It even upset me to hear people comfort *me*. Even Budgie, who was trying only at kindness, telling me not to worry about him. She lumped him into a category, *men like him*. She talked about how free I'd be without him. She tried to help me find the unhappiness that had existed with him, all of the unrest. But I knew it was all crap, all platitudes. I had loved Mick. We had been lucky. He was not a man like *them*. He was my *Mick*.

We had always been each other's.

And then these outsiders came in trying to comfort us away from our division like it made any sense, and it didn't.

"The second she tried, I understood what was going on. I know how meaningless that sounds, like some epiphany. You always see things coming a mile away—"

I scoffed. "Not this time."

"That's not even true. You never liked her."

"Yeah, I never liked her, but I never saw this level of manipulation coming. Never saw us getting divorced."

He winced at the words.

"How does Nicole fit into this?"

His lip curled. "She and Regan are friends. Nicole's publicist is with Regan's firm."

"Ah."

"I'd run into her when I met Regan for dinners. Regan would meet up with her before she met with me, and Nicole always hung around some. Stuff like that."

"*Stuff like that.*"

My heart ached, and yet my tongue was sharp and poisonous with hate.

"Regan kept hyping her up like maybe she was what I needed. Someone who had been through fame," he looked at me, and one of his dimples showed, "I know, I-I get it. Fame. That's how she phrased it."

I wanted to explode and scream, *don't tell me how she phrased anything!*

"I was not lying when I said nothing happened with her, of course nothing happened—"

"It's not an *of course*, Mick, nothing is."

"It is to me, and not that there aren't a hundred other reasons, but for one thing I was never attracted to her. I felt sorry for Nicole. She seemed broken, and I sort of became her friend when we were all out together. It was me, though," he squinted his eyes. "I did it to myself. I was thinking too much, Dahl," he said in an almost gasping apologetic tone.

He had said those words to me many times about the game—my reply was almost Pavlovian. I moved toward him and then covered it up by sitting across from him. This show had made me paranoid about being caught and misunderstood.

I knew him so well that I could hear every unspoken thought. His eyes were red with the pain. His body was facing mine, every part of him reaching, whether he knew it or not, like a tree reaching for the sun.

"I thought we were thinking about starting a family. I thought we had a five-year plan. But you couldn't open up to me. When I heard you tell Sabrina, about the pills, I felt betrayed and humiliated. But the more I thought about it the more I realized, that's on me. My wife can't even confide in me because of who I am or who she thinks I am."

He hung his head, wrinkled his brow, and looked back at me with all the earnestness that a man could.

"What are you asking me for, here?"

"I want to pretend *this* never happened. I'll deal with the lawyers," he looked like the word made him sick, "I'll make it like none of it ever happened."

"You can't make it like it never happened. You can censor it all you want, but you already did this to me. On camera Mick. You can't undo everything that happened with the show."

We looked at each other.

He stood from his chair and came over to me, where he knelt on the ground, taking my hands in his—which I nearly pulled away. He stared up at me, needing me, but trying to look strong for me too. Trying to look reassuring.

"I will spend the rest of my life making it up to you," he shook his head, "that's such a cliché. I'm, I know you hate clichés. I will, though, Dahlia, I will never forget you again. I'll do all the stuff I stopped doing. I won't put the walls back up. Whatever it takes. Anything. Dahlia. Anything."

I paused, my mind swirling.

"How did Regan know about the show?"

To his credit, he did not look annoyed with me for asking more, for ignoring his begging.

"Zoe. I guess they knew each other from school, from NYU." He let out a breath.

"Ahh. Okay then. Gee. Didn't they play us so well," I was angry, but swallowing tears. Anyways, tomorrow's the last day of filming. It'll be fine. I'll be fine. I've survived. I guess we didn't."

Removing my hands from Mick's grasp, I drew a deep breath and blew it out with a quiver.

I will not cry. Do not cry.

"But the truth is Mick we didn't lose because of what *they* did to us. We lost... because *we* weren't good enough to win."

38

Zoe

Zoe had picked up smoking again, and from the first drag she had no idea why she had ever stopped. She was in her shitty car; the weather was terrible, overcast, and spitting rain. The exhaust from her Newport smelled different in the closed walls of her trashy clunker, and it reminded her of high school. Of course it did. It was the same old Corolla. Instead of homework, binders, folders, and used-but-unopened textbooks in the back, it was her equipment and a bunch of books that had promised to teach her how to become a real Hollywooder.

The six-disc changer had the same old albums that had been in there forever, since she usually used the cassette adapter and dongle to connect her phone. But that had stopped working, and now she had six albums to choose from:

- An old EDM mixed CD she had burned
- *The Queen is Dead* by The Smiths
- The *Moulin Rouge!* Soundtrack
- The Who's *Who's Next*
- A horrible pop mix CD she'd made that had songs of the likes of Maroon 5, Fallout Boy, Green Day, Foo Fighters, and even a Nicole Trace song, among others.

She had burned all these CDs in an attempt to be retro. She thought she was being cool. Now she was a twenties-something girl with a broken adapter, forced to listen to the soundtrack of her optimistic youth. Funny. She would never have thought of herself as optimistic, not ever, but in retrospect, she had been something close to hopeful at some point.

Now her career was crumbling, and she was trying to feel anything but empty.

She was supposed to care about everything she had done. No, worse than that, she was supposed to have earned something by pushing herself and everything at her job to the utter *fucking limit*. Didn't people get rewarded for going out on ledges? Didn't they get celebrated for pushing boundaries?

She picked a random disc on the radio, knowing somewhere in her brain that it was going to land on The Smiths album, but still allowing herself to feel like *it fucking figures* that it came on.

Her phone buzzed on the passenger seat beside her, and she ignored it. Eventually it stopped. She lit another cigarette. It made her feel both jittery and calm.

She got out her trusty bottle of car whiskey from the glove compartment and took a swig.

Aleksandr wanted to talk to her. Legal wanted to talk to her about the accident last week. The participants were whining like babies in dirty diapers, and she was the one who was screwed. She was supposed to get all the credit, not the blame.

Zoe laughed.

It was funny, right? Someone somewhere would find it funny that the water banana was what happened to Sabrina. Right?

The laughter spilled out of Zoe as she sang over the jaunty beat of "Frankly Mr. Shankly."

She sang along, still laughing, still inhaling smoke from the cigarette, and then from that which bounced off the torn upholstery of the car.

By the second verse she was cracking up. She belonged in the cuckoo's nest. She was positively hysterical.

She remembered when her parents tried to get her on medicine, and she had thrown it down the toilet, one pill at a time, not being forced to do a tongue check like in the movies.

She could take them now. The pills were little oblong pink things. She rattled them around like she used to do with skittles in a custard cup in her old kitchen.

No one was here to protect her, no one was here to protect Zoe from herself, no one was here to call an ambulance and get there in the nick of time. If she took them, she'd be dead.

"Some Girls Are Bigger Than Others" began. She leaned back, head on the rest.

Self-righteousness bloomed in her struggling heart and mind as she insisted silently and to no one that she had only tried to create art; she had only tried to do what no one else would: get her ahead. Get Zoe to success. Get Zoe to a place of comfort.

She poured all the pills out into her sweaty palm and tried to imagine what it would feel like to take them. It was a dark version of playing pretend that she had done a thousand times in her life.

She imagined taking them with a swig of whiskey, and she wondered if she'd feel every part of her die before her brain shut off.

A big bleeding ink blot of rage spread through her mind as she thought again of Sabrina and all those women. They would be some of her last thoughts. Not even her own life flashing before her eyes. Perhaps because there was so little to think of.

Perhaps because some girls *are* bigger than others.

She didn't want to think of how it had always been a gasping *try* to get by. She had never been alive. She had been dying, always. Her death, would that even be hers?

She funneled the pills back into the prescription bottle, closed it, and threw it onto her passenger seat. She tilted her head back and her idea—the idea she had implied had potential but was secret—began to take form.

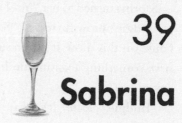

39

Sabrina

Strapping into an evening gown was no small task. Sabrina had opted for a dress with a corset-like bodice, the form of it giving her bruised torso some support. The relief from the reinforcement was not unlike the time she sprained her ankle, and her foot was in pain when it was bare, but it was okay when it was in a pair of structured shoes.

"I don't know how you've done it without medicine, Sabrina, I broke a toe a few years ago and lived off this stuff. I was asleep for a week." Budgie set down the bottle of Vicodin on the bedside table.

"I hate how they make me feel," said Sabrina. "Do up the back, will you?"

Budgie zipped the back up slowly. "Are you sure you're up for this?"

"No."

"Ah, well then."

"It's fine. I'm not through battling them. Ed says he thinks he can skew the edit if need be."

Budgie zipped the last two inches with one final lurch. "Sorry, too tight."

"It's alright."

"You're the only person I know who would wear one of these. You were blacked out with a concussion a week ago, and now you're in four-inch stilettos and a corset."

"You've got dancers who perform on broken shinbones."

"Yes, but those kids are unable to feel pain due to youth and the blind and desperate desire for fame."

Sabrina turned to her. "Yes, I remember that particular impairment."

Budgie's brow furrowed. "Sabrina, I'm sorry that I suggested you come on this show. It's been such a mess. I thought Aleksandr must have something exciting up his sleeve, but this has played out like any old—"

"Budgie, please. It's okay. If anything, this was a part of my unending pattern, I was the one who thought it would be the big fix-all. I'm going to do something different after this. I have to make a go of it on my own and I haven't figured out what that looks like yet, but I will."

"You and Dahlia both seem to be looking to find a new dream."

Sabrina shook her head. "I've been meaning to call her. How is she?"

Budgie shrugged. "She's alright. You know what it's like. I'm surprised Mick wound up being such a bastard."

"I feel awful for her. At least I didn't love Robbie at the end. At least you didn't love any of your husbands. Well, except one."

"Now is not the time," said Budgie. "Come on, we'll be late."

She opened the bedroom door, and the two of them walked the marbled hallway to the foyer. Zoe was there, zipping up the last of her equipment. Sabrina's hair and makeup team and the rest of the crew had already left. They had filmed Sabrina and Budgie discussing her injuries, and Zoe had guided the conversation to bring up every negative subject of Sabrina's life.

Zoe had a habit of coming in smelling like a dirty night out. Today was no different. Cigarette smoke was trapped in her hair and old booze poured out of her pale flesh.

Zoe sort of lingered, like they all might leave together, but in truth Sabrina needed a moment to prepare for the last night of filming. Something told her that it was not going to run smoothly.

Zoe headed to the elevator, and right as the doors were about to shut, she stuck her arm out to stop them and said, "You know what, I got a text about a missing boom cover maybe left behind in

your room when we were filming. Can I run and see if it's there?
Do you mind?"

"No, no, of course," said Sabrina.

Zoe zipped out and turned the corner headed toward the
bedrooms where they'd been filming earlier.

Budgie seemed annoyed, but Sabrina stared after her.

"Strange girl."

"I fear it's worse than that."

There was something about Zoe—besides her absolute
loathsome personality—that Sabrina didn't like. She reminded her,
in a way, of Robbie. They were both snakes, but different kinds.

When Sabrina had met and fallen in love with Robbie, she had
reported drunkenly, happily, to a paparazzi with a handcam that he
was handsome, rich, and lethal. She had chosen the word because
it felt accurate but hadn't considered how strange a word it was to
use until much later.

She had learned how right she was.

And Sabrina had a sick feeling she was right about this
one, too.

Zoe returned to the elevator with an apology and a long story
about crew losing these dead-cat covers all the time.

The doors began to slide shut with Zoe on the other side of
them and Sabrina watched her become a sliver and then vanish.

"Quick drink?" asked Budgie.

"Yes, but nothing too strong."

"Negroni? I make a mean negroni."

"That's not exactly weak. Yes, please. I haven't had a drink since
all this happened."

And in truth, she was starting to feel a thousand times better.
Perhaps all her coping-drinking was catching up with her. Perhaps
it had stopped being a reasonable part of wallowing and it had
gotten bad.

Budgie laughed. "I'll meet you on the terrace, if you want to
have it out there."

"That sounds lovely."

Sabrina looked out over the city that she loved, that she knew, that was hers and not Robbie's, and for the first time in as long as she could remember, she felt good. Pain in her side notwithstanding. She felt optimistic. She felt energized. She felt independent. This show had been something of a mistake, but nothing had gotten too bad, had it?

Perhaps it was asking for trouble to even wonder.

Budgie appeared in the doorway, sun caught in her eyes, which were the same shade as Sabrina's.

"What's wrong?"

"Nothing." She shuffled to the settee and handed Sabrina her cocktail.

Sabrina took it, grateful, and saw that Budgie had an iPad under her arm.

"What's that? Is that yours?"

"No."

"Is it ... whose is it?"

"I think it's that little monster's."

Sabrina looked toward the elevator, as if Zoe might come back in on cue.

"You're not going to look through it are you?"

"I am."

"Why?"

"Because something is not right about her."

"Where was it?"

Though speaking with a punishing tone that implied she wanted nothing to do with Budgie's snooping, she sat down beside her and stared at the tablet.

"Do you think she left it behind on purpose?"

"I have no idea," said Budgie.

She tapped the screen. It lit up. No passcode.

It opened straight up to the Notes app, which had a note named for each of the women.

Budgie clicked on her own.

Married several times
Gay? Reason for so many marriages?—imply
Interviews with former students/cast members—DONE
Resents Sabrina?
Childless
Fat—insecure?
Doesn't get serious much—sociopath?

Then, under a subheading called **in phone**:

Wears real fur
Texts with ex-husband (x2) reconnect?

"What's that mean, *in phone?*" asked Sabrina.
"Not sure."
Sabrina reached across and tapped her own name and a far, far longer list revealed itself.

Self-obsessed
Former drug problem—exploit?—DONE
Daughter issues—DONE
Contact Robbie?—4 attempts made
Resents Budgie?—interview
Anorexic?
Drinking problem—exploit
Conflict with Dahlia—not working
Conflict with Mariana—working
Contact famous exes—attempts made
Greedy, shows off her money—in edit/interview
#Metoo—full of shit?—edit

Under **in phone**:

Multiple contacts to daughter, unsuccessful
Phone album filled with Robbie/Aubrey family photos—(still in love with him?)—exploit/edit

Texts with Budgie about Robbie—hates him blah blah blah
Researched rehab—push push push

Budgie hit away to another tab called Ep 2.

PICK UPS—EPISODE 2

SCENE—MARIANA AT WINE BAR WITH DAHLIA
PICK UP—*"I wasn't going to drink, and she was furious."*

SCENE—LEXI AT HOME WITH SUGAR DADDY
PICK UP—*"...I get what I want."*

SCENE—DAHLIA AND MICK DATE NIGHT
PICK UP—*"It's pretty obvious we have a great relationship."*
PICK UP—*"I wish we could both be in the city again."*

They continued to glance through the other episodes. All the manipulation was there. All of the small exploitations.

"She can't have meant us to find this."

"I don't know," said Budgie.

"Wait...," said Sabrina, tapping on *EPISODE 8*, including some scenes which had not yet been filmed.

PICK UPS—EPISODE 8

SCENE—BUDGIE AND SABRINA AT PENTHOUSE
PICK UP BUDGIE—*"She hasn't been herself lately."*

SCENE—MARIANA'S CHARITY PARTY
DETAILS—Sabrina + Mariana fight
PICK UP MARIANA—Something like: "Sabrina has been acting irrational tonight."

SCENE—HOSPITAL
DETAILS—Mariana & Lexi @ Sinai discuss Sabrina + pills
PICK UP LEXI—"I feel like we should have seen this coming."

"Sabrina plus pills?" said Sabrina. "What does that mean?"

Budgie looked toward the apartment. "Wait a minute."

She stood up, tossing the iPad onto the cushion beside Sabrina, and then went inside. Sabrina stood, but waited for her.

"They're gone," said Budgie when she returned.

"Who's gone?"

"Your pills."

"Gone?"

"Yes."

"They were right there."

"Sabrina, don't be thick. She was in your bedroom. She must have taken them."

"But ... why?"

"I don't know. But something is wrong. She's going to do something."

40

Dahlia

Mick arrived to pick me up at six o'clock on the dot, like a prom date looking to impress my parents. We were going together to the finale filming tonight because we had agreed that even though we weren't going to win, we were going to *get out there and show them what we're made of*. We had agreed to appear to be the old ourselves.

I looked my absolute *effing* best. The glam team Budgie recommended had been outstanding. She also referred me to her stylist who had me in Saint Laurent. Younger Dahlia would have seen me and thought, "that woman is fancy and beautiful, and one day I will be like her."

With great hesitation and with a beastly heartache, I had also slid back on my engagement ring and my wedding ring. It felt like a warm bath. When doing this, I refused to cry off all of my expensive lashes and makeup and let out a Shwarzeneggerian roar to stop myself from erupting.

The doorman rang and told me Mick was there.

I went down after one last look in the oversized hallway mirror. We had bought it in LA on Melrose and had almost broken it moving it within our condo, after having had it survive a hero's journey across the country—we laughed about it a lot; it became something of a running joke.

We'd still wound up with the bad luck.

He met me in the lobby. No cameras.

"You look beautiful."

I gave a curt head-tilt of thanks and followed him to the car. The driver held the door for us, and we climbed in.

Since we were not being filmed, we were sitting as far apart as two strangers might.

The air on the seat between us seemed to contain a magnetic pull that I—perhaps we both—resisted.

Staring out the window, trying to act like he was not there, I felt him do the same. At one point he cracked the window before looking to me with a lingering gaze and then looking away. I pretended not to notice.

We pulled up at the event venue—some deserted Upper East Side consulate. He got out first and held out a hand. Anticipating the contact of his skin on mine, I hesitated, then took it and stepped out.

The production photographers were there, waiting, and they got pictures of us right away, me under his arm like everything was normal.

I wanted to fold into him.

I could and would not.

"Is Sabrina here yet?" I asked Milo when I saw him.

He shook his head, "Zoe is coming now with her," and he directed us to an alcove where we were mic'd. For whatever reason, Mick looked nervous.

Milo then bustled us through the party to get the footage they needed. I kept an eye out toward the entrance for Sabrina, Budgie, and Zoe.

I was so alert for them, in fact, that when we were set up to film with Nicole, I didn't even notice.

"Nice to see you guys," said Nicole. "You guys know Regan. Obviously, Mick, *you* do."

Regan was in a sleek navy jumpsuit that I recognized as being advertised on Instagram.

"I didn't know *you* were coming, Mick," said Regan, like the passive aggressive girlfriend.

He squeezed me and gave me a kiss on the top of the head.
"I couldn't miss a night out with my girl."

Regan looked like she'd watched a spider give birth.

Nicole looked like the spider.

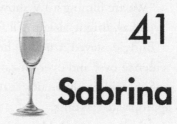

41

Sabrina

Budgie and Sabrina arrived and upon getting out of the car, Zoe was there looking frantic.

"Hey ladies—did you—did you happen to see an iPad lying around at your place?"

The look on her face told Sabrina it was no ploy. She had not meant to leave that.

"No, I didn't," said Sabrina, convincingly, she hoped, as she was being outfitted with her mic pack.

"We left right after you," said Budgie, also being set up. "She'll look later."

"Okay…"

Budgie said, "Now, Zoe, I will repeat these words, until someone finds me Aleksandr: *we are filming a TV show, we are filming a TV show, we are filming a TV show.*"

"Budgie, I'll find him but he's sort of hard to track—" Zoe started.

"We are filming a TV show," said Budgie.

Zoe laughed. "You're a riot. But yeah, I'm not sure if—"

"We are filming a TV show."

"You're making this impossible, are you going to—"

"We are filming a TV show."

Zoe stared at her, polite smile fading into a grimace. She got on her two-way radio and said, "Aleksandr, are you on set?"

There was silence.

Zoe made a helpless face and then said, "Budgie, I'm not sure if—"

"We are filming a TV show!"

"Okay, alright, alright, I'll find him."

Budgie stayed true to her promise and repeated the same sentence over and over on camera until they found him.

She said it differently each time, adopting the tone of the appropriate response.

Sabrina was a child again, unable to keep a straight face while Funny Budgie Got Her Way—she could have written a children's book about it.

Finally, Zoe arrived with Aleksandr, who ushered them into a side room alone.

"Hello, Verroye girls," he said, gently closing the door behind him. "How can I help you today?"

"Aleksandr," said Budgie, undoing her own mic and reaching across to do the same for Sabrina. "This is a shit show."

He nodded. "Welcome to reality TV."

"There's a reason you did this. Why? I find it a little hard to believe you did it to get a taste of the world."

"I don't know what you mean."

"When I did *Chicago*, for example, I didn't do it to do a show that had been done a hundred times before. I did it so that I could cast an entirely Black ensemble, with the hopes that I might illuminate how differently that story plays out. I didn't want to tell the same story, you know, I wanted to do something different. I have always admired your work and thought you and I might be somewhat similar."

He considered her, intensely for a moment, as Sabrina looked on.

"Am I wrong?" pushed Budgie.

After a pause, he said, "No. You're not wrong. I am aiming to do something—different."

Budgie nodded. "And Zoe, is she your errand girl or a loose cannon?"

"To be honest, Ms. Verroye—and Ms. Verroye—Zoe is the least admirable iteration of heartless I've ever had the displeasure of knowing."

"Why don't you take a look at this?" Budgie handed him her phone. Before leaving the house, she had screenshot everything she could find.

42

Dahlia

"**S**abrina!"

I screamed for her, interrupting whatever the hell Nicole was talking about, my voice carrying across the room.

She turned, and I let go of Mick to go to her.

He followed me, I didn't even have to look back to know.

"Sabrina," I said, when I got to her. A pro now after these eight weeks, I rubbed the head of my mic as I whispered in her ear. "Something's wrong. Zoe knew Regan and I think this whole show has been—"

"I know," she said. "I know."

In overhearing this, Budgie tilted her head. *How does she know?* She seemed to ask.

"It's alright," said Sabrina. "Don't worry about Zoe."

I nodded. Mick pulled me back in protectively, and I sensed he had landed eyes on Zoe.

There was a frenetic air of confusion among the crew. They usually looked passive and blank, like flies on the wall.

Lexi was being filmed with her oaf, Tom. They were fighting. Milo and Fiona were directing them, pausing them every few moments.

Mariana was holding court over Regan, Nicole, and some sycophantic friends who looked desperate for airtime. Zoe was close by with a headset.

What had I done? What had I gotten myself into? What had *Mick* gotten us both into?

I squinted my eyes and saw Nicole pointing not at me, not at Mick, but at Sabrina.

At nearly 8 p.m., they had us sit side by side at two U-shaped tables. It looked almost medieval. The event was hosted by Mariana to raise awareness for one of her charities.

The guests, we were only fifteen in total, were served a round of cocktails in small Nick and Nora glasses and were told to wait for a toast, to be given by Mariana. A tray of drinks came to us, and Zoe appeared in time to distribute them herself.

"Alright now in a minute, Mariana's going to do her toast about—"

"Zoe," said Sabrina, with projection that quieted the room. "Given this is our last night of filming, before we 'do this,' I wonder if you might join us for a drink?"

Zoe looked confused, going still as a frightened cat.

"Sabrina, we—you can't—I can't be…"

"No, no, I think it's fine. Aleksandr?"

Zoe's perennially scrunched face screwed up even further as she looked past the crew to Aleksandr, who was standing with his arms crossed.

"It's fine, Zoe, go ahead," he said.

She tried to look cooler, shaking her hair and licking her lips. "Okay, sure."

"Here, have mine," said Mick, sliding his cocktail toward Sabrina and Zoe. "I've got conditioning this weekend, I really shouldn't anyway."

"Okay then," said Zoe.

Zoe picked up Mick's glass.

"Mariana, do you mind if I say a few words?" Sabrina asked, moving around the table to stand next to Zoe.

Mariana looked annoyed but said, "Sure, why not?"

"Thank you. I wanted to say, we've been doing this show for the last several weeks, and the more I think about it, the more I think how we have only Zoe to thank." Sabrina indicated that there should be a round of applause, and so there was. When it subsided, she went on. "You know, my whole life I have been in the spotlight, and it's been this sick, pallid spotlight that seemed to *hate* me for even existing. Maybe there's a different spotlight for other people, or maybe that's what it's always like. And as I've gotten older—*way* older, as some might point out...."

There was a trickle of laughter.

"As I've gotten older, I've learned how true it is that there would be no celebrity without the people behind the scenes. Some of you may know about my recent time in the press. Culture is determined by the decisions of those who go unseen."

Zoe's teeth were all starting to show as her understanding continued to dwindle.

"I don't want that to be the case anymore," said Sabrina. "*This* is Zoe, and she has made this show possible. My god, you've done a lot, haven't you. Aleksandr would not have a show without you, would he? You'd turn a body to a corpse before risking bad ratings, wouldn't you?"

Sabrina glistened a pearly smile that seemed without malice.

"Please, let us give a toast to those working behind the scenes to make sure that the world has a show to watch. Shall we?"

The room, and we, lifted our glasses.

Zoe had lost all the color in her face.

Sabrina rested a hand gently on Zoe's.

"But I wonder," said Sabrina, "if you might not mind switching?"

Zoe's head cocked like a dog hearing a whistle.

"Switching?"

"Drinks." She grinned again. "You see in our family—Budgie, I'm sure you remember this—we have a fun custom. Whenever you toast to someone, we switch drinks." She directed her gaze to the rest of the guests. "It can be a bit of a strain if you love champagne, and the stranger has whiskey." Back to Zoe. "But it's a bit of a tradition for me. For us." She nodded toward Budgie.

"You should have seen her father when someone refused him," said Budgie.

"Won't you switch with me, Zoe, as I toast to you and all your brilliance? You do it all so well."

Zoe's eyes had grown to the size of quarters—this was wide for her, as she had very small eyes.

She paused and cleared her throat. "Yeah, for sure, Sabrina. Let's do it."

They swapped drinks.

Zoe grimaced, but I think she was trying to smile. "You know what my nickname was in college?"

"What's that?" asked Sabrina.

"Rasputin. I could take or drink anything." She laughed. "I'll always drink with you, Sabrina."

"Don't kid yourself," said Budgie. "You're not the kind of person who is liked enough to get a nickname. Not the kind you'd take any pride in anyway."

There was a small ripple of gasps and then laughter.

"Cheers," said Sabrina, holding up her glass, and then clinking it with Zoe's, "Bottom's up…"

They both downed their drinks.

Zoe's teeth scraped against her bottom lip. Sabrina glared at her and then cleared her face of anything but amenity.

"Thank you all! Mariana?"

43

Zoe

It tasted like hell, but then, it was Fernet, muddled mint, and a bit of honey. Fernet is bitter, intense, and hard to hide. Luckily, she was not the only one in the room who looked like they'd swallowed poison.

The servers cleared away the empty glasses, Zoe handing hers to one of them herself.

She returned to the back with the rest of the crew.

"What the hell?" she asked Aleksandr. She turned to see Jason was filming her. "Why are you filming me? Why is he filming me?"

Aleksandr shrugged. "Some behind the scenes stuff."

Zoe's heart pounded. "I have to run to the bathroom."

"No, Zoe, we're in the middle of filming here. Please stop talking and put your headset back on."

"I feel sick," she lied.

"Suck it up," he said. "I'm sure you'll be fine ... Rasputin."

Zoe's heart was not merely pounding, but racing.

Did Aleksandr know? He couldn't. He couldn't know what he was doing.

"Aleksandr..." she started.

He raised his eyebrows. "What?"

"I–I had Sabrina's ... Sabrina's drink." She glanced at Jason's camera. She'd talk to him later, get him to cut this. "She had sort of ... a plot twist in her glass."

He nodded.

"I really have to go to the bathroom."

She'd always been invincible, but there was no telling what was about to happen if she didn't resolve this.

"Headset on, Zoe," said Aleksandr. His voice was already sounding fuzzy.

44
Dahlia

My hand was on Mick's thigh. All thoughts of our divorce far from my mind. I didn't care if I touched him like normal. Even though, tonight, when this was over, I was pretty sure we would go our separate ways again, marriage dissolved.

Sabrina sat down after her toast, as Mariana—irritated Mariana—began hers.

"What was that?" I asked her.

"I have a feeling," said Sabrina. She leaned back in her chair. "I have learned my lesson. I trust my instincts now, and I don't care what happens as long as I follow them."

I took my hand off Mick's leg.

***

Within fifteen minutes, an ambulance took Zoe away. I stood beside Sabrina with Mick behind me. Aleksandr stood beside Budgie.

"Has there ever been a reality show about women in prison?" Aleksandr asked no one in particular.

Budgie laughed as the sirens wailed.

The crew never stopped filming.

45

Dahlia

I surveyed the space and took it all in. My bedroom floor was covered in canvas tarps, and all the furniture, also covered, was moved to the center of the room; the walls were halfway to a deep jewel turquoise. For some reason, at some point, my taste had gone from bold to bland, and Mick and I had decorated this place like we modeled it off a teenager's notion of an adult's house.

It's amazing how a new coat of paint can conceal years of bad choices.

For the first time in a long time, I was spending my own money however I felt. Yes my *own* money because, while I knew it was not entirely independent, I had landed a book deal and a cohosting spot on a morning talk show. The book was based on my experience of filming reality TV, and perhaps I had gotten both opportunities because of Mick, but the book was all mine. There had been lots of posturing at wine bars and coffee shops and trying to look like a writer but blending in with everyone else, nonetheless I had done it. And it was good. I knew it was good. It was being published in the spring.

Aleksandr's show, of course, had never aired. Or at least not how we had thought it would.

A documentary was released to quite a dramatic and eager fanfare.

It was called *The Day Reality Died*, and it focused on the behind-the-scenes footage with Zoe at the center. There were all these slow pans over her high school photos, like she had committed a mass shooting or something. And yes, she had tried to kill Sabrina Verroye.

Maybe not kill her, but when she ground up painkillers and put them in her drink (only to consume them herself), she showed that she was willing to let her die if that's what had to happen.

Instead, she was the one who collapsed and took the ambulance ride. I didn't know too much about the lasting effects of what happened, but I knew she was more broken than even before and was embroiled in court cases while I was picking wallpaper for my entry way.

The footage of Zoe made me sick. Seeing what she had been willing to do. What she had said. And how chilling it was to see her celebrating her achievements. I yearned to find a way to pity her but found that the empathy would not come.

The rest was every bit as unnerving to watch. Hard to see myself drunk like that, hard to see the distance between Mick and me.

Aleksandr Borrow got credit, the industry assuming the exposition had been his plan the entire time—show how far a young, hungry PA will go to get ahead.

No one—save for perhaps Budgie, Sabrina, and myself—seemed to notice that if that *was* the case, then he was as complicit as if he had told her what to do.

But it didn't matter. We had all got out as unscathed as possible. We were bruised but not beaten.

Sabrina was happy now, I thought. Aaron Sorkin had cast her in a quiet, nuanced comeback role in his upcoming film. She was still with Leo, though Budgie believed the novelty might wear off at some point. The two of them were gallivanting around the globe studying holistic wellness. She had gained a little bit of weight, which made her look far more beautiful, even. She smiled all the time and didn't wear makeup in half the pictures on her feed. Her last post was with Aubrey, from an ashram in Phuket.

Budgie was working on a new project—a musical stage performance about the making of a reality TV show. She sent a video the other day of the Not-Nicole-Trace character doing a gaudy dance and singing brassily in a sparkling leotard.

Lexi was the same, but with more followers. She had dumped Tom though and kept "joking" that Sabrina and Budgie should set her up with a "rich guy that isn't a total douche."

Mariana got her own show interviewing experts in porn, sex toys, and every other facet of the sector. She hosted it with her husband, and I had to admit, it was good content. She was funny. I sort of wished I'd gotten to see that side of her, but neither of us felt the need to reach out and give it a try.

Nicole Trace relapsed and wound up in rehab, and Mick and I never heard from her or Regan again.

Mick and I were … well. It's hard to say. We were divorced. But we still saw each other. I guess you could say we were dating. If that's what you call it when your ex-husband—whom you still love to pieces—refuses to let you go and has regained something he had lost. After much back and forth and a tendon surgery on his knee, he decided to stop playing and ended up being the funny former athlete who did analytics, commentating, and cute TV spots. I knew he was having fun with it, which made me happy.

He was back in the city. He had rented a place nearby. And now we packed bags and had sleepovers. We made new friends again. He took me to dinner. We did galleries on weekends. Every now and then we went on a trip. We had sex. I loved him. He loved me. And I was starting to believe he'd do what he promised, which was to love me forever.

I still wasn't sure. For now, the place would stay my own.

In fact, everything would stay my own.

When the topic arose, and it did quite often, I shared that I thought the title of the series got it wrong. Reality hadn't died, it had been regenerated. My life became real. The other women say the same thing.

I never wanted fake again.

I craved the real, even if it hurt.

I was hungry for the actual.

I was made sick at the idea of smoke and mirrors.

I would never settle for anything less than sincere, genuine, verifiable reality.

I left my work-in-progress place and headed back to shower at the Crosby Street Hotel, where I was living during the renovations. I was meeting my friends for a drink there later. My friends, Sabrina, Budgie, and Lexi.

It turned out we all got along quite well when undocumented, like Mick and I recovered without the papers. I was learning, slowly, that life is much better, without any proof that you actually lived it.

Acknowledgments

There are many people, instrumental in bringing this story to the page, who are Most Loved, Most Treasured, and Most Appreciated.

First of all, thank you READER. It is my sincere hope that you were entertained.

Thank you to my family. You have been there at my side the whole time, and I am forever grateful. You have cheered me on, given the best input, left me notes by my bedside, in my purse and on my phone, encouraged me, and kept both my popcorn bowl and wine glass topped up.

Thank you to my study group. You are the best and bravest women I've ever met. Thank you for letting me be the "e." You were generous beyond measure with your stories, time, and insight, and I remain humbled by your graciousness. Kaley, Melanie, Diane, Jessica, and Georgie, thank you for sharing.

Thank you, Don, for being the first to believe in me.

Thank you mom, for finding the ideal home for my work.

Thank you Anita, for being there so I could do this.

Thank you Luciana, for being the sweetest, chattiest EMS worker.

Thank you Kitty for ensuring I wrote that scene just so.

Thank you Karine and Cece, for your warmth and reassurance.

Thank you LeeAnne, you are generous to the core.

Thank you to everyone who stopped me on the street, at the club, in a restaurant, at the grocery store, or at the airport. If you see me, please stop me. Meeting you is an immense pleasure.

Thank you, Deanna. No words for your patience, talent, and support.

Rebecca Eckler—you are spicy, kind, funny, and a true inspiration. Thank you for taking a risk on a debut writer.

Thank you to every Real Housewife past or present. No one outside the sorority will ever truly grasp what we go through in the name of good content.

Finally, thank you to Dr. Phyllis Chesler. Your book *Woman's Inhumanity to Woman* (2009) helped me immensely. It ought to be required reading for every sixteen-year-old girl.